D1561847

THE GUEST

THE GUEST

Hwang Sok-yong

Translated by
Kyung-Ja Chun and Maya West

Seven Stories Press
NEW YORK · TORONTO · LONDON · MELBOURNE

Copyright © 2001, 2004, 2005 by Hwang Sok-yong
English translation copyright © 2005 by Seven Stories Press

English translation rights arranged through agreement with Zulma.
Published and translated with kind support from the Korean Literature Translation Institute.

A Seven Stories Press First Edition

Seven Stories Press
140 Watts Street
New York, NY 10013
http://www.sevenstories.com/

In Canada
Publishers Group Canada, 250A Carlton Street, Toronto, ON M5A 2L1

In the UK
Turnaround Publisher Services Ltd., Unit 3, Olympia Trading Estate,
Coburg Road, Wood Green, London N22 6TZ

In Australia
Palgrave Macmillan, 627 Chapel Street, South Yarra VIC 3141

College professors may order examination copies of Seven Stories Press titles for a free six-
month trial period. To order, visit www.sevenstories.com/textbook/, or send a fax on school
letterhead to 212-226-1411.

Cover design by Jess Morphew
Book design by Jon Gilbert

Library of Congress Cataloging-in-Publication Data
Hwang, Sok-yong, 1943–
[Sonnim. English]
The guest / Hwang Sok-yong; translated by Kyung-Ja Chun and Maya West.—1st U.S. ed.
    p. cm.
ISBN-10: 1-58322-693-1 (hardcover : alk. paper)
ISBN-13: 978-1-58322-693-3 (hardcover : alk. paper)
1. Korean War, 1950-1953—Korea (North)—Hwanghae-do—Fiction. 2. Exorcism—Fiction.
I. Chun, Kyung-Ja, 1945– II. West, Maya. III. Title.
PL992.29.S6S6613 2005
895.7'34—dc22
                                        2005006794

Printed in the USA
9 8 7 6 5 4 3 2 1

CONTENTS

Author's Note

❖

WHEN SMALLPOX WAS first identified as a Western disease that needed to be warded off, the Korean people referred to it as "*mama*" or "*sonnim*," the second of which translates to "guest." With this in mind, I settled upon *The Guest* as a fitting title for a novel that explores the arrival and effects of Christianity and Marxism in a country where both were initially as foreign as smallpox.

As smallpox reached epidemic proportions and began sweeping across the nation, shamanic rituals called "guest exorcisms" were often performed to fight against the foreign intruder. *The Guest* is essentially a shamanistic exorcism designed to relieve the agony of those who survived and appease the spirits of those who were sacrificed on the altar of cultural imperialism half a century ago.

This twelve-chapter novel is modeled after the Chinogwi exorcism of Hwanghae Province. The ritual consists of twelve separate rounds. As is the case during an actual exorcism, the dead and the living simultaneously cross and recross the boundaries between past and present, appearing at what seem like random intervals to share each of their stories and memories. My intention was to create an oral discourse in which a type of time travel provides the latitudinal coordinates of the story, with the longitude provided by the individual characters' first-person narratives, revealing a wide range of experiences and perspectives.

If it is true that trying to rid yourself of residual memories inevitably results in a clearer and more solid memory, then the spirits of the past must be impossible to escape, regardless of whether they are alive or dead. At times, these apparitions can be more than mere phantoms: they are sent to us by the tragic wars of the past as a form of karma we must deal with—they are facets of the burden of history, a vivid reality.

In Gabriel García Márquez's *One Hundred Years of Solitude*, the reader is exposed to the ghost of a forefather who inexplicably returns to life. In that text also the ghost is more than a mere magical phantasm. A reality rife with exploitation and repression had weighed upon the people of Latin America for countless years. A product of the pressing actuality that freedom is an impossible dream, the phantom is one that history itself must face down, fight, drive out, use, and conquer. Countless souls have been lost to the blind inevitability of history itself; dismantling this structure and returning to a state in which time belongs to the people is a goal of this novel.

I began work on *The Guest* in 2000, the fiftieth anniversary of the Korean War. The September 11 attacks a year later came directly after *The Guest* was first published, and the onset of this new "Age of Terror," along with the inclusion of North Korea in the so-called Axis of Evil, and the beginning of a whole new war, made the fragility of our position clearer than ever. It was a chilling experience to be so reminded that despite the collapse of the Cold War infrastructure, our small peninsula is still bound by the delicate chains of war.

Because of Korea's identity as both a colony and a divided nation, both Christianity and Marxism were unable to achieve natural, spontaneous modernization; instead, they were forced to reach modernity in accordance with conscious human will. In North Korea, where the legacy of class structure during the traditional period was relatively diluted compared to the South, the tenets of Christianity and Marxism were zealously adopted as facets of "enlightenment."

During the Korean War, the area of North Korea known as Hwanghae Province was the setting of a fifty-day nightmare during which Christians and Communists—two groups of Korean people whose lives were shaped by two different "guests"—committed a series of unspeakable atrocities against each other.

Today, in a district known as Sinch'ŏn in Hwanghae Province, there stands a museum that indicts the American military for the massacre of innocents. The literal translation of the museum's name is "The American Imperialist Massacre Remembrance Museum." Many years ago, when I visited the North, I was given a tour of this museum as a matter of course.

Later on, during my stay in New York, I met a Korean minister named Ryu and heard the eyewitness account of his childhood in Hwanghae Province. Not too long afterwards, in Los Angeles, I was lucky enough to meet another survivor who shared with me her detailed firsthand account of the actual wartime incident that led to the founding of the aforementioned museum.

As it turns out, the atrocities we suffered were committed by none other than ourselves, and the inner sense of guilt and fear sparked by this incident helped form the roots of the frantic hatred that thrives to this day. Less than five years ago, when I first completed *The Guest*, I received fierce attacks from both Southern and Northern statists.

The scars of our war and the ghosts of the Cold War still mar the Korean peninsula. I can only hope that this particular exorcism helps us all move a step closer to a true, lasting reconciliation as the new century unfolds.

I

The Exorcism

WHAT REMAINS AFTER DEATH

REVEREND RYU YOSŎP had a strangely distinctive dream a few days ago.

It might have been the day before he went to New Jersey to meet his older brother, Ryu Yohan, a presbyter of his church—or maybe it was the day he first heard the news that he could now visit his homeland for the first time in forty years. He wasn't sure.

The dream was in pieces, disjointed and divided, but each scene remained as vivid as the moments that were passing.

❖ ❖ ❖

A murky day. A black-and-white photo almost: trees, branches, earth, all black through and through, set against a sky in chalk-white. Something flutters in the wind—a rag, perhaps, or a piece of laundry. Could that black bird be a crow? From the corner, underneath a patch of distant darkness, a human figure slowly approaches. One shoulder drooping lower than the other, the figure limps up to the middle of a latticed screen. It is carrying something over its left arm, and every now and then the faint cries of an infant can be heard. The baby is wrapped in a billowing bedsheet that trails down to the figure's calves. A wind passes through and away, shaking the trees, but the birds in the air merely quiver in silence. The figure lifts the baby onto the first branch

11

and begins to wind the rest of the sheet around it. The soft, squeaky crying continues, growing fainter and fainter, until gradually it dies away.

❖   ❖   ❖

Again, but this time different segments. This time the sound comes first. The delicate trembling of a violin floats up from the depths of a dark, hollow pit. Barely audible, like a breeze escaping from a deep cave. It is the song called "Touch-me-nots." No doubt about it. And then, perhaps because of the song, a vision of red petals, slowly swirling by like bits of colored paper.

❖   ❖   ❖

At the mouth of a village in early winter an overcast sky hangs low and heavy over a mountain ridge. Whitish pellets of soft hail float through the air. A man rushes down the hillside, and as he enters my field of vision, I recognize him: my older brother. He looks exactly the way I saw him last, a head of white hair and a bent back. In one hand, he holds a pick, dragging it behind him as he comes down the hill huffing and panting and letting out long gasping breaths. I am dreaming, yes, but even so I can't help but wonder what my brother might have been doing beyond the hill. Up front, up closer to the screen, he is searching for something; he kneels down swiftly, his backside jutting up—ah, he means to drink some water. He gulps it down like an animal. Suddenly he lifts his head; a bell tolls nearby. Still kneeling, he raises his upper body, and clasping both hands, he lets his head drop to his chest as though he is going to pray.

❖   ❖   ❖

Completely incoherent, totally disordered, and yet each scene was somehow familiar to Yosŏp. It was a mystery to the Reverend—his life was in America, but the dream fragments that greeted him every morning upon waking were invariably about Korea. A full twenty years since he'd immigrated, over ten years since he first became pastor of an American church, but the big, foreign noses had yet to show up in a single dream.

Despite the twenty years, however, Yosŏp still lived in a humble Brooklyn apartment. His brother Yohan, on the other hand, had long since moved to a white residential area in New Jersey, as befitted a true immigrant of the sixties. It was an unremarkable place—a small, wooden house of the kind commonly found in the suburbs of New York: it had a garage, a deep basement, a living room, and bedrooms of indifferent size, a backyard just spacious enough to hold a barbecue, and a white wooden fence out front.

The heat was stifling. Yosŏp drove to his brother's in the old minivan he usually used to shuttle around the members of his church. On this day, of all days, the air-conditioning in the tired van had finally failed, so he was driving with all the windows down. He made a point, however, of rolling up both windows whenever he hit a red light on a secluded street. He knew better than to ignore the advice of his faithful churchgoers. If you simply stood at an intersection with your windows open, they'd say, a black man would be sure to materialize, gun in hand, and hop in. One church member, on his way home from work, had been subjected to just such an ordeal. He and the black man had driven all the way home together, and he'd ended up simply leading the burglar up to his apartment, opening the door, and obediently inviting him in. By the time Yosŏp finally arrived at his brother's house, the back of his dress shirt was drenched in sweat, and he was ready to collapse from exhaustion.

Every visit to his brother involved something of a production. There were a number of motions one had to go through before one could be admitted into the house itself, the inside of which was always dark. Such darkness might have been considered routine in the dead of winter, but in this, the height of summer, Yohan actually had to employ wooden pincers on either end of the heavy curtains to keep them tightly closed.

Yosŏp pressed the doorbell. No sign of life. A home-security company sticker was plastered on the front door, advertising to all that this home was, electronically speaking, decidedly secure. Most likely his brother was examining the security monitor that would now be displaying the upper half of Yosŏp's body. He heard a clicking rattle and then, "What brings you here?"

Yohan's voice was always the same. He was getting on in years but he still spoke as if he were in a great hurry, biting off each word. Under it all lay the constant suggestion of cold irritation.

"I just came by to see you."

"Alone?"

Never mind the fact that they both knew he was watching the

monitor. The whole exchange was so ingrained in Yosŏp that he answered automatically, his "Yes" obedient. For quite a while, as was customary, he was left standing on the landing to stare at the unresponsive front door. At this point, his brother would be peering out of the French window in the living room, the one situated to the left of the door where he could check the front yard and street. Yosŏp saw the curtains move. Then, only then, did he hear the sound of the inner door being opened, followed by the turning of each lock in the outer door, one by one, and lastly the removal of the iron chain. The door opened a tiny sliver.

Ryu Yohan, a presbyter of his church and Yosŏp's older brother, lived alone. Well, to be more precise, he shared his house with a cat. No one knew how old the cat was exactly, but it had already been getting on in years when one of the churchgoers had given it to Yohan's wife half a decade ago. It was probably safe to assume that the cat was older than its current master, at least in cat-years. Yosŏp always found it sleeping on an old blanket spread out by the fireplace in the living room. It was black and white: white belly and legs, coal black everything else. Only its eyes were visible when it crouched down in the dark. Yosŏp's sister-in-law, dead these past three years, had loved the cat intensely—so much so that she had always insisted on keeping it in the bedroom itself. When she died, Yohan gave the animal to the owner of a hardware store several blocks away. Less than three days passed before it found its way back home. After attempting to return the cat to its new owner on multiple occasions, only to have it come back time and time again, Yohan washed his hands of the matter. Now, each completely indifferent to the other, they simply shared the house. The only light in the darkened living room came from the cable TV. A cartoon flitted across the screen—one of those involving a coyote that continually got itself in hot water for chasing after some sort of wild hen—and the volume was too loud. Yosŏp immediately reached for the remote and unceremoniously turned it down.

"Big Brother, it's such a fine day. Why not go for a walk or something instead of just watching TV day in and day out?"

"With the ache in my legs, even walking is a pain. What did you come for today?"

Instead of answering, Yosŏp simply lowered his head and began to pray. Being a presbyter himself and so unable to protest, Yohan pretended to lower his head along with his younger brother. Yosŏp prayed in the name of God for the good health of his brother, living all alone, and for the safety and prosperity of his two nephews now working and living in different cities.

"Actually, the truth is . . . I'm going home."

"To Seoul? Why?"

"No, not Seoul. I'm talking about our hometown in the North."

"The North . . . you mean Hwanghae Province?"

"Yes, exactly. I've been given a chance to go to Ch'ansaemgol—to Sinch'ŏn."

The moment he uttered Ch'ansaemgol, Yosŏp realized that some forty years had passed since he'd last mentioned the name of his hometown. Ch'ansaemgol. The word started out with the scent of a mountain berry, lingering at the tip of one's tongue—but then the fragrance suddenly turned into the stench of rotting fish. It was as if a blob of black paint had been dumped on a watercolor filled with tender, pale-green leaves, the darkness slowly seeping outward towards the edges.

"You're . . . so. I guess you're involved with the Commies now."

Big Brother was anything but delighted. The glance he shot his younger brother was full of suspicion, the kind of look one might expect from an old man who lived alone.

"There's an association called the 'Committee for the Promotion of Reunions for Separated Families.' If you pay a small fee for service and travel expenses, they help you get permission from the North Korean government to visit your hometown. They have such businesses now in Canada and L.A."

"Do you think it likely that God will allow you to go back to North Korea?"

"It is through the grace of God that things have worked out as they have. But never mind that—Big Brother, don't you ever think of your wife? Of Daniel?"

Yohan betrayed no sign of emotion and continued to stare blankly at the television. He wiped his two palms over his face in one smooth motion.

"All dead, probably. If Uncle is still alive, he may at least know where they've been buried. Don't you think so?"

Presbyter Ryu Yohan had certainly changed a great deal since the old days; even his legendary stubbornness was beginning to lose its edge. These days, at best, he simply fell silent or began to digress.

"If you go there . . . look for them."

Yosŏp, tempted to ask outright why his brother wouldn't go look for them himself, decided to keep his peace. Until now, the two brothers had never discussed the subject of "home" at any length. It was likely that Yohan had already noticed how his younger brother found it difficult to forgive the man he had been in those days.

"What do you think about ghosts?"

The question had neither head nor tail. A presbyter asking a minister's opinion on ghosts, of all things! Of course, Yosŏp knew that his older brother was asking him about phantoms, not demons.

"They appear in the Bible many times. That is, the possessed do."

Yohan lowered his voice, as if someone listened nearby.

"I've seen ghosts. Many, many times."

"This is talk I haven't heard before."

"I just never told you. Even in Seoul I saw them every now and then. Then, all these years in America, they didn't show—not once—but now they're back again. Ever since Ansŏng-daek* died."

Ansŏng-daek had been Yosŏp's sister-in-law. She was Yohan's second wife, the woman he married after he crossed down into the South by himself, the woman with whom he had lived in America until three short years ago. Not once had Yohan ever referred to her as "your sister-in-law" or "my wife."

"You don't go to church these days, Big Brother, do you?"

"Look, just drop it. The festive mood rubs me the wrong way. Those people just muddle through the church services—their hearts aren't in it. All they really want is an excuse to use the chapel to drink tea, eat food, and brag."

"That's just the way they do things here. Do you still pray?"

"Sure. I pray and read the Bible everyday."

"That's good. It so happens that I've been visiting with church members today. Why don't we hold today's service here in the house, Big Brother?"

---

* *Ansŏng-daek*: traditionally, women who married into the family from a different area were referred to by their place of origin instead of their given name—Ansŏng-daek would originally be from Ansŏng.

"Did you bring your Bible and hymnbook?"

"I'll go get them from the car."

"Don't bother. We've got mine, Ansŏng-daek's and even the kids'—we have sets to spare."

They began. Yosŏp opened the Bible and began with a passage from 2 Corinthians:

> Now I rejoice, not because you were grieved, but because your grief led to repentance; for you felt a godly grief, so that you were not harmed in any way by us; For godly grief produces a repentance that leads to salvation and brings no regret, but worldly grief produces death. For see what earnestness this godly grief has produced in you, what eagerness to clear yourselves, what indignation, what alarm, what longing, what zeal, what punishment! At every point you have proved yourselves guiltless in the matter.

Trying his best to ignore his brother's presence, Yosŏp began his sermon.

"We left our home forty years ago. Despite the unhappy events we faced there, we left because our faith allowed it, because our belief in the Lord taught us that we would find a new place, a place to build a heaven on earth. War was waged in our home as we left. Many, many innocents died. To live, people killed and were killed. In the book of Deuteronomy, Moses reminds his people of the promise made to their ancestors regarding the land of Canaan. He delivers the law, teaching them how to win a life of victory in the land of promise. They said, Jehovah, let all the enemies of the Lord face this same end. Do not pity them or offer them promises, only annihilate them all. And yet, Jesus taught love and peace. I say again—those left behind in our hometown had souls, just as we do. It is we who must repent first."

His reading glasses on, his Bible open, and his head down, Yohan seemed to be making a valiant effort to sit through the service. Yosŏp went on to speak of the peace that came with old age and what one must do to endure loneliness.

Unable to bear it any longer, Yohan cut short Yosŏp's mumbling.

"Well now, how about a . . . why don't we sing a hymn?"
His voice, piercing and powerful as he sang, hadn't changed a bit.

> A mighty fortress is our God,
> A bulwark never failing;
> Our helper He, amid the flood
> Of mortal ills prevailing.
> For still our ancient foe
> Doth seek to work us woe;
> His craft and power are great,
> And armed with cruel hate,
> On earth is not his equal.
>
> Did we in our own strength confide,
> Our striving would be losing;
> Were not the right man on our side,
> The man of God's own choosing.
> Dost ask who that may be?
> Christ Jesus, it is He;
> Lord Sabaoth His Name,
> From age to age the same,
> And He must win the battle.

The hymn complete, Yohan took charge and began the final prayer that would bring their little service to a close. He didn't mention a word about his younger brother's upcoming journey. He did pray, however, for the health of his children and of Yosŏp— even that of his sister-in-law. He then added abruptly, "Please protect the souls of my wife, of Daniel, and of my daughters, and help me to join them in the Kingdom of Heaven. In the name of Jesus Christ, our Lord, amen."

With that, the two brothers finished their family service.

❧ ❧ ❧

It is around supper time so the air hanging low above the thatched roofs of the village and out over the alder forest on the hill is thick with the smell and smoke of fresh pine twigs set ablaze. Bluish tints still cling to the sky, but darkness has already begun settling in all around, hugging the earth.

I've just finished up my business in the outhouse next to the hedge-gate and am about to pull up my pants. I can see the itsy-bitsy apples dangling from trees in the orchard and can just make out a cabbage field straight ahead of me. A boy is running towards the orchard, leaping over furrows in the field. He jumps over another. If he keeps it up, he'll squash all the cabbages for this winter's kimchi.

Hey you! What do you think you're doing!

Uh . . .

Oh, it's you, Yosŏp. Get on over here.

Realizing it was my younger brother, I slowly make my way towards him. Turn around. Let me see. What have you got there?

I snatch up the bundle he has hidden behind his back and open it up. Out comes a gourd containing some cooked rice and a little china bowl filled with pickled radish and bean paste.

I just brought it out to eat with my friends while we play.

You little brat—tell me the truth! Where are you taking that food?

Big Brother . . . this is a secret just between us, okay? Promise you won't tell.

❖   ❖   ❖

I didn't think much of it at first when Yosŏp came by and started talking about Ch'ansaemgol. Let me see, I wondered. Where was Ch'ansaemgol again? But then he started in with the let's-have-a-service, let-us-repent, Commies-have-souls-too spiel, and so on and so forth, and later, after he finally left, I suddenly remembered the dead villagers. Out of all of them, Illang's face was clearest—and he looked exactly the way he did back then. He'd been approaching forty. If he were still alive, he'd be over eighty by now. I had that bastard's nose pierced with an electric wire, and we dragged him all the way to town.

The TV was off. Slowly, stealthily, the face of that son of a bitch, Ichiro, began floating up out of the black blankness of the screen. It was the same face that had gradually come back to life so long ago, the one that slowly regained consciousness after I cracked his skull with a pick handle and knocked him out. The wretch must have been strong as an ox, no doubt about it—I hit him on the temple, right above the ear, and it didn't even take him that long to wake up.

Eyes out of focus, he sat back on the ground and swayed his upper body back and forth, as if his head felt too heavy.

Get up, you stupid piece of shit!

I struck him again, this time on the back, again with the pick, but Illang just kept on swaying. He wouldn't fall flat. Ready to burst with rage, I put a bullet in my pistol, cocked it, and placed the muzzle against his blood-drenched head.

You son of a bitch, you took our land—thought you'd be Party chairman for a thousand, ten thousand years, didn't you?

I was right about to pull the trigger when the boys stopped me and said we should really take him to town for investigation. So I ordered them to pull him up by the armpits to get him to his feet, but the bastard suddenly rose by himself, mumbling, Believe in the God of Chosŏn* . . . .

Goddamn bastard. Still have breath to spare, eh? An illiterate fool, but now that you've listened to a couple of lectures you talk ready and smooth, is that it?

That very face from that very day—that was the face reflected in the blank TV screen. Not that I found it particularly frightening. Faces I could recognize never did scare me as much. I asked Yosŏp what he though about ghosts, but his answer wasn't good enough.

A long time ago in Chinatown, I saw a shadow play at a Chinese pub. It was built along the same lines as the revolving lanterns we had back in the old days, but this device involved the addition of a painted scroll that slid back and forth in front of the light. At night, when I lay in the upstairs bedroom, the window facing the street lets in a faint light, and the headlights of the cars that speed by shine in, touching the ceiling in a flash before they fly away. Depending on the speed of the car and the size of the headlights, the shape of the reflection on the ceiling varies. Even with my eyes shut, I can feel the movement. That night, dozing off and on, in that strange place between wakefulness and sleep, I was awakened by the sirens and red blinking emergency lights of a passing ambulance. Clustered around the foot of my bed, I saw them, a group of people looking down on me. They came in every shape and size: Chungson's wife, always out and about with one breast

---

* *Chosŏn*: Korea.

hanging low under her *chŏgori*,* constantly jiggling the baby on her back as it slipped down her hip; the female elementary school teacher who used to live above that store at the mouth of the village; a fiddler with bobbed hair in a People's Army uniform; the six little daughters of Myŏngsŏn's family; and so on. Anyway, they were all women and they all just stood there. They stood with their backs to the window, and because of the darkness I shouldn't have been able to recognize their faces—but somehow I did. I recognized them at once. I caught myself mumbling aloud in spite of myself.

"I speak in the name of the God Jehovah! Away with you, Satan!"

And with that, I was wide awake. The mattress was soaked in sweat where my back had touched the bed. It was a pain, but I was so thirsty that I went downstairs to the kitchen. I turned on the light above the steps, but the living room remained completely dark. Whenever I climbed up or down the stairs, I was struck by the thought that no one should ever live in a two-story house in their old age. Meanwhile, I'd developed a habit of stretching my stooped back and pounding it a couple of times every time I reached the first floor. While stretching at the bottom of the stairs that night, I thought I saw someone sitting on the sofa in the darkened living room that faced me. I let it be and went to the kitchen. I opened the refrigerator. The light came on. I was gripping the plastic water bottle and taking it out of the door rack, when I was so startled that I almost dropped it entirely. An eye was staring up at me. Hey, you, what are you looking at? A fish head left over from lunch. The croaker's gills were a little blackened from being fried, and only the sockets were left—no eyeballs. Slowly, deliberately, I closed the refrigerator door and turned to walk back toward the living room. That's when I saw the thing still sitting on the sofa.

Who are you?

The black thing answered, its speech thick, hoarse, It's me. Don't you know me?

Who are you, I say.

In a voice that sounded caked with charcoal, it said, I'm the mole that used to hang about Ŭnnyul.

---

* *Chŏgori:* a short, blouselike top, tied with a long ribbon—part of the traditional Korean costume known as *hanbok*.

"Uncle Sunnam?"

Forgetting everything for the moment, excited and delighted, I quickly flipped on the light. The cat was out enjoying its nightly excursions, and there was nothing in the living room except for the furniture and TV set. In a corner near the hallway stood the wooden coat stand carved in the shape of deer antlers. Only then did my legs go limp. Sunnam had been about ten years older than myself, which would have put him somewhere in his mid-thirties back then. He worked in Ŭnnyul as an excavator in the Kŭmsanpo mines until he returned home after Korea's liberation from Japan. He was good at singing and gambling, and when it came to drinking he'd always been one to do it by the barrel. In the winter of that year, I finished him off. In those days, there was a utility pole that stood at the crossroads where the thoroughfare leading into town from Ch'ansaemgol met with the farm road. It was to that same pole that I eventually had Uncle Sunnam's neck hanging by a wire.

❖ ❖ ❖

Word came that the list of names had been announced by the Office of Representatives. The Reverend Ryu Yosŏp met Mr. Kim at a shabby diner in Manhattan. The junky old air conditioner was making a huge racket, but the table directly underneath it was the only one available. Mr. Kim, like Yosŏp's older brother, was an elderly man approaching seventy. He'd been a journalist in Korea, he said, before he immigrated to America, but for someone with that kind of occupation he didn't seem quick enough. He took an envelope from his wrinkled briefcase and placed it on the table. Rummaging through it, he produced several pieces of paper.

"Let's see, this one here is your invitation, Reverend Ryu Yosŏp—and now, take a look at this."

Yosŏp glanced down at the document he'd been handed. The title printed along the top, "Homeland Visitors Group: Approved Applicants," caught his attention.

"I see that it's no longer the 'Reunions for Separated Families' program."

"Oh, yes. You see—well, they had some problems with the 'Reunions for Separated Families' project, so they no longer call it by that name. They now use names like "Homeland Visitors" and "Tour Group" instead. In any event, Reverend, I seem to remember that you never did submit a list of family members you hope to find."

"Yes, that's right."

"Well, it's not too late. As long as you make the request here, there's always a way to get around the red tape once you get there . . . and you also need to fill in the name of your hometown."

Yosŏp hesitated a moment. He was in a difficult spot. Identifying his hometown as he set off to visit the North would hardly be advisable, and yet without doing so it would be impossible to find out what had happened to his relatives.

"So, where is your hometown again?"

Ballpoint in hand, Mr. Kim peered at Yosŏp over his reading glasses.

"Pyongyang . . . it's Pyongyang."

"Where in Pyongyang?"

Yosŏp blurted out the first thing that came to mind.

"Sŏn'gyori in Pyongyang city."

"And the address . . . ?"

"Well . . . the address I can't remember, but once I'm there I'm sure I'll be able to recognize the place."

"Yes, of course, of course. It's been over half a century, after all. Leaving the street address blank shouldn't be a problem."

Collecting the various papers and his plane ticket, Yosŏp paid Mr. Kim a lump sum to cover the airfare, travel expenses, and service charge.

Yosŏp called his older brother as soon as he got home. The phone rang for a long time before Yohan finally picked up. His voice was calm and rather subdued.

"It's me, Big Brother. What took you so long to answer?"

"Um, I was sleeping."

"What are you doing at night that you should be sleeping now?"

"I don't know. I can't get to sleep at night these days."

"You should read the Bible, pray, and go to sleep."

"Why did you call?"

"Ah, yes. How was Daniel's name recorded in the family registry?"

"Well, I imagine it would have worked the same way as yours—we called you Joseph when you were young, but changed it to Yosŏp in Chinese characters for the official records. Likewise, Daniel's name should just be Tanyŏl. Ryu Tanyŏl."

Yosŏp told his brother that he understood and was about to hang up when he was seized by the urge to add one last thing.

"Big Brother, do pray to God for forgiveness. Then the dead, too, will be able to close their eyes in peace."

"What did you say!"

Yohan began to shriek. Considering how poor his health had been of late, it was a wonder where so much energy could possibly have come from.

"Why should I beg for forgiveness? We were the Crusaders—the Reds were the sons of Lucifer! The hordes of Satan! I was on the side of Michael the archangel, and those bastards were the beasts of the Apocalypse! Even now, if our Lord were to command it, I would fight those devils!"

"Brother, disputes between the powers that be are different from those among men in this world."

"Nonsense! The Holy Spirit was upon us back then!"

With the resounding crash of a receiver being slammed into its cradle, the line went dead.

❖ ❖ ❖

Three days before he set out for the land of his birth, Yosŏp had an odd encounter.

It started raining in the afternoon. Judging from the fierce way the raindrops were slamming against the windowpane, it didn't look like the kind of rain that planned to stop any time soon. The sheets of rain thinned out a bit as night fell but showed no real sign of letting up.

A call came from New Jersey. It was the minister of the church that Presbyter Ryu Yohan attended. He was young, the graduate of a first-rate seminary, and because his family had immigrated when he was still a child, his English was fluent and his sermons sophisticated. He was named successor and brought to the church when the previous minister retired and moved to Boston to be with his children. Ryu Yohan had served with the old minister for decades as a presbyter and continued to be revered for his long-standing service. For some reason, however, he and the new minister were simply not compatible. Gradually, Yohan lost heart with the whole institution and, as Yosŏp had been told during his last visit, became fed up with the Western way in which the church was run. Yosŏp, on the other hand, had studied for a second degree in the States. So despite the fact that he had actually been ordained in Seoul, he understood the young minister and had a favorable opinion of him and his ways.

"Something . . . something awful has happened to Presbyter Ryu."

Anticipating what might be wrong, Yosŏp made an effort to calm his voice.

"Everything is as God wills it, and I am not easily surprised. Feel free to tell me what happened."

"I'm so sorry. Presbyter Ryu passed away today at around 9:00 p.m. We were with him till the end."

"I'll be there soon. Have you notified the funeral home?"

"Please don't concern yourself with that—our church has a steward who handles funerals. You can trust him to take care of all the necessary details."

Yosŏp woke up his wife. She burst into tears and said again and again that they should have visited more often and that she felt guilty. Yosŏp left the packing to his wife and contacted his nephews, Samyŏl and Pil-lip, who lived in Washington, D.C., and Detroit. Luckily, Samyŏl was home, and Yosŏp asked him to call his younger brother to pass on the news.

It might have been on account of the rain, or maybe that it was the middle of the week—whatever the reason, the streets were practically empty. Yosŏp stuck to the main roads whenever possible and drove much faster than usual. By the time he pulled up to his brother's home, a sizeable gathering of Yohan's fellow churchgoers had already arrived. A good twenty people or so were crowded into the living room, sitting in the various chairs and milling about on the carpeted floor. The young minister sprang to his feet and greeted Reverend Ryu and his wife. Seeking out familiar faces, Yosŏp greeted several acquaintances. A bit dazed, he looked around.

"My brother . . . ?"

"He's upstairs."

This time Yosŏp led the way and started up the stairs. A great deal of time had passed since he'd entered his brother's bedroom. Like the miser he was, Yohan had apparently kept on using the same metal bed he'd bought years ago at a used furniture sale in his neighborhood. A cardigan sweater was draped neatly across the back of a chair, and a pair of dress pants lay on the seat. The late Presbyter Ryu Yohan was lying on his bed, covered entirely by a white sheet. Yosŏp went over to the head of the bed, pulled down the sheet, and looked at his dead brother. It might just have been the fluorescent light, but Yohan's face looked to be made of old paper, discolored to a faded yellow; his white hair seemed nothing more than a fistful of tangled old yarn. A veteran of countless encounters with bodies of the newly dead, Yosŏp had come to believe that he was capable of reading the various expressions of death. Looking at his brother's face, Yosŏp read a sensation of relief, of lightness, as if Yohan had finally set down some heavy load. Drawn towards it, unable to stop himself, Yosŏp reached out and felt his older brother's cheek and traced the cheekbone with his hand. Cold, but not stiff—it was still soft. Could it be that his brother had actually known peace? He prayed for a moment and pulled the sheet over his brother's face. The young minister and Yosŏp crouched down, facing each other as they squatted on the carpeted floor by the side of the bed. The young minister began to explain.

"Presbyter Ryu called me early in the evening, saying he didn't feel well. He asked if I could come over and pray for him. I suggested that we go to the hospital together, but he insisted that wasn't necessary—he said a plain service with me was what he'd like to have."

❖ ❖ ❖

We're off to the stream—I'm tagging along after the older guys from the neighborhood. The banks are sandy, the water crystal clear as it gushes through the jagged rocks. Uncle Sunnam is leading the way, dragging a yellow mongrel along by a length of string. Odds are that he's caught the bitch that wandered over from the other side of the hill—I bet it's the same dog that was playing about in our village.

His swift tongue and practical jokes have long since established him as *the* man at our village *sarang*.* Until Uncle Sunnam starts going off to work the mines over in Ŭnnyul, we go hang around outside the *sarang* every afternoon just to see what the older guys are up to. Ichiro, the long-

* *Village sarang*: a communal room or meeting area used primarily for recreation.

standing neighborhood servant, is always there. Even we young ones use the casual, low form of speech to Ichiro. In the wintertime, everybody brings their work to the village *sarang*; they boil sweet potatoes to eat with cold *tongch'imi** juice while they do their work. Sometimes the little ones, pressured by the older guys, brave a taste of *makkŏlli*.† In the summertime, plans for stealing chickens and pilfering melons are cooked up in that room. One time, trailing after Uncle Sunnam's gang on a river-fishing trip, I even learn—among other things—about masturbation.

In the shade of the trees along the stream, they boil water in an iron cauldron usually used for boiling cattle feed. For the first time in my life, I witness the killing of a dog—exciting and cruel enough to make your blood boil. They tie the dog's neck with hemp string, winding it round and round many times over, then they throw the other end of the string over a tree branch and pull. As the string becomes taut, the dog's eyes roll back into its head, flashing white, and its four legs flail frantically, suspended in midair. Then the older guys circle around; armed with wooden clubs, they beat it all over as hard as they can. The dog can't make a sound. All it can do is rasp out a choking noise and thrash about until it shits all over the place. Once it's over, the dog is almost formless. They singe its hair over a bonfire down by the edge of the water. Our eyes gleam eerily, filled with murder and appetite.

❧ ❧ ❧

Ah, why does that particular summer day come back to me now? It must be because I saw the phantom of Uncle Sunnam on the same night Little Brother came to see me. All day long I've had a splitting headache, chills running up and down my body—maybe I'm coming down with some sort of flu.

It started pouring in the afternoon; the rain was thick and intense. The sound of thunder tore through the house. I turned off the TV and lay down on the sofa in the living room. Feeling wretched and sullen, I rifled through the kitchen cabinet and found a bottle of cognac. When was the last time I touched alcohol, I wondered. This bottle was the one Samyŏl

---

* *Tongch'imi*: a pickled radish side dish that is stored and served in its own juices.
† *Makkŏlli*: a thick, unrefined rice wine.

brought home at Thanksgiving. I must have been just lying in the darkness, dreamless. Someone shook me by the arm.

Hey. Hey, Yohan. Get up. Get up.

Slowly, I opened my eyes. Someone in black, squatting down by the sofa, was shaking me awake. I wanted to sit up, but somehow my body wouldn't budge.

Who are you?

It's me, Uncle Mole.

Uncle Sunnam.

That's right. Aren't you going to pester me for tales about the old days? Go ahead . . .

This tale, that tale—even the cow in the field has its own tail.

As if I'd been waiting for the joke all along, I snickered. The black thing giggled, too.

That was why I hanged you on the utility pole.

The black thing fell silent. It moved over to the chair facing the sofa. It sat down and crossed its legs.

I've come to take you with me.

Can't I go tomorrow instead?

Doesn't work that way.

I flew into a temper.

I'm not the one that made you join the Communist Party, am I? I will not go with you! I am a presbyter in the church!

The black thing rocked his legs back and forth and muttered a response: There aren't any sides over there—no my-side-against-your-side.

Well, I killed you, so I'm definitely not on your side.

No such thing as living or dying, either.

What about forgiving and repenting?

Certainly not.

Where is 'there,' anyway?

Where you were born . . .

On the brink of losing consciousness altogether, I staggered to my feet. I moved closer to the chair and was about to lay my hand on Sunnam's body when, with a flicker, the phantom disappeared.

It was still raining incessantly. I opened every lock in the front door to give everything inside me—not to mention everything inside my house—a chance to get out. I was getting over my flu symptoms, but I still felt drained. I wanted to wash myself clean. I went upstairs, filled up the bathtub, and immersed my body. It felt as if my whole body were dissolving, melting into the water, leaving only my soul floating on the surface. Gradually, I felt more comfortable. As soon as I got out of the bathroom, I called the new minister and asked him to visit me. I took off the robe, changed into clean underwear, took out a new pair of pajamas, and put them on. The sound of the rain grew fainter and fainter.

❖ ❖ ❖

"We came in here and found him sleeping quietly. We weren't sure what we should do, so we began to pray. We thought the Presbyter was still asleep all through the prayer, but when we said amen, he joined in and said it with us. We asked him whether he was feeling unwell, but he told us he felt fine and that he was quite comfortable. He said he wasn't in any pain but that it was time for him to go to sleep."

The young minister stopped himself, removed a notepad from the inside pocket of his jacket, and inspected it for a moment.

"I had a feeling that something unusual was going on, so I wrote down what he was saying. He said that he was returning to his birthplace, that his body should be cleansed by fire after his death and placed in a cinerarium—he also said that there's a bankbook in a basket under the bed and that the money in the account is to be used for expenses. Soon after that he was quiet, and when we looked closely, we realized he'd stopped breathing."

Following the minister's directions, Yosŏp took a look underneath the bed. There was indeed a basket. It was square, like a box, and had a padlock—most likely something left behind by his late wife. He opened the lid and found a Chemical Bank bankbook wedged between a small pile of photo albums and day planners. The bedroom door opened and the deacon poked his head in.

"The people from the funeral home are ready with the coffin, sir."

"Tell them to bring it up here, please."

Two men from the funeral home entered, carrying the coffin over their shoulders, and Yosŏp directed them to put it down by the bed. He then began to wash and shroud the body with the young minister. The whole procedure must have been a first for the young man, but for Reverend

Ryu Yosŏp it was familiar territory; his experience with such matters dated all the way back to his days in Korea—and after all, it was his own brother. Yosŏp went to take a look in his brother's wardrobe. There were several suits, but he needed to find the *hanbok** that he remembered Yohan owning.

He found them, together with some winter underwear, in the bottom drawer of the wardrobe: Yosŏp took out the *chŏgori*, *paji*,† and *magoja*‡— the *durumagi*,§ he set aside. With the help of the young minister, he took off Yohan's pajamas, and they wiped down his face, arms, and chest with gauze steeped in alcohol. The abdomen, legs, feet, and toes, too, received the same treatment. Yosŏp knew well the entire panorama of events that had left his brother's body so small and shriveled. After he finished dressing Yohan in his *hanbok*, Yosŏp wrapped him in a cotton sheet and, together with the minister, lifted him up by the head and legs to lay his body in the coffin. He then stuck a bundle of cloth underneath the head to steady it and filled up the space around the body with crumpled rice paper, packing it in to keep the body from jostling around. Yohan's fellow churchgoers were called upstairs, and they all held a small service together.

At dawn, Yosŏp and his wife decided to return home for the time being, leaving the crowd of churchgoers behind. It was agreed that the wishes of the dead ought to be honored in terms of the funeral service, but they decided to put aside any further discussion on that point until Samyŏl and Pillip arrived.

❖ ❖ ❖

On his way driving home to Brooklyn, Yosŏp had a rather bizarre experience. At some point on his route he turned the usual way, only to realize several blocks down that the street, lined by tall, dark buildings on either side, was completely dead. He sped up, expecting that normal, brightly lit streets would appear soon enough—only to find himself wondering whether he

---

* *Hanbok*: the traditional Korean costume consisting of a blouselike top, vest, pants, and coat for men and a top, skirt, and coat for women; although only worn now on special occasions, hanbok was once worn daily.

† *Paji*: pants.

‡ *Magoja*: vest, part of the full hanbok costume.

§ *Durumagi*: coat, part of the full hanbok costume.

wasn't just going deeper and deeper into this inexplicably alien place. As a three-way split in the road came into view, he slowed down and tried to sort out his thoughts.

His wife, her head thrown back against the headrest, was fast asleep in the passenger side. Yosŏp, having just spent a sleepless night himself, was finding it difficult to think clearly. It would be best to turn back, he finally decided. He turned the car around—and soon realized that he couldn't recall the spot where he'd turned onto this street. He drove very slowly, thinking that he'd eventually have to ask someone for directions.

All of a sudden, out of the corner of his eye, he thought he caught a light shining down an alley on his left. Feeling rather reluctant, Yosŏp turned the wheel once more and entered the alleyway. The light turned out to be a small bonfire. It was quintessential New York: buildings abandoned when the last shops went out of business and the last legitimate tenants took off, now used as shelter for garbage, homeless alcoholics, and squatters. Thinking to himself that he'd wandered into the most dangerous of traps, Yosŏp tensed and gripped the steering wheel tight with both hands.

Squatting in front of the fire was a shadow of no discernible gender, tearing up cardboard boxes to feed the flames. It was still summer, yes, but a concrete forest on a rainy night can be chilly in any season. Yosŏp brought the car to a stop. This is probably how they make it through the night, he thought. The shadow turned in his direction, but the front steps of a building blocked the nearby light and he was unable to see the shadow's face clearly.

"Excuse me!" he called out in English as he rolled down the window.

The shadow slowly sauntered out onto the sidewalk. It was an old hag with a shock of white hair, draped in a huge man's coat long enough to almost graze the pavement as it swung to and fro.

"What, got yourself lost?"

"Yes. Right. I'm trying to get to Brooklyn."

The hag burst into a cackle.

"What are you going there for? It's no use, you know, even if you get there."

He shouldn't have even bothered responding—he should have just turned his car around and gotten out of there—but instead, in spite of himself, he blurted out, "I'm going to my *house*."

"That's no house of yours. Your house is the Kingdom of Heaven. I know very well where you're coming from."

"And where might that be?"

Again the old hag cackled.

"You know very well, too. You're coming from the house of the dead."

With a thud, Yosŏp's heart sank. The hag moved even closer, practically leaning her chin on the edge of the open window.

"Buy this, and I'll tell you the way."

She held out something that looked like a small bundle of yarn.

"How much?"

"Ten dollars."

"Too expensive."

"Well, five, then . . . that's as low as I go."

Yosŏp fished a five-dollar bill out of his wallet and gave it to the woman. She placed the small bundle in his hand.

"Keep this on you, and something good will happen. Now, go out to the main road, and turn right after three blocks. That'll put you on the road you're used to taking every day."

Eager to get away from there, Yosŏp turned the car once more in a rough swerve. For a split second, his headlights illuminated the old hag as she waved her hand. Awakened, perhaps, by the sudden turn, his wife opened her eyes, looked around, and asked, "What's going on?"

"I got lost."

"Did you talk to someone?"

"Yeah, a homeless person, I guess. I asked for directions."

Yosŏp looked again at what the old hag had deposited in his hand. He couldn't tell what kind of animal skin it was, but it was a leather pouch—something you'd see for sale at a Native American tourist trap.

❖ ❖ ❖

The family of Presbyter Ryu Yohan decided to follow his wishes and put his remains to rest in a cinerarium. His two sons, Samyŏl and Pil-lip, both led busy lives in different cities, and they seemed rather relieved by the idea. Before they actually pushed the coffin into the mouth of the furnace at the crematory, they held another service. Afterward they stayed on to listen to the flames as they burned away inside the furnace. Later, the relatives moved over to one side and began separating the bones from the big pile of ashes that had been dumped out on the broad wooden counter. The four men, Yosŏp, Samyŏl, Pil-lip, and the young minister, each held a receptacle that resembled a deep porcelain bowl, and used tongs to pick out pieces of bone. The ashes were still warm. The bones were white. They looked clean. There really weren't many, in terms of quantity. All the bones collected by the four men, if put together, would probably have amounted to a few handfuls at most. Before he poured his share of the bones into the urn, Yosŏp, without really thinking, quietly picked up one of the pieces and slid it into his suit pocket.

2

Possession

TODAY IS TOMORROW FOR THOSE
WHO DIED YESTERDAY

◈

STARTLED BY THE ALARM, he got the distinct impression
as he fumbled for the clock that something had just fallen to the floor. Even
after he succeeded in quieting the alarm, however, Yosŏp chose to bury
his head back in the pillow and stay in bed. The sound of a drill, driving a
nail into some far off wall, pounded through his skull. Someone's moved in
again, he said to himself. Lying on his stomach, he doubled up the pillow
to cover his ears. Bit by bit, though, he was waking up—his mind kept
getting clearer and clearer until finally he could no longer stay in the sweat-
drenched bed.

Sitting up on the edge of the bed, Yosŏp looked at the clothes he had
so carelessly tossed over the chair. He opened the curtains to check the
weather and turned on the table lamp. The window offered a view of the
building next door, close enough to keep the room perpetually dreary and
dark; but if you pressed your face right up against the glass and looked up,
you could see the line of sunlight that touched the top of the neighboring
structure. He noticed the thing that had dropped to the carpet.

It looked like a small, black book. Picking it up, he saw that it was a
palm-sized day planner. Ah, that's right. Yesterday, Big Brother Yohan
passed away. He remembered giving the bankbook to Samyŏl at the

crematorium, but he must have forgotten about the little planner and brought it home.

He opened the planner and began flipping through it, one page at a time. The first few pages were full of phone numbers, written down in no apparent order. There was the number for Yosŏp himself, followed by numbers for the church, for Samyŏl and Pil-lip, for a Chinese restaurant, a garage, a dry cleaner's, the social security office, and a hospital. There were also names and numbers of Yohan's friends, fellow senior citizens whom Yosŏp had no way of knowing, and, every now and then, some dates and memos. Most of the pages were left unused, but near the middle of the book Yosŏp found several notes that had been written only a few days earlier. "Call Pak Myŏngsŏn tomorrow," declared one recent scribble.

Yosŏp got up, turned on the air conditioner with the remote control, took some water out of the refrigerator, and drank it from the bottle—all wearing nothing but his underwear. He sat down at the table and thought for a while. The only sign of life in the apartment was the whirring of the air conditioner; his wife must have left already, off to her job at the hospital. Who was Pak Myŏngsŏn, again? The name was only vaguely familiar, but he got the feeling he'd be able to put his finger on it if he tried. Several young maidens clad in white *chŏgoris* and black *mongdang chi'mas** flitted through Yosŏp's head, but his fuzzy memory was unable to match any satisfactory names to the faces. He thumbed through the planner and located the phone number under Pak Myŏngsŏn's name. The area code alone was enough to show that the woman lived in Los Angeles. Tomorrow, Yosŏp would be boarding a plane to Los Angeles. The Homeland Visitors were assembling first in L.A. and going on to Beijing from there.

Holding the planner open with one hand, Yosŏp used the index finger of his other hand to dial. He listened as the phone rang on the other end of the line. He was about to hang up on about the tenth—or maybe the fifteenth—ring, when he finally heard a faint voice.

"Hello ?" A woman's voice answered in English.

"Hello," he said in Korean.

"Who's this?"

---

* *Mongdang chi'ma*: a short, traditional skirt that falls just below the knees.

"Ah, well . . . may I speak to Ms. Pak Myŏngsŏn?"

"Speaking. What can I do for you?"

"I, ah . . . I am the younger brother of Presbyter Ryu Yohan."

The other end of the line fell silent for a moment. Yosŏp could still hear her breathing, but he cleared his throat just to make sure. She spoke up.

"He said he'd come himself . . . but it seems he's changed his mind."

"I beg your pardon? My brother arranged to visit you? When?"

"Next weekend."

Once again Yosŏp cleared his throat then said, rather nonchalantly, "My brother passed away yesterday."

An outburst of emotion, something close to a laugh, was immediately followed by a resounding click. The line was dead.

❧ ❧ ❧

It's something you go through every time you pack. You take all the things you're going to need, and then you spread them out on the bed and across the floor. Then you try to fit it all into one suitcase. You end up taking some of the stuff out, and then you repeat the whole process all over again. You cut down on the clothes and remove what you can from the shaving kit, and in the end you just barely manage to fit everything in. Before changing your clothes, you go through all your pockets and empty their contents: wallet, passport, tickets, planner, loose change, and car keys. Before changing his clothes, Yosŏp took all his sundry items and put them in a little heap on the bed. Then, one by one, he put each item in its place: the wallet in the right inner pocket of his jacket, the passport and tickets in his left inner pocket, the car keys on top of the dresser for his wife. He was reaching for the coins when something, something resembling a warped *tojang*,* caught his eye. He picked it up for a closer look, holding it before his eyes and turning it over a couple of times. Suddenly realizing what it was, he clenched his hand around it and looked around the room. What on earth was he going to do with it? Also on the bed, he noticed something that looked like a small lump of yarn. He opened the soft, strong leather pouch and put the sliver of

---

* *Tojang*: a small, cylindrical personal stamp used to sign or authorize official documents.

bone in it. A thin leather string dangled from the pouch, so he pulled. Its mouth squeezed shut.

On the plane, Yosŏp got the impression that he was chasing after time itself. As he was boarding he'd been struck by the notion that since he was heading westward, the sun would simply continue to hang behind him—but somehow, time had not only caught up, it had left him behind. The screen at the front of the cabin was down; a movie was playing. He hadn't rented a headset, so all he could do was watch the silent pictures move about. He'd had about three glasses of wine. A Chinese woman in her fifties sat next to him. With a rustling noise, she fished something out from under her seat. Through the open plastic bag, he spotted something mysterious and red. She tore off a strip of the red stuff, about the size of a finger, and held it out to him. "Chicken, chicken," she mumbled. It appeared to be some sort of boiled chicken dyed red.

With a shudder, Yosŏp shook his head violently and said in English, "Oh, no, no thank you." The foreign syllables felt raw, lingering about his ears. The voice didn't sound like his own.

Yosŏp was sitting in an aisle seat, facing the curtain that hung at the far end of the cabin to screen the entrance to the toilets. Someone behind the curtain was moving around. As the top of the curtain shook a little, the person's lower half came into view: a pair of trousers and dress shoes. All at once the curtain was parted, and the man behind it was now looking in Yosŏp's direction. Staggering every now and then to the rhythm of the plane, Big Brother Yohan was walking directly toward Yosŏp. Yosŏp closed his eyes. No one passed. When he opened them the aisle was empty, the screen still flickering. He stood up, holding onto the back of the seat in front of him. Making his way out into the aisle, his step a bit unsteady, Yosŏp wondered where Yohan might be sitting.

Turning this way and that, Yosŏp peered back into the faces of the passengers he'd just passed. Well, he's not sitting on that side of the aisle. Yosŏp drew the curtain aside and walked into the darkness. A gleaming blue light showed the toilet to be vacant. He pushed the door open and entered. The deafening roar of the plane filled his ears. The tired face of an elderly man floated on the mirror's surface. He washed his hands and face. He scrubbed his face dry with a paper towel then ran his two palms down across it, from forehead to chin. Turning around to face the door, Yosŏp suddenly felt like he was a stranger to himself. He glanced back at the mirror. Looking back at him was his brother. Frantically, he threw the door open and stumbled out. He yanked the curtain aside and came out into the aisle, only to see Yohan sitting in his seat. After a moment's hesitation, Reverend Ryu Yosŏp stepped forward, looking his brother straight in the eye as he made his way back to his seat. When he got to it, however, it was empty. As he turned to sit down, he looked behind him and saw his brother's face appear in the back of his seat. He went ahead and sat down. Crushing his brother's phantom with his body, Yosŏp leaned back into the seat.

Yosŏp, Yosŏp!

Startled, he jumped up, then sat back down, mumbling to himself, Don't do this—it's futile. Once you're gone, you're gone—that's all there is to it. What reason do you have to keep showing up like this?

I want to go home, too—that's what.

The plane seemed to drop all of a sudden, and the cabin shook a few times. Yosŏp hastily fastened his seat belt and sat up straight. Maybe I had a little too much wine. He felt as if he and his brother had become one and the same being. His mind grew hazy and soon only his brother's murmurs were audible:

I want to go to our hometown with you, to Ch'ansaemgol, to the old days. Look over there, you can see the nettle tree. We never could get our arms all the way around its trunk. They said it'd been there forever, since long before we were born, so it must be hundreds of years old.

❧   ❧   ❧

The tree stood strong all throughout the war, so it'll probably still be the same as it's always been. Roots that look like the fingers and toes of some giant would crawl out above the surface at the base of the trunk, stretching out in all directions. The scars here and the gnarls there, the bark, wrinkled like the skin of an old man—all inspire awe. The tangled mass of branches looks like a head of hair, the strands reaching up towards the sky. The pieces of cloth the villagers have knotted onto almost every branch all billow together in the wind, a rainbow of five colors—yellow, blue, red, white and black. It will be dusk soon, and under the tree a woman in white sits with her back against the setting sun. She has a bowl of clear water set on a little table before her. She is praying fervently to the divine spirits. Big Brother Yohan whispers nearby. Look—it's Great-grandma. The woman in white, her hair white, and the band around her head white, too, is Great-grandmother. At home they call her Big Grandma. I'm on my way back from the fields, and Big Grandma motions to me, calling me over.

Little One, Little One!

My name's Yosŏp, not Little One.

Big Grandma gestures wildly, as if something is wrong.

Your pa and grandpa will be punished—the heavens will punish them. Possessed by the Western spirit, they gave you and your brother such hideous names!

They say God is one and the same everywhere, in all countries.

Well, I know everything, everything from the very beginning. Those big noses just came here with their books and spread them all over the place. Our ancestor, the founding father of our race, was Tan'gun. He came down from the heavens a long, long time ago.

They say that's not so. They say that Jesus Christ is our Lord and Savior.

People should worship their ancestors properly if they want to be proper human beings. Our country has gone to the dogs because so many have started worshiping someone else's God.

Big Grandma wraps up the water bowl, the little wooden table, the candle, and the incense burner in a square of cloth. Then, facing the *changsŭng pŏpsu** chiseled into the stone post along the road, next to the cairn, she says, Come, Little One—bow to him.

Pah, what's it even supposed to be?

The spirit of Mount Ami, of course. The honorable spirit who protects children from catching the Guest. Worship him well and you won't get sick. You'll live a long, long life.

If Father finds out I'll be in big trouble.

Tell them Big Grandma told you to, and neither your pa nor your grandpa will dare lift a finger—don't you worry. What are you waiting for? Come on now, quit dawdling and bow!

I'm a bit frightened and I feel kind of strange, but Big Grandma has

---

* *Changsŭng pŏpsu*: an iconic representation of a local deity.

given me an order, and I'm tempted by the guarantee of protection against smallpox, the Guest that could leave my face ugly and pockmarked. The *changsŭng pŏpsu* has a tiny nose and eyes that poke out like a pair of glasses. Its mouth is a slit stretching from cheek to cheek, with fierce looking canines sticking sharply out at each corner.

Big Grandma, if this *changsŭng pŏpsu* helps children, how come it looks so scary?

Ah, that—that's to scare away the Guest, the barbarian spirit from the faraway lands south of the sea. Come on now, hurry up and bow.

I finally give in and bow, but it's the kind of bow I'd give to a Japanese teacher who has a sword at his waist—my heart shriveled with fear. I am so sick with dread that as soon as I finish bowing I take off running for our neighborhood. It isn't just frightening, it's unfamiliar. Big Grandma may be friendly with it, but I can't shake the feeling that the heavens will punish me for what I've done. The incident stays with me for a long time.

❖   ❖   ❖

Again, Big Brother's voice:

You know, the day I was named deacon, I took the young men in the church and we uprooted that thing. We threw it away in the thicket along the stream. That hideous monster lay there in the grass for a year or two before a flood finally washed it away.

Again, I heard myself answering.

Well, I don't think what I did was right. I bowed in spite of myself because I was afraid of the Guest—because even if you survive you're scarred for life.

Unlike the rest of the family, who were all busy in their own way, Big Grandma and I didn't have much to do. We spent hours together in her room across from the main wing. With nothing but sisters and a ten-year difference between Yohan and myself, there was no one around for me to play with. Whenever I dropped by Big Grandma's room she offered me all kinds of goodies—the grown-ups brought her all the best seasonal foods and she always had some hidden away for me. Melons, watermelons, and peaches in the summer; chestnuts, dates, and apples in the fall—which were too common to be really inviting—and honeyed wheat cakes and even baked sweet potatoes in the winter. Grandma told me all kinds of stories.

"If you go fifty *ri** from our village towards the setting sun, you can see Mount Kuwŏl. At the top of Sahwang Peak, there is a rocky cliff that looks like a paneled-wood door. In the olden days Grandfather Tan'gun— he's the one that founded our nation—would come down and stay there sometimes, and whenever he went back up to heaven they say he hid his sword and armor behind that stone door. That's why that rock's called the Armoring Stone. Some time ago the Japanese came and cracked that cliff trying to steal away the hidden sword and armor, but they just ended up spending a whole lot of money for nothing. Here in our Chosŏn, we say the son of God is Tan'gun, the Honorable Grandfather. When I was young, I, too, once climbed all the way up Mount Kuwŏl. There's a temple there called P'aeyŏpsa, and on the peak across from the temple you've got the Tan'gun Platform. They say that was where Grandfather Tan'gun, standing on the flat stone, looked down to choose the very best place for his people to settle. That very best place is the place we call Changjaeibŏl today. They even have writing there that says 'Tan'gun Platform,' and you can see the equipment the Honorable Tan'gun used to shoot arrows, and even the spot where he placed his knee when he took aim. Tan'gun's footprints, the ones he made when he crossed from Siru Peak in front of the temple all the way to Sŏngdangri—you can see those, too.

"Your Big Grandma grew up in Namuribŏl in Chaeryŏng, and your great-grandpa and I are both from families that never had to worry about putting food on the table. Both our families worked as agents for the landowners— we farmed the land that belonged to the palace. In the very beginning, all of Hwanghae Province belonged to the palace. Your grandfathers were all diligent workers, and they even managed to buy a bit of land—and back then there weren't many landowners to speak of, you know. But after the Japanese took over, all the land belonging to the palace was given to the Oriental Development Company, the Financial Union, or the Industrial Bank—that's why your grandpa's the only one still farming our land and why your pa has to work as a clerk for the Oriental Development Company.

"Your grandpa ended up believing in those Western ghosts all because he made the wrong kinds of friends. I hear that those big-nose missionaries,

---

* *Ri*: a Korean unit of distance equal to 393 meters.

the ones who keep spreading the tales about those ghosts, I hear they first got into Chosŏn through Sollaep'o, in Changyŏn. Ever since then, everybody in Changyŏn, rich or poor, believes in those Western spirits. That boy from Changyŏn, the one who made friends with your grandpa—the one who became an elementary school teacher—he's just like his crazy parents— he's a Western-spirit freak. In the town of Sinch'ŏn, too, I hear they built a mission home or a chapel—whatever it is they call it—and every day the young ones gather there to talk about who knows what. How can a mother win over a full-grown son? Even the ancestor tablet that stood in our living room has been smashed, though it was terrible for me to bear.

"The village women came and said something awful was happening, and I asked what. They said, 'Your son, your son is in the chapel, and he's doing the rite of receiving a spirit.' 'Receiving what?' I asked them, and they said, 'It means your son, he's being possessed.' I ran like hell, let me tell you. When I got there I found them asking this and answering that and rubbing his head with water. They told me that was the sign a Western spirit has come into your body. It reminded me of my husband and how he wailed his heart out when he got home, after they chopped his topknot off in the marketplace. I cried and cried and beat the ground with my fists. After that your grandpa became a very high shaman of the Western spirit. And now, now, how can I stop him from turning his own offspring into Jesus freaks? You tell me! Your own father aside, even the girl he brought into this family under the name of daughter-in-law was the child of a Jesus shaman . . . so, there, you listen well—never forget what I'm telling you now.

"Your grandpa wasn't really the first son in the family. In fact, he was the youngest of my three sons—his two older brothers died, and then he was my only son. You, too, have to be careful. You don't know how scary the Guest can be, do you? Just over the past few years, in this valley alone, hundreds of children have died from it. Even if you survive, I'm telling you, it's no use—the Guest scars you, it scars your face, leaves you marked for life.

"Once the Guest started spreading, the doctors would only visit the rich—in the countryside you couldn't even get hold of a blind medicine man. Consulting a shaman was the best you could do. But wine and meat were impossible to find, and unless you had offerings or money you couldn't even dream of having a full exorcism. You could place a gourd down on top of the water jar and chant a sutra while beating it. When more and more people started falling ill, they built a makeshift shelter outside the village to house them, gave them rice, soy sauce, and salt to live on by themselves. Even family members weren't allowed to go near them. They were mostly children, you understand, but there were a few adults, too—when a grown-up died the oldest child would take care of the family. And, well, who wouldn't cherish their own flesh and blood? So some people would keep their sick child until they just couldn't hang on any longer, and then they'd wrap it up in a skirt or cloth and go up to the mountain in the middle of the night. In the mountain they'd find a tall tree and tie the child to one of the branches, and then they'd come back down. Heaven only knows where all the crows came from, but they'd flock to the babe and peck out its eyes. Sometimes, though, the child wasn't dead yet—so the parents would stay all night long to keep the birds away. If the death was a long one, the parents would have to guard the tree night after night for days on end. Ever since we were children we have known that the Guest is a Western disease. A barbarian disease, they call it, from the Western country, so it's certain that it came from the land where they believe in the Western spirit, you see? I had to send away two sons, your grandpa's two older brothers, with the Guest. So would I be overjoyed, would I be ready to believe in the Western spirit like my one surviving son—or would I be angry at it—angry forever? You tell me. I'm telling you, a man needs to understand where he comes from in order to be truly human, to be blessed."

Over the years, my grandfather doubled the land he inherited from my great grandfather, and my father managed the orchards of the Development Company very well. By the time we were liberated from Japan, we were one of the richest families in the village. My grandfather and my father, together with the Christian landowners in the neighboring village, went on to build a church in Ch'ansaemgol—Kwangmyŏng Church. It was much bigger and had many more believers than the one already in town. My great-grandmother passed away before the liberation.

◆ ◆ ◆

Reverend Ryu Yosŏp waited in the front room of the nursing home—it resembled the lobby of a small hotel. He drank cold water from a paper cup. A number of potted ferns lined the hall, and there was an aquarium, too. A middle-aged woman was tapping away at a computer, behind a counter that looked exactly like a hospital reception desk.

Immediately upon his arrival in L.A., Yosŏp had contacted the travel agency to confirm the arrangements for his visit to North Korea, and then he called Pak Myŏngsŏn. Despite some initial hesitation, she gave him the visiting hours and address of the nursing home in which she lived. After arranging to spend the night with a close friend, a younger minister, Yosŏp unpacked his luggage and headed straight for the nursing home. According to one of the attendants, she'd gone out for a walk in the park and was due to return in about twenty minutes.

Tucked in the middle of the rectangular main building was a cozy little garden with a fountain. A line of palm trees stood in single file, their long leaves drooping down low. Every now and then an elderly woman would pass by through the corridor. It was probably some sort of condominium-style nursing home.

"So. Here you are."

At some point a Yorkshire terrier had sauntered up to him; it was sniffing his knee. Yosŏp lifted his head and saw the old lady who held the other end of the leash. She wore a patternless baggy brown dress and a pair of glasses tinted slightly red. The dog wagged its tail and busily scurried back and forth between its owner and Yosŏp. He got up slowly and bowed to her, bending deep enough at the waist for his hair to fall forward.

"How do you do? I am the younger brother of Presbyter Ryu Yohan."

Holding the rim of her spectacles in one hand, the old lady slowly scanned Yosŏp from head to toe. Gesturing for him to follow, she led the way to the elevator.

The place was quite large for a studio apartment. The kitchen and living room were essentially part of the same space, but the table and chairs, as well as an armchair and a TV set, had been placed a small distance from the rest of the living area—an arrangement that kept the place from feeling too crowded. There was a door next to the kitchen, and the front part of the living room was screened off with a curtain. Behind it would probably be the old lady's bed. She seemed to have had a perm some time ago, but now her white hair was cut short, right under the ears, and looked quite tidy. Yosŏp looked around the room, and then, as was his habit, gathered both hands between his knees and said a short prayer under his breath. Standing in front of the sink, the old lady looked at Yosŏp, who was sitting in the armchair, and asked, "Are you praying?"

Without answering, Yosŏp kept mumbling and finished the last phrase before lifting his head. The old lady was looking at him, a curious smile hovering over the corners of her mouth.

"I beg your pardon?"

"I asked if you were praying."

"Yes, I am a . . . minister. Aren't you Christian?"

"I'm not sure if you people have the right to ask such questions."

Pak Myŏngsŏn, took out some chilled corn tea from the refrigerator and poured it into a glass.

"Well, would you like a cup of coffee?"

"No, but I would like a glass of water, please."

She placed the glass of corn tea on the small table in front of him and returned to the dinner table to sit down.

"So. What was it that you wanted to see me for?"

"Do you know my brother well?"

The old lady turned slightly away from the table and took off her glasses.

"I know both Yohan and you very well."

Something behind her wrinkled face was vaguely familiar to Yosŏp, but he couldn't quite place it.

"Have you forgotten the family from Palsan that was so rich with daughters?"

In his mind, Yosŏp tried to clothe this tall, skinny old woman in *hanbok*. Ah, this was none other than that girl, the lady evangelist, the tall, older girl who'd been the vice chair of the youth group at Kwangmyŏng Church. Palsan was a neighboring village. It leaned up against a different mountain ridge, but the fields of the two villages were connected, so the people of both shared their sorrows and joys through all four seasons. Yosŏp managed to recall the name of a girl his age.

"Now I remember, you're . . . In . . . Insŏn's big sister."

"Yes, Insŏn was our fourth."

A summer day full of towering cumulous clouds. Cicadas drone atop the willow trees as a group of naked children line up to jump from a hillside into a stream, wetting their ears with saliva and holding their noses shut with one hand. There, mixed in with all these boys, is a girl—Insŏn. Evening comes and we're absorbed in a game of "catch-the-thief," when suddenly we hear, loud enough to ring through the entire field, "Hey, Insŏn! You're gonna get it from Mom! Get your butt in here and eat your dinner!" The voice of the older sister, Myŏngsŏn, the eldest in a family teeming with daughters.

"Where's Insŏn living now?"

Reverend Ryu Yosŏp was smiling at the aged Pak Myŏngsŏn as if they were children once more, but in lieu of an answer she took out a pack of Lucky Strikes from a cabinet drawer. She pulled one out—it had no filter. Lucky Strikes had been an established favorite among soldiers during the Korean War, and even though Yosŏp's chair was on the other side of the room, he recognized the red circle logo at once. Myŏngsŏn lit the cigarette and exhaled a couple of times.

"My oldest lives in Philly, and the younger one is here in L.A."

His question forgotten, Yosŏp merely listened to the sound of her voice. It was, in fact, Myŏngsŏn who continued, asking him, "You say that Yohan died?"

"Yes. The day before yesterday, in the evening. It was peaceful, as if in his sleep. I saw your name in his planner, so . . . I called you. You said he arranged a visit?"

The old lady was still puffing away—a long, deep exhalation.

"Well, all things come to an end when you die, don't they," said the old lady, as if to herself. She turned to Yosŏp.

"How old were you during the war?"

"Thirteen or fourteen, I think"

"Insŏn died a *while* ago. Chinsŏn, Yŏngsŏn . . . and the youngest, Tŏksŏn, too. They all died."

For a fleeting moment Yosŏp's dream came back to him, and the countless deaths from the winter of that year whizzed by in front of him like a slide show.

"So it happened during the war. But . . . didn't your family attend church?"

"Just mother and me," Pak Myŏngsŏn murmured. "I wonder how it ever occurred to Ryu Yohan to come and see me."

"You never had any contact with him before then?"

"He might have kept in touch with the father of my children."

"Where does he live?"

"In Seoul. You'd probably recognize him if you saw him."

Nothing surprised Yosŏp any more. Sangho had been best friends with Yohan, and he had a younger brother named Sunho who was around the same age as Yosŏp: two families, two sets of brothers. Back then, Sunho's family had owned an orchard.

"Didn't Sangho come to the States with you?"

"He didn't want to. He's still living in Seoul."

For quite a long while the two sat apart from each other, neither one saying a word. Pak Myŏngsŏn glanced at the digital clock that hung on the wall opposite the dinner table. Yosŏp got to his feet.

"You see, the thing is, I'm actually going home, to visit."

"Where . . . to North Korea?"

"Yes. If you have anyone you'd like to send word to . . . "

The old lady shook her head faintly. Yosŏp turned to leave, but stopped short at the door. Myŏngsŏn didn't follow him out; she simply got to her feet and stood in front of the table.

"Do you not go to church anymore?"

In answer to Yosŏp's question, she shook her head. It was the most definitive motion she had made throughout the course of their half-hour meeting.

"No. Never again."

❖ ❖ ❖

Icy mist slides slowly down the black hillside, twirling around the naked branches, and settles down on the ground. I shoulder a knapsack pieced together from an old army uniform and follow him. The first group, the ones lucky enough to make it onto a truck, have already left earlier in the evening. Those who lagged behind have been told to get to the ocean to hitch a ride on a boat. My man is wearing a winter cap and, like me, he's got a knapsack on his back. My Sangho is carrying his carbine upside down—he's still in his field jacket with the Youth Corps armband. With two *mal** of rice on my back, it's tough for me to keep up with him. Every now and then he turns around and hurries me along with an irritated grunt. Our village finally comes into view. We enter a narrow alley and find the whole place blanketed in silence. Taking his carbine off his shoulder and holding

---

* *Mal*: unit of measurement for grains and liquid; two *mal* equals about ten gallons.

it at the ready, Sangho slows his steps. This time, I lead the way—I know the shortcut to my house better. We turn at the stone fence and as I open the bush-clover gate my foot catches on something. My breath catches in my throat and I just stand there nailed to the ground, unable to stop trembling—it's Sangho who kneels down to try shaking her awake. Even in the dark Mother's white *chŏgori* is clearly visible. As if nothing is out of the ordinary, he calmly turns the flashlight towards our little two-room house, sweeping the beam of light into every nook and cranny. I look, too. My younger sisters lie side by side, all dead. The room reeks of blood. Hastily, he turns off the flashlight and the figures vanish, buried in the darkness. Over the years, only the image of Tŏksŏn will stay with me. Her thin wrist rests on the doorsill. Motionless, she is looking in my direction with her mouth slightly open. I try to stifle my cries, to keep from screaming out loud, and Sangho drags me back out into the front yard. Mother, lying prone on the ground, stirs ever so faintly. Mother! Wake up! She motions for me to leave, to run away. Who, who's done this to you?

❖   ❖   ❖

It was around ten o'clock when Yosŏp returned to his lodgings. From the nursing home he had gone to Koreatown for dinner. There, for the first time in a long while, he drank some *soju** all by himself. The younger minister had been waiting for him. Opening the door to let Yosŏp in, the man seemed somewhat bewildered at the smell of alcohol that accompanied his arrival.

"Did something happen?"

Yosŏp answered with a smile, saying nothing. To the "Good night" that floated up from the bottom of the stairs, Yosŏp simply raised one hand and graced his host with a grand little wave.

Collapsing into bed, Yosŏp was overcome by a rather pleasant, hazy sinking sensation—a feeling that was soon interrupted by the realization that something was prodding him in the behind. He rolled over on his side and reached back. The instant he took it out of his back pocket he realized what it was—the leather pouch. His heart pounding violently, he untied the string wound tightly around its mouth and removed the sliver of bone.

---

* *Soju:* distilled grain-based Korean liquor known for its potency.

It was about as big as the joint of a finger and shaped like an ivory *tojang*, though only half the normal size. Yosŏp held the thing between his thumb and forefinger, turning it this way and that, examining it from every angle. It looked like a compass you might read about, the kind one could use on a journey in some fairy tale. He put it back in the pouch, refastened the string, and tossed it on the nightstand.

Yosŏp got out of his clothes and slid underneath the sheet. He was right on the verge of falling asleep when something inside his throat suddenly rose up and passed through his neck to his skull, and suddenly Yohan's soft voice was with him again.

You knew, you knew all along, and you just kept quiet about it, didn't you?

What do you mean I knew? Knew what?

The things we did during those forty-five days.

I only know what I saw.

You've been to see Myŏngsŏn, haven't you? Her family, every last one of them—I did them in. What do you have to say to that?

What could possibly make you do something that hideous?

Just . . . well, you'll understand it all later.

Sangho, wasn't he your close friend?

He was. That little shit took out more people than I did.

But you two were on the same side, weren't you?

Hey, hey, enough of that. We're not on any side.

❧   ❧   ❧

Long, long ago, an American ship called the *General Sherman* sailed out of Tianjin harbor in China. The owner of the ship, a man named Preston, had heard rumors that precious treasures were buried in the royal tombs of Pyongyang in the Chosŏn kingdom. Acting in concert with a British firm, Meadows and Company, he set out for Chosŏn on June 18, 1866. His ship carried Western goods popular in China at the time and an assortment of weapons, not to mention nineteen sailors, two friends named Wilson and Hogarth, a Danish man named Page who acted as captain, and a Protestant minister of Scottish origins known as Thomas—the designated interpreter and guide.

Prior to this journey, while doing missionary work in Shandong, Thomas had encountered two men from Chosŏn who claimed to be believers of the Catholic faith. The Reverend Thomas longed to spearhead the first Protestant mission in Chosŏn, known then as a mysterious hermit nation. Setting out with this goal in mind, he eventually reached Paengnyŏng Island, off the west coast of Hwanghae Province. There he remained for two and a half months, handing out sixteen copies of the Bible (translated into Chinese) to the islanders. Apparently under the impression that Chosŏn was some kind of tiny, feudal realm, Thomas reportedly tried to meet the king in person in order to get direct permission to carry out his sacred mission. He was, however, unable even to find his way to Seoul. As it was his first time in the country, he promised himself he would one day return and headed back to China. With that first event serving as the impetus, the Reverend Thomas applied himself to studying the Korean language. Eventually, he became competent enough to communicate directly with native Koreans. He even gave himself a Korean name, Ch'oe Ranhŏn, using Chinese characters.

Due to a minor disturbance caused by the invasion of a French fleet a few months before the *General Sherman*'s arrival, the royal court of Chosŏn was adamantly against the entry of foreign ships into any of the nation's ports. On the night of July 11, the *General Sherman* sailed up the Taedong River and dropped anchor at Sinjangp'o in Ch'oribang, Pyongyang Prefecture. A great commotion ensued, as the general populace understandably assumed that the French fleet, which they heard had retreated, was mounting another attack. The governor of P'yŏngan Province dispatched his number one man to ascertain the purpose of the ship's visit to his shores and to observe its general movement. When the man arrived, Ch'oe Ranhŏn, that is, Reverend Thomas came forth to act as the interpreter. Thomas introduced his company, explained that their sole aim was that of commercial trade, and suggested the friendly exchange of various Western goods with Chosŏn articles such as gold, ginseng, paper, and fur. In addition, Thomas clarified that his party consisted not of troublemaking Catholics but of peaceful Protestants. The governor's man replied that Chosŏn law not only prohibited trade with all Westerners, it explicitly forbade the presence of Protestants as well as Catholics. He asked for their immediate departure, even supplying food to replenish their stores, as per their request, in the hopes that this would send them on their way. On July 13, however, the *General Sherman* simply sailed farther up the river and dropped anchor again at Turodo, slightly below Man'gyŏngdae, and sailed up and down along the river in a small boat, observing the state of affairs in the city of Pyongyang.

The official Protestant stance, however, is slightly different. They insist that from the outset, they mistook the Taedong River in Pyongyang for the Han River in Seoul. Upon his arrival, they say, the Reverend Thomas came ashore at Changsap'o, in the vicinity of Sŏkhojŏng, and began handing out Chinese translations of the Bible along with various missionary pamphlets to a crowd who had gathered on a hillside to get a glimpse of the *General Sherman*. It is likely that the governor's men, who had a duty to fulfill, felt the need to put a stop to this activity. On the sixteenth, these Korean officials were taken aboard the *General Sherman* and held as hostages.

On this last point, too, the Protestants have their own story. The Reverend Thomas, they say, tried to reason with the governor's men, reiterating the purpose of their visit to Chosŏn: "We did not come to your nation to do harm; we have no underhanded schemes. We only aim to, first, share Christianity with you. Second, we hope to trade wonderful goods with you, and third, we wish to appreciate the beautiful scenery and famous historic sights of your land."

It was during this discourse, according to the Protestants, that an official document was found on one of the governor's men, a document containing an order to the effect that the crew of the *General Sherman* was to be lured onto land and massacred. They say the crew was so outraged by this discovery that they took the men hostage, and not for any other reason.

Greatly dismayed, the perturbed provincial governor dispatched an officer in an attempt to conduct some sort of negotiation, but the Westerners refused to settle for anything less than open trade. On the nineteenth, the *General Sherman* set sail once again, traveling even further up the river to Hwanggangjŏng, where they dropped anchor once more and took to smaller boats so that they could move up the Crow Rapids. The populace, shocked and enraged by this inexcusably rude behavior, gathered en masse along the riverside. The people chanted in unison demanding the release of the hostages and mounted an attack built around the legendary Pyongyang stone-throwing technique, whereupon the government soldiers joined in, doing their part by shooting arrows and firing guns. In the midst of this pandemonium the hostages somehow managed to escape from the ship.

The Western ship, far from turning back, responded by raiding the village along the river, looting food and cattle and killing people.

On the morning of July 22, an intense battle broke out. Chosŏn government troops began by showering artillery fire. The *Sherman* countered with its two cannons. Though the *Sherman* was able to block her opponents' artillery fire for a time and employed the use of both cannons and rifles, the limited gunpowder and manpower on board was exhausted by the end of a full day's combat. On the following day, the twenty-third, the *General Sherman* started its retreat downriver. Downstream, however, the Chosŏn soldiers that had been ambushed earlier lay in wait, ready to carry out what would prove to be a virtually ceaseless series of attacks. Meanwhile, the river itself, which had been swelled by a particularly rainy spell, was growing shallower; at the end of an ongoing offensive-defensive battle that lasted three days, the ship became stuck in a sandbank. At this point, the people of Pyongyang set fire to several boats and sailed them down the river. As intended, the *Sherman* caught fire and its crew, no longer able to resist, came out on the bow to plead for mercy. The ship's remaining gunpowder exploded and its barrels of oil burned fiercely. Some of the crew jumped into the river and drowned; those who reached land were slaughtered by the murderous crowd. The Protestants remember the scene of the Reverend Thomas's martyrdom as follows:

"The Reverend Thomas did not consider running away to save his life. Instead, he did his utmost to save the Bibles he had brought with him from the flames and deliver them to the people of Chosŏn. He carried a box full of Bibles on his back, and, avoiding the fire, climbed up a low hill along the shore. We are told that he took out the Bibles one at a time and tossed them to the people standing along the hillside.

"'Oh, Lord, bless these poor souls who do not yet know the Gospel!'"

It is said that even as he was dragged to Yanggakto along the Taedong River, Reverend Thomas never ceased calling out the name of Jesus Christ. On September 6, at dusk, the twenty-seven-year-old Thomas was beheaded. Thus was the first seed of Protestantism sown in the northwest region of the nation. Church history states that Pak Ch'un'gwŏn, a Chosŏn government military officer, was Reverend Thomas's executioner. It is claimed that this man later repented and was baptized, becoming the first Protestant believer in Pyongyang.

The first Protestant church in Chosŏn was established in Hwanghae Province in the 1880s, when Protestant ministers who had settled in China began traveling back and forth across the border to Ŭiju, spreading the word of God. One of Chosŏn's first Protestant believers, a man named Sŏ Sangnyun, later left the area to avoid government persecution and went into hiding with relatives. It was Sŏ who would eventually become the founder of the Protestant church in Hwanghae Province.

Sollae in Changyŏn is a beautiful place—a stream flows down from Hunam, running through a luxuriant forest of pine trees and into the ocean. Kumip'o, too, is lovely, with its gold and silver sands that stretch out for miles on end. Fifty-eight households were then living in Sollae; fifty of them became believers. In 1887, the Reverend Underwood visited Sollae. He chose seven among the believers and baptized them. Over the seven years that followed, the villagers put enough money away to build what would be the first church in Chosŏn.

In old photographs, the church appears to be nothing more than a rundown tile-roofed house of about a dozen square yards. In front of the latticed sliding door a small, covered porch has been built in place of the usual wood *maru.** That would have been where they took off their shoes when they entered the church. A tall zelkova tree stands behind the house, big enough to cover the roof; more likely than not, it had served the entire village as a shrine before the arrival of Christianity. Neat rows of perennial plants line the front of the yard.

After Underwood came Appenzeller, who passed through Sollae on his missionary journey across the northwest region, and after him was the Reverend Gale, who stayed for a while to learn the language and customs of Chosŏn. Gale, in turn, was followed by Moffett, a missionary. The one who actually settled down in Sollae for life was a farmer-turned-missionary named Fenwick, but it was the Reverend McKenzie who ultimately formed the deepest ties with the Ryu family. McKenzie had been working as a minister in a Presbyterian Church in Labrador, Canada. In the fall of 1893, he just happened to come to Chosŏn.

Cho Pansŏk, a childhood friend of Yosŏp's grandfather, was three years

---

* *Maru*: a raised wooden floor; the main communal space in a traditional Korean house, sometimes opening onto the yard.

his senior—which would mean that he was born in 1877. Cho's folks were originally a tenant family, but with the money they saved from croaker fishing at Yŏnp'yŏng in Paengnyŏng they were able to buy a boat and some rice fields, elevating themselves to the status of middle-class farmers. It was after Reverend Underwood's visit that Cho's father, one of the founding members of the church, first became a zealous believer of Jesus, and it is said that he was baptized immediately upon the church's completion. Later on, when the Fenwicks and Underwoods took up residence in Sollae, Cho Pansŏk's father not only arranged for his son to participate in their Bible studies, he also insisted the boy run errands for the Westerners and frequent their homes. Yosŏp's grandfather first became acquainted with the young Cho Pansŏk at one of the annual farmers' gatherings in Sinch'ŏn. Pansŏk had learned a method of tomato and cabbage cultivation from Fenwick and was traveling around the Changyŏn area to teach this new method of farming and, of course, hand out copies of the Bible in vernacular Korean. As luck would have it, this was around the same time that Yosŏp's grandfather Samsŏng had started opening his eyes and embracing the word of God. Before long, they say, Yosŏp's grandfather was always at Pansŏk's heel, trailing after him as if he were a real, blood-related big brother.

"Samsŏng, would you like to visit our village?"

"Do you mean it? Oh, Brother Pansŏk, I can't wait to see the church in Sollae!"

Grandfather's heart was filled with excitement at the prospect of finally seeing it all: the picture of Jesus, the globe that was said to show the world in one glance, the Bible with the leather cover, the cross figure on which Jesus was crucified, and, most of all, the real, live Reverend Mae Kyŏnsi.

In Korean, the Reverend McKenzie's name was spelled Mae Kyŏnsi. He was known to go through his daily routine in a coarse, cotton farmer's outfit, even wearing ordinary straw shoes. He only wore his suit and tie on Sundays for worship. This was probably due to the influence of his predecessor, Fenwick. Fenwick had been known as missionary P'yŏn Wiik. Right at the outset, Missionary P'yŏn had chosen the outer wing of Cho Pansŏk's house as his residence. Because of this, Pansŏk was able to learn English and read the Bible from a very early age; he came to realize that the world outside of Chosŏn was enormous, not to mention enlightened and civilized. Pansŏk's knowledge of such things would no doubt have impressed

Yosŏp's grandfather immensely. In his youth, Yosŏp's grandfather, Ryu Samsŏng, had attended the Confucian academy in his village and studied very diligently, all in accordance with his family's hopes that he would pass a provincial examination offered in Haeju and perhaps even earn a low-level government position someday—a dream born of the fact that the Ryus had lived in servitude for generations upon end, harboring resentment and envy of anyone with a government post of any kind. By the time Yosŏp's great-grandfather had started following the Eastern Learning movement, however, it is likely that his son Samsŏng had already given up on the idea of taking the government examination. It became clear afterwards that in the Year of the Horse, the year Grandfather first met Cho Pansŏk and became a believer, the Eastern Learning rebellion was already sweeping through the nation; this fact greatly increases the likelihood that Yosŏp's great-grandfather either dropped dead on the road from some random disease or was beaten to death somewhere along the way. In any event, by that point the Ryu family was by no means financially uncomfortable: they owned acre upon acre of rice fields, fields they had hoarded for untold generations, a little bit at a time, as they managed the land in the name of the royal family.

❖　❖　❖

Yosŏp and Yohan, listen carefully.

I will always remember the first time I visited Sollae with Presbyter Cho Pansŏk. Reverend Mae Kyŏnsi was living in front of the church in a mud hut with a thatched roof. Brother Pansŏk told me a thing or two before I went to see him, so I bought two dozen eggs in Changyŏn. Western people like eggs, pheasants, dried fish, flour, and things like that. The Reverend Mae was about thirty or so. Brother Pansŏk went up to the wooden porch and said, "Are you in, Reverend?" Then the Reverend said, "Come in, please"—all in our language, perfect and clear. He was wearing round glasses and he was wearing *hanbok*, woolen vest and all. When Pansŏk said I was someone who studied the Bible with him, Reverend Mae nodded and held my hands—his hands were warm. He had a calendar on the wall. It was a solar calendar, they tell me. Also on the wall was a wall clock. I'd never seen a wall clock before, and every time the pendulum swung back and forth I couldn't help swinging my head back and forth along with it.

Reverend Mae Kyŏnsi showed us the Bible with the thick leather cover, then he showed us a picture framed in glass. That was the first time I saw Jesus. The first Jesus I saw looked like Reverend Mae in many ways—you see, both had brown hair on their heads and grew hair under the nose and chin. Jesus had his hair grown long, like a woman, but he, too, had a big nose because he was a Westerner. Reverend Mae Kyŏnysi asked me, "How long have you been studying the Bible?"

Pansŏk answered for me, saying, "We read the Korean version together from cover to cover—I did the explanations."

Tenderly, Reverend Mae looked me in the face. "Is that so? Which part do you like best?"

"I remember the scene where Abraham offers his own son as a sacrifice and then receives the revelation of faith in God."

Hearing my answer, Reverend Mae nodded slowly.

"Abraham was a chosen man. God chooses with love all the Christians who believe in Him."

My dear grandchildren, Yohan and Yosŏp—mind my words. That day I received many blessings from Reverend Mae Kyŏnsi. His voice still rings loud and clear in my ears. Do you know what I learned that day? The mission of the believer and the great love of our Father in Heaven. Reverend Mae Kyŏnsi visited the Bible reading group we organized in Sinch'ŏn. He baptized me, and in the summer of that year he died of sunstroke during his mission tour. Brother Pansŏk and I went to Pyongyang to attend a revival service—I'm sure you heard all about what happened then. That was when I returned home and smashed our ancestral tablet, the false idol your great-grandmother worshipped. I graduated from the Pyongyang Seminary and became a minister. Your mother is the daughter of a minister who went to school with me—both the families of your mother and your father are people who have been chosen by God.

❖ ❖ ❖

You see, Big Brother, rather than ruthlessly destroying Nineveh, God spared the people—so He Himself told Jonah. Now it's time for you to let go of resentment and hatred, time to enter heaven. Our ancestors would wish that for you also.

Hey, hey, there isn't an iota of resentment left in me. Life itself is a curse, isn't it? Damned if I know why the hell we were so frantic about everything back then.

Let's go visit our hometown together. After that you should go where you're supposed to go.

No place to go. We're just floating around together.

Who is "we"?

Oh, quite a bunch of us, really. Uncle Mole, Ichiro, and plenty more.

The girls I used to fetch rice for—are they there, too?

We're like particles of dust. There are many, many here.

The voice was gradually dying out, turning into other sounds. The faint ticking of the clock's second hand was growing more distinct, the fluorescent hands already pointing to three in the morning.

3

Keeper of the Netherworld

SWITCHING ROLES WITH THE DEAD

OVERNIGHT, LIKE SOME STORYBOOK adventurer, Yosŏp flew over the ocean in an enormous, bird-like Boeing and arrived in an entirely different world.

Waking up from a short nap, he found himself in China. At the hotel, the tour group was handed over to a North Korean travel agency. Their North Korean flight bound for Pyongyang was scheduled to leave the following day, so the group was on their own until the travel agency bus came to pick them up the next morning. On this tour, the group numbered thirty-six people. Twenty-five were from the U.S. and eleven were Korean-Japanese. They did no more than glance at each other's faces once or twice in the hotel lobby.

Two people were assigned to each room, and Reverend Ryu Yosŏp was no exception. His roommate was an old man, half bald, who looked to be about the same age as Yohan had been. It took a handshake and a couple of introductory niceties for Yosŏp to realize that the man was actually closer to his own age—only three years his senior. Now a professor at some university out West, the man said that Pyongyang was his hometown. Sitting on the two beds that were bolted to opposite walls of the room, the two old men rambled on about their lives in America and about their hometowns.

"People kept saying they were going to drop an atomic bomb on us, so we left, left without having any idea how we were going to make a living—we barely knew which way was south—we just dragged the entire family out onto the road."

The bald professor went on with his story.

"Rather than lose our entire family to the bomb, Grandfather decided that the oldest grandson, at least, should be taken down south to carry on the family line—that was the reasoning. The rest is history. I was just the second son, attending junior high school. Still, I was old enough to know what was what, and I resented the fact that Father was only taking my older brother to safety. I'd visited my aunt quite often over the holidays, so I figured I wouldn't have any trouble catching up to them on my own. I snuck out of the house without saying a word to Grandfather or Mother. Later, when Seoul was reclaimed, I ran into some people from my hometown who said they'd run into my father and older brother. Apparently Father turned back, worried about leaving the rest of us behind. My aunt's family probably went farther south for safety—I never was able to find them. All those years of suffering, alone, drifting all over the world, and it's only now, when I'm over sixty, that I get to go home and search for what might be left of my family. What kind of fate is this?"

Stories of families being separated during the war were so common that hearing only a few lines for each case, like the quick report you might catch on a TV newscast, was almost always enough to get an idea of what happened. And yet, despite the overarching similarities, there was always something about hearing it firsthand, directly from the lips of the survivor, that tugged at your heart. At around the same time the professor's family had been separated, Reverend Ryu Yosŏp's family had also been in the vicinity of Haeju. It was later on that Big Brother Yohan took a boat and retreated to Anmyŏn Island. Most of Yohan's friends had either enlisted on the spot or been transferred to a special unit.

"You said that your hometown is Pyongyang as well, Reverend, isn't that right?"

"Uh . . . yes, that's right."

"Any members of your family still around?"

"I was never able to find out. They're probably all dead by now. . . ." Yosŏp's words trailed off.

"I don't trust these guys. I can't even imagine how my family back home must have changed."

Yosŏp almost blurted out that maybe the professor ought to consider how much he himself had changed. Instead, he said, "Well, they probably don't trust us, either. After all, we did abandon our homes."

"No, no, I don't think so. They are the ones who harassed us—they wouldn't leave us alone. From the very beginning they refused to believe in anything other than the so-called fundamental class."

Yosŏp responded with a vague nod. Even among the North Koreans who ended up in America, there was a distinct trend: the more successful one was, the stronger his or her resentment towards the North. Yohan's case was understandable, to a degree, since he'd actually been involved in the fighting. This man, on the other hand, had never wronged his own people; judging from his story, he hadn't done much of anything but fall victim to a stroke of bad luck that landed him far from home. And yet, here he was, criticizing the North before they'd even arrived. Maybe it was all the time they'd spent living in such a different world—maybe time was to blame.

"Aren't you hungry? I'm thinking about going out to grab a bite to eat. Would you care to join me, Reverend?"

"Sure. The hotel food here will probably be just like the food on the plane; there must be a Korean restaurant somewhere around here."

Yosŏp and the professor left the hotel and wandered out into the business district. There they eventually discovered that restaurants in the immediate area would not be opening until dinnertime. With some help from a taxi driver, they made it to an alley crowded with small eateries, a touristy neighborhood. There were more than a few signs in Korean: Sŏrabŏl* Restaurant, Pubyŏngnu† Eatery, Moranbong‡ Restaurant, Koryŏ§ Restaurant, and so on. The professor had a thing or two to say about this, as well.

"Look at them. You see, even the restaurant signs here have political leanings."

"Well, then . . . perhaps Koryŏ Restaurant would be something neutral?"

---

* *Sŏrabŏl*: another name for the Silla period (57 B.C.–A.D. 935), which was located in a southern region of the Korean peninsula.
† *Pubyŏngnu*: a well-known pavillion in Pyongyang that overlooks the Taedong River.
‡ *Moranbong*: a mountain situated slightly to the north of Pyongyang and famed for its beauty.
§ *Koryŏ*: the Three Kingdoms were united at the beginning of the *Koryŏ* dynasty (918–1392).

The two men exchanged looks and went into the restaurant; as they'd expected, the place was run by Chosŏn folk whose families had immigrated to China several generations ago. The place was quite spacious. The tables were empty, but that might just have been the time of day: a bit too early for dinner and a lot too late for lunch.

"Let's see, what do I want?" the professor mumbled to himself, perusing a menu that consisted of pieces of paper pasted to the wall.

"I don't see any *toenjang tchigae** . . . excuse me, can you make the *nakchi pokkŭm*† very spicy?"

Hearing Yosŏp's order, the matronly server approached the table with a pretty little smile on her face.

"You, sirs, you're from America, aren't you?"

"That we are! How did you know?"

"People always ask for dishes they haven't had in a while—not to mention the way you're dressed."

"Well, what do people from Seoul do?"

"Oh, they just order anything, like soup and rice."

"Then we'll have that, too," said the professor cheerfully. Then, out of nowhere, he turned back to the woman. "Ma'am, which do you prefer, the South or the North?"

She flashed her friendly little smile again.

"That's the kind of question you ask to tease small children. 'Who do you like better, Mommy or Daddy?' It's the big nations that carry the guilt. After all, the ordinary, common folk haven't committed any crimes, have they?"

The professor laughed out loud.

"You have a way with words that would put a politician to shame."

Walking away from the table, the woman muttered under her breath, "I was wondering when you'd ask."

"I beg your pardon?"

She turned her head and spoke again in the way Chinese people speak, her words unhurried.

"I've repeated that same answer so many times it hurts my lips to say it."

---

* *Toenjang tchigae*: a stew made from *toenjang*, a soybean paste.
† *Nakchi pokkŭm*: sautéed octopus.

At any rate, Yosŏp's overall mood at the restaurant wasn't bad at all. The professor ordered a bottle of *chugyŏp ch'ŏngju** to accompany their meal, and the Reverend, unable to turn him down, ended up emptying three whole glasses. It didn't take long for him to start feeling the alcohol take effect.

Yosŏp returned to the hotel by himself. The professor wanted to have a look around the business district, but for Yosŏp the combination of a midday drinking bout with his already low tolerance had been more than enough to completely drain his body of any energy he might have had. He told the professor that he needed to rest. The fatigue, in part, was due to the three straight nights he had gone without sleep during his brother's wake in America. It occurred to Yosŏp that China was in the midst of a whirlwind of change, exactly the way Seoul had been long ago, around the time he immigrated to America. That was why the place felt so familiar. Beyond the main street, lined on either side with apartment complexes and random buildings, there would be back alleyways of old neighborhoods where screeching children black with dirt would run wild and old men would sit around in groups of three or four, maybe playing Chinese checkers. In a way, Yosŏp felt close to home already.

❧   ❧   ❧

Before my eyes I can see twinkling lights—they shatter like frog eggs, starting out garnet and then brightening into orange, then, slowly, a pale green, then yellow, and then finally blue—and all the while they are merging into one, these twinkling dots, undulating gently like a jellyfish. The thing moves away, fading into the darkness beyond. It is pitch black. Following it, I am sucked up into the darkness, breaking through to the other side. At the far end I can see a pinpoint of light; it grows bigger and bigger as I get closer and closer. Now I'm stepping down into a green meadow filled with sunlight. Each step I take feels nimble on the cushiony grass. There's a narrow path and the grass stretches all the way out to the top of a little hill, but I can't see anything beyond that from where I stand. A whitish gray trail of something, maybe fog or maybe smoke from someone's kitchen fire, is winding its way round and round the hilltop. As I walk up the narrow

---

* *Chugyŏp ch'ŏngju*: bamboo-leaf wine.

path the white fog-like stuff envelops me—it's everywhere—I can't see a thing. Then, straight ahead, something faint—it resembles a house. As I get closer I realize it is a wooden pavilion, bare, without a trace of lacquer or paint. The dark figure of a man is standing before it, facing me.

Who—who are you? I ask, stuttering in fear.

Me. It's me.

He takes a step forward, out of the fog, and suddenly I see him clearly, as if he alone has walked into a ray of sunlight. I recognize him at once. It is Uncle Sunnam, a field hand who once worked in our orchard.

Uh, what brings you here, Uncle?

I've come to accompany your older brother.

Big Brother Yohan has left already.

He's still wandering about, like me.

Then you should both repent and hurry on.

Ah, why don't you go look and see what's over there.

Through the stark, naked apple tree branches, I see a snow-covered field and a frozen brook glittering under the winter sunlight. It is Ch'ansaemgol, back in the old days. I feel like he is carrying me piggyback.

❧ ❧ ❧

"The Song of the General" filtered through the speakers as the Chosŏn Minhang airplane took off—just the melody, without the lyrics. The tempo quick, like a marching tune, it had been sung day in and day out at the People's Elementary and Middle schools in the years that followed the liberation. Maybe that was why it made Yosŏp's heart convulse. The professor who'd shared his room had trailed after him and taken the neighboring seat. Now, craning his neck, he peered past Yosŏp at the view out the window.

"Would you like to switch seats?" asked Reverend Ryu Yosŏp, not meaning a word of it.

"Oh, no, no thank you. I'll take a good look around later, when we're off the plane."

Despite his protests, however, the professor continued to strain himself, trying to look out the window over Yosŏp's shoulder. Judging from the panorama of wrinkled mountains that rolled out beneath them, the plane must have been flying over Manchuria. They might be near the Liaodong area. The voice of the captain filtered out from the loudspeaker.

"You are now entering the skies of our mother country. From now on, please remain seated and fasten your seat belts."

As he gazed down at the mountains and forests that looked so much like miniature models, at the tiny houses in the city, studded here and there like tiny grains of white sand, tears welled up in Yosŏp's eyes in spite of himself.

The plane flew low, so low that it actually seemed to graze a small hill covered in red soil and stunted fruit trees, and finally landed on the runway. Yosŏp looked out the window and saw a group of elementary school children, each one holding a bouquet, and some personnel from the Koreans Abroad Relief Committee, all lined up and looking bored.

❧ ❧ ❧

The Homeland Visitors were taken to the Koryŏ Hotel and, in the lobby, introduced to their guides: two men and one woman. The first man, in his fifties, was rather fat and had beady eyes; the other, in his forties, had oiled and neatly combed every last strand of his hair all the way back. This second man was extremely thin and looked particularly high-strung. The woman looked suave, though she, too, was somewhat on the plump side. She had a high soprano voice, took noticeably large steps when she walked, and also seemed to be in her forties. Although they'd all been introduced, Reverend Ryu Yosŏp knew there was no way he would remember their names, so he categorized each one in his mind under a nickname. Number one was "Fatty," number two was "All Back," and number three, the woman, was "Soprano." Fatty didn't talk much, and whenever his already small eyes happened to meet those of a visitor, he'd squeeze them shut altogether and smile gently. All Back was the one who came forward and handed out the day's agenda.

"First, everyone will go to his assigned room and unpack. After lunch, you will have one hour in which to rest. In the afternoon, we will go on a tour through downtown Pyongyang, and when you return from the tour you will have dinner. This evening, to help you relax and get over the fatigue of such a long journey, we will take you to the Kyoye Theater. Please complete your luncheon between one and two, and be back here by three o'clock."

This time, fortunately, each person was assigned a separate room. It wasn't that Yosŏp actively disliked the professor who'd been his roommate in Beijing—it was just that inconveniences became unavoidable when men of that age were forced to share a small space together.

The hotel itself consisted of a set of twin towers, each about forty stories high. Considering the huge number of rooms available, there seemed to be very few guests in residence. The lobby and the coffee shop were bustling with people, but when Reverend Ryu got out of the elevator on the twelfth floor to find his room, not a single trace of human habitation could be seen anywhere. He was hesitating in the dark corridor when a young woman in an apron suddenly poked her head out of a doorway and rushed over to him.

"What room number?"

Instead of answering, Yosŏp held out his key. The young woman led him to his room. To his amazement, the room was quite luxurious. The front door opened onto a living room and the bedroom was further inside, separate from the main room. In place of carpeting, the floor had been covered with patterned mats—a famous Kaesŏng product—and a stream of cold air flowing down from a vent near the ceiling revealed that the entire place had central air-conditioning.

"If there's anything you need, just give us a ring."

After the woman left, Yosŏp sat down on the sofa in the living room, held his hands together, and said a brief prayer to himself:

Our Father in Heaven, I am now back in my homeland. Though these people may be different from us, though they may be a crowd of heathens, please, God, help me to overcome any hatred in my heart towards them. Give me the power to have confidence as a Christian without ever trespassing a whit upon Thy will. Might Thou be with me until the day I leave this place to return home, and through the Holy Spirit, I implore thee, allow Thy humble servant the blessing of faith. In the name of our Lord, Jesus Christ, amen.

Inside the Ch'ŏlima* refrigerator Yosŏp found an array of drinks including a pear-flavored soft drink, omija† water, Ryongsŏng Beer, Kŭmgang Draft Beer, mineral water, and Sindŏk Spring Water. On the dinner table lay two melons, two apples, a glass, a thermos made in China, green tea, a box of milk crackers, and a bag of old-fashioned candy. The bedcovers had a bluish design and looked like silk, but they were probably synthetic.

---

* *Ch'ŏlima*: this brand name translates to "horse capable of traveling one thousand *ri*."
† *Omija*: fruit of the Chinese magnolia vine, often used in Korea to brew tea.

When it was all said and done, every object in the room struck Reverend Ryu as being somehow unfamiliar—each item seemed like a physical testament to all the lives that had lived in this place over the past forty years during his absence. The doorbell rang. Yosŏp went to the door.

"Who is it?"

"It's the guide, sir."

Yosŏp thought the sudden visit odd but opened the door. All Back stood in the doorway. Uninvited, he entered the room as brazenly as if it were his own and sat down, straddling the arm of the sofa.

"Why don't you have a seat?" he said, as if he were the host. And so, their roles reversed, Yosŏp took the chair opposite All Back and sat down rather tentatively.

"There are a couple of things we need to check with you."

All Back took out a document from one of his inner pockets and opened it.

"Ryu Yosŏp . . . you are a minister, correct?"

"That's right. How do you know that I'm a minister?"

All Back glanced up at Yosŏp for a second then returned to his document.

"At the time of application, you put down Sŏn'gyori, Pyongyang, as your hometown, correct?"

"Well, yes, but I've forgotten the exact address."

"Is anyone in your family still living in our republic?"

Reverend Ryu shook his head firmly, although, in that instant, it occurred to him that his uncle, one of his older sisters, his sister-in-law, and his oldest nephew, Tanyŏl, might still be alive somewhere in Sinch'ŏn.

"No."

"Not a single one?"

"No, not one. Our entire family moved to the South."

"What is the name and age of your late father?"

"Let me see, if he were still alive, he would be over ninety. His name was Indŏk. He passed away in the South."

"Ryu Indŏk? He, also, was Christian?"

"He was a Protestant presbyter."

"I see. And there's no one, no relative or friend that you are interested in being reunited with?"

"No," Yosŏp answered curtly.

"Ah, well, that is all. Please excuse the interruption. Get some rest."

"Actually, I was just about to leave. Isn't it time for lunch?"

"So it is."

Yosŏp left the room with All Back and got on the elevator. Leaning against the opposite wall of the elevator, All Back stared Yosŏp directly in the face.

"I don't quite understand the purpose of your visit to the motherland."

"I'm old. I just wanted to come and see my hometown."

His expression icy, All Back grinned, the corners of his mouth curving slightly up.

"And yet, you say that you have no one, no one at all, to go and *see* in your hometown?"

— Yosŏp stood quietly, his eyes burning a hole through the elevator doors.

The restaurant was bustling with people. Aside from the Homeland Visitors the hotel apparently had guests from Japan and Europe, as well as a number of technicians from Russia. The menu, a traditional Korean lunch, was the same for everyone in the group; it had been planned that way in advance, a typically North Korean way of doing things. The food was a little bland—not spicy enough, but tolerable. When Yosŏp sat down, the professor, who'd been sitting at a different table altogether, sprang up and hurried over to take the seat across from him. Lowering his voice, he whispered to Yosŏp, "Someone

— searched my bag. I say, these guys really are keeping a close eye on us."

"What do you mean?"

"When I came out of the shower, I found the zipper on my bag open and my underwear all crumpled."

"They probably just did a thorough inspection when we passed through customs."

"It was my carry-on bag—I've been holding onto it ever since we got off the plane." The professor shook his head in indignation. "I specifically requested to be reunited with my family members. I think that might be why they're watching me like this."

"Well, then your family must be alive and well. It's only natural that they would try to find out everything about you before they allowed you to meet them, don't you think?"

The professor nodded. "Ah, you do have a point there, Reverend."

❖ ❖ ❖

Reverend Ryu had entertained the notion of leaving the hotel, just walking out through the main doors and taking a stroll down the street, but he soon thought better of it and returned to his room. He felt somehow that he and this street were not a part of the same reality. As a minister with his own parish, Yosŏp hadn't really traveled much. He had, however, visited Europe on several occasions to attend some church-related conferences, and, naturally, he'd been to different parts of America. Finding himself in a faraway, unfamiliar city like Amsterdam or Copenhagen, he would wander through the streets by himself and sometimes go into a restaurant and enjoy a delicious meal all alone. If he had time, he might visit a museum or an art gallery. So why did this place strike him as being so strange? He felt as if he were being observed, examined from every angle, right, left, above, below, front, and back—all by another version of himself. He dropped his hand just as his finger was about to touch the elevator button, fancying that he heard the murmurings of his other self, that it was right beside him. He took one last look around before finally stepping into the elevator. It was only after he reached his room, locked the door, and sprawled out on the bed that he was able to calm himself down a little.

That afternoon, the group of Homeland Visitors boarded the tour bus that would drive them around downtown Pyongyang and stop at several historical sites. Yosŏp ended up sitting by the professor, who had claimed the seat with the best view, the one directly behind the driver. The professor was already waiting and saving a seat for him by the time Yosŏp climbed aboard. So, what sights did Yosŏp see? He began by reading the strange signs and billboards, muttering to himself the way he did in any new city when he spotted something written in English, Japanese, or German. It was his way of trying to reconcile himself to his alien surroundings, to avoid a sense of disharmony

Industrial Products Store, Agricultural Products Store, Fish Market, Vegetable Store, Butcher Shop, Dog Meat Shop, Noodle Shop, Rice Cake Shop, Ice Cream and Soda Shop, Barbershop, Beauty Parlor, Bathhouse, Bakery, Home Appliance Repair Shop, Clothing Store, Tailor Shop, Rice Soup Restaurant, Bookstore. Then there were all the propagandistic slogans spelled out with crude neon letters in primary red and blue, as yet unlit.

Live Life Our Way! Mobilize, Annihilate, Expedite! Beautify Pyongyang, Capital of the Revolution! Long Live Our Great Leader, Comrade Kim Il Sung! The Party Decides, We Act! Revolution and Construction, Anti-Japanese Guerrilla Style!

The bus coasted through the sparsely peopled streets at a leisurely pace. Every now and then it would stop in front of the Arch of Triumph, the Tower of Self-reliance, the People's Palace of Culture, or the Pyongyang Department Store. The Homeland Visitors, listening to their guides and lecturers, were forced into single file and stood in vacant admiration before these impressive buildings and monuments, these heaps of marble, cement, and tile.

Reverend Ryu much preferred to simply sit by the window and watch the passersby. An old grandmother walked by carrying a bag and in a great hurry to get who-knows-where; young people in twos and threes crossed the street chattering back and forth; groups of students marched by all lined up with a gait that spoke of having places to be and things to do. It was a weekday, and most people wore working clothes, their collars buttoned up at the neck. Every now and then a man in a suit would come into view. High school and junior high school students' uniforms were the color of persimmons, complete with hats that resembled Lenin caps. The elementary students walked by in orderly lines wearing jumpers, overly colorful shirts with huge red ribbons, or red Boy Scout kerchiefs tied around their necks. The women all wore fairly similar two-piece outfits— the only noticeable difference between old and young was that the younger women's dresses were slightly brighter and their heels slightly higher. Every now and then you might spot a young woman with a stylish hairdo wearing a short skirt or a Western-style dress and holding a parasol, but then there were also some women still in their work clothes, wearing sports caps with long visors. Weighed down with sacks of green onions and vegetables, they were probably on their way home from the grocery store. A housewife, carrying one child on her back and holding another by the hand, hurried towards a streetcar stop.

The streetcars were shaped like buses, complete with rubber tires, and were connected to a system of electric wires that hung suspended in the air. They passed by every now and then. Each streetcar was made up of two compartments connected together by something like an oversized accordion. Citizens were lined up at every stop. A truck sped by carrying men and women in work clothes, not one of them standing or sitting, all just squatting there in neat rows, staring straight ahead. A young female traffic officer whizzed by on a streetcar, brandishing her baton. For one fleeting instant, her green uniform and the white face underneath her cap were frozen in the windowpane. She disappeared.

The city was like a cinema screen; a flat square of life lay out there. Watching it made Yosŏp himself feel as if he were no longer quite three-dimensional. The multitude of people who had created this movie for themselves had singled out Ryu Yosŏp, and they had no intention of ever letting him in, no matter how desperately he tried to climb into the screen.

That night Yosŏp went with the group to the Kyoye Theater, where they watched a performance that involved all kinds of acrobatics, not to mention somersaults and seesaws, tightropes, balls, horses, and even magic tricks—and yet he remained decidedly unexcited. The buildings, the monuments, the milky light of the streetlamps and all those passersby— they were still all too vivid. He felt as if he had walked into some sort of surrealistic painting.

A cylindrical aquarium slowly rose up over the round stage, followed by a translucent veil of artificial fog. Inside the cylinder were a number of dancers clad in bathing suits; their undulating movements made the red, white, and blue sashes tied around their waists billow out like fish fins. With the colorful lighting that was projected on them from above, the dancers appeared to be fluttering in midair. As the lights were gradually dimmed and the fog floated further upward, the dancers, too, slowly ascended. Right as they were about to disappear completely behind the curtains that hung above the stage, the lights all went out at once. Immediately, the room was filled with thunderous applause. Then, in that very instant, the hazy figure of a man rose from that darkness. By and by, the figure became distinct, its mouth spreading sideways into a grin. What on earth . . . who *is* that? Is that the Mole? Uncle Sunnam? The moment passed and Yosŏp found that he wasn't even that startled. Doubtless he had simply imagined it.

When Yosŏp, fumbling in the darkness, came out of the aisle between the seats, the female volunteer who'd been standing at the rear of the theater approached him.

"Where are you going, sir?"

"Ah, I . . . don't feel too good."

The attendant led him to an emergency exit at the left corner of the theater and cracked it open.

"There's an infirmary that way, at the end of the corridor. When you return, come in through this door," she whispered.

Out in the corridor, Yosŏp loitered aimlessly for a while before turning in the opposite direction, away from the hall with the bathroom. He ended up in the theater's spacious lobby. The room was completely empty: nothing but unoccupied sofas and mirrored pillars. He couldn't quite tell which pillar it was, but someone emerged from behind one of them and weaving his way in and out between the other pillars, cast a quick glance back in Yosŏp's direction. Without realizing what he was doing, Yosŏp followed the shadow's trail. Passing the mirrors, Yosŏp ran into countless reflections of his own torso, stopping him in his tracks over and over again.

❖ ❖ ❖

Pushing through the big glass doors at the front of the theater I walked out onto the street; a cool breeze enveloped me for a moment before it moved on. I began to stumble down the slope of the cement sidewalk. In the darkness, someone approached me.

Where are you going? Come with me.

I turned and saw the white figure of Uncle Sunnam, looking the same as he had so long ago, the year he returned to his hometown. He'd been in his early forties then, and he always wore the people's uniform with all the buttons and his hair cut short. He was younger than me now, it seemed, but despite my seniority I couldn't help but feel like a child.

How come you keep showing up by yourself? What happened to Big Brother?

I came to see you 'cause Yohan asked me to. There's something I want to show you.

He led me past an apartment complex speckled here and there with lit windows and took me out to the riverbank. I went over to sit on a wooden bench underneath the thick willow trees that lined the bank. I could feel Sunnam standing right behind me.

Now, look. You see? It's my hometown.

There appeared a scene of rice paddies and fields stretching out before a ravine where thatched huts sprouted up like tiny mushrooms amid the forests along a mountain ridge.

That's the village I used to live in. My real hometown is Changjaeibŏl. It was only after Father lost our land to the Oriental Development Company that we moved to Mŏbaugol as a family of tenants.

Three oxcarts stand under a ginkgo tree in a vacant lot in the village. A man holding a ledger is shouting—he's a Japanese officer. Beside him is a Korean agent, one who specializes in dealing with tenant farmers. Big, tough-looking men are emptying one of the houses. The pile of rice that sat in the front yard is carried out in sheaves. They take the dresser and the trilevel chest that Sunnam's mother brought with her as part of her dowry—everything: the clothes hanging on the wall, the bedsheets and covers. The cast-iron pot cemented to the kitchen floor and even the water jar are emptied of their contents and rolled out. One of the brutes has taken down all the china neatly stacked up in the kitchen cabinet and carries it out in a huge wicker basket. Father tries to snatch back the bedcovers, but then he's kicked down by the men. Mother is clutching at the basket full of dishes. The agent tears it away from her and pushes her away. Sunnam is ten years old. His eight-year-old brother and four-year-old sister have long since plopped themselves down on the ground, crying their eyes out. Sunnam picks up a stone and throws it at one of the big men. It bounces off his back and falls to the ground. The man turns around with an angry frown on his face and glaring. Sunnam jumps to hide behind the earthen wall.

Sunnam turned to Yosŏp, Your father managed to secure himself quite a bit of land, but he started out as an agent for the Oriental Development Company, too. You know what an agent does? He raises the taxes that tenants have to pay and he makes them pay for his own tax, and if the tenants don't obey, he just terminates the contract and transfers their tenant rights to another farmer. The Oriental Development Company and the Financial Union, not to mention the landowners—they liked the go-getters, you know. They'd trade their best agents with each other, so after being transferred to a different area, these new agents could simply refuse to acknowledge the tenants' claims to taxes they paid the previous year. Sometimes they'd raise the taxes for new tenants, or fix an arbitrary quota for the coming harvest and collect money in advance. Our family had to deal with it all—depending on the season, we would take them the bass, catfish, or carp we caught in our nets, pheasants or a roe deer we'd been able to trap—we even made them rice cakes and presented them with bolts of cotton and muslin. None of it mattered, though. If the harvest was under quota because of cold weather or a typhoon, our tenant contracts would be taken away on the spot. Some of the villagers just filled their stomachs one last time and fled to Manchuria in the dead of night. You can't blame them, really. The price of rice was about as good as the price of shit, and after you paid off the expense of your irrigation system and fertilizer, what with the fees for Financial Union, you could have sold every last thing you owned and you'd still be in debt.

In a ravine along the mountain ridge in Mŏnbaugol, dugouts built by tenants who have lost their tenant rights begin to appear, one by one, until one day there are scores of families living there. Sunnam's family moves in, too. They eat bark off the pine trees, wild berries, and arrowroot. Sometimes they make cakes, mixing millet with the sticky part of the red and white soil they dig out of the earth. Other times, they have soup with millet powder, mixing it with radishes and greens they find in the fields after the harvest is over. How sweet and tasty the cabbage roots are! They eat anything—bean leaves, bellflower roots, bonnet bellflowers, buckwheat hulls, acorn liquor lees—and when there's nothing else to be had, they grub up wild greens from the mountains and mix them with water that's been used to wash rice hulls—it makes a sort of gruel.

Sunnam continued, One night, my younger brother and I—he's dead now—snuck out into some bastard's field. We stole a bunch of sesame seeds that had been covered in night soil. We ate them all. We were sick for three, four days with constant diarrhea. That was actually what sent my brother up to the heavens. We all moved to a construction site along the Chaeryŏng River, and my older sister was sent away to work as a nanny. Within a few years our family was scattered all over the place. I was already twenty years old by the time I ended up working for your folks.

I was born the year after Uncle Sunnam came to work for my family, so that would mean that he was our handyman for about five years. By then, Yohan was already about ten years old. Sunnam disappeared later, some six years or so before liberation. I can still remember Sunnam carrying me piggyback on the path we took home from the marketplace. His back was solid, firm as a wooden plank, and his sweat-soaked cotton top smelled something like burnt pine needles, or maybe the kind of moss that gathers on rocks. The moon had risen early, hanging a span or two above the village hill, and his song floated out amidst the white reed blossoms and eulalias as they swung gently with the breeze along the stream:

> Bellflowers, bellflowers, bellflowers,
> In Kŭmsanp'o, Ŭnnyul, white bellflowers—
> Just one root and the basket's overflowing,
> *Ehe ehee heya eya*, I say—*diyarah*
> The sight of you melts my heart.

If Sunnam hadn't returned after liberation, he might have remained a total stranger to me. Yohan, though, would have remembered him. He was already nearly grown, old enough to follow the field hands around and frequent the village *sarang*.

❖ ❖ ❖

It was all thanks to Mr. Kang that I was finally able to leave Presbyter Ryu's house. Mr. Kang was one of those intellectuals, and he'd come home a few years earlier from Manchuria—his health was terrible. His family was pretty well-off. They used to run a Chinese medicine shop in town, but then they all turned Catholic. The whole family kind of fell apart when the brothers left for China to work for the Independence Movement. Some say that Mr. Kang himself went to Manchuria to join the Independence Army, but the point is that the man practically had one foot in the grave when he finally came home. He had tuberculosis. He was just about to keel over, really, but his father and his wife—they'd stayed home to raise the children—they took real good care of him. They gave him Chinese medicine and brought him back to life. When he finally got better and could leave the house again, he turned the old Union warehouse into a night school. Young men who'd never even seen a school and little kids—they were the first ones to attend. They learned *han'gŭl** there, and hearing them all read out loud

---

* *Han'gŭl*: the Korean alphabet.

made me so jealous I actually got myself a seat in the back row. He never specifically said we should strike down the Japanese beasts, not in so many words, but I learned phrases like "the world of the proletariat," "equality," and "capitalists and landowners." I'll tell you, though—I didn't quite know what those phrases really meant at the time.

Come to think of it, Kwangmyŏng Church, the church my master's family went to, was a place someone like me wouldn't dare go near, not once. Those who had families, even if they were tenants, invited or persuaded each other to attend, and some of them became regular churchgoers. A hand like me, though, and the other servants—we just worked all year round, filling up our spare time with chopping wood, feeding cattle, or baling hay. All we could do was listen to the hymns or the bells tolling in the distance.

I left Ch'ansaemgol and moved out to Ŭnnyul because of a fight with the Union. All the big landowners in the county had gotten together and formed this so-called Union, and their agents would handle the tenant contracts any old way they pleased. They had full control of all the farming expenses and tenant fees, and the landowners just managed the Union to their own advantage, taking a heavy commission. In Ŭnnyul they had to form a Farmers' Mutual Aid Association because it was so bad—and since all the land was owned by the Company, all the tenants could unite without any internal conflicts. In our village, led by the people who'd gone to Mr. Kang's night school, we set up our own mutual aid association, modeling it after the one in Ŭnnyul—but the Union bribed and threatened our members, one or two at a time, and pretty soon everyone left. It all came to nothing. I was sick and tired of living in that kind of place anyway and planned to move to Ŭnnyul to find some work, but then *their* Mutual Aid Association got rounded up. All the members were dragged all the way up to Haeju and . . . punished. Severely, for two months. They were all crippled and maimed when they finally came home.

Anyway, the comrades I'd befriended in Ŭnnyul introduced me to a subcontractor in the mining industry, and the whole lot of us ended up going to work at Kŭmsanp'o. The work was hard but living with friends, eating, and sleeping together in the barracks—it was ten times better than living alone in somebody else's house as a servant. Right before liberation, all of us, not just the miners but the Japanese foremen, too—we were all having a hell of a time. Everybody was so tense that we'd frighten ourselves with the sound of our own breathing. Still, those first three years I spent there—those were the days. The blood in our veins boiled back then, hot and wild. Once every ten days the *Workers' Bulletin* would circulate through the barracks, and a kid would come by to explain what was in it. Just like the weekly church bulletins, they were printed on cheap, coarse paper with a mimeograph machine. Through those bulletins I learned words like "socialism" and "class."

On Liberation Day, I was coming out of the mine shaft with my fellow workers to have lunch—we were riding in the cart. The bell started tolling like crazy, and the Japanese foreman came out to stand in the yard, waiting for us in front of the office. The bastard mumbled, suddenly all humble, not at all like he used to be, and said that the mine was closing, that Japan had lost the war. Some of the men jumped up and down, shouting hurrah, hurrah, but most of us just stood there, bewildered, then slowly wandered back to the barracks. The subcontractor was there, handing out chits and telling us to go to the office to exchange them for money. He said that he, too, was leaving for good. I turned to a comrade who used to read the *Bulletin* with me, and said, "This mine, the rice paddies, the fields—all of it—it belongs to us now."

❖　❖　❖

"What are you doing here?"

Startled, Reverend Ryu Yosŏp recoiled and looked around. He had been sitting on a bench by the riverside. The owner of the abrupt voice had come up from behind, but now he was coming around the side. He sat down next to Yosŏp. It was the guide, Mr. All Back.

"Ah, well, you see . . . I wasn't feeling very good, so I came out for some fresh air."

"You've come quite a distance to get your fresh air, haven't you?"

Yosŏp didn't respond, turning instead to gaze quietly in the direction of the river. The hill beyond the far bank was thick with willow trees and covered in darkness, but the walkway along the water's edge was bright enough thanks to the intermittent streetlamps. A man and a woman walked by, discussing something with their heads hanging low.

"Let's go. Everyone's been waiting."

Pressured by the guide, Yosŏp got up from the bench. As they walked up onto the sidewalk, he could see a car waiting, its headlights on. Yosŏp got in the back seat—All Back had opened the back door and held it for him—and the guide took the passenger seat. As soon as Yosŏp got inside, Fatty, who'd been waiting in the car, spoke up.

"We've been very worried about you."

"But why?"

Fatty's good-natured face looked even more bloated as he laughed, his eyes looking pretty much closed.

"Reverend, you must try to understand our society. I guess this is what they call liberalism. You are a tourist, and you came here with a group."

All Back turned around in the front seat and added, "We've been circling round and round this whole area looking for you."

"I'm sorry," said Yosŏp.

He meant it.

4

From One Generation to Another

YOSŎP GOT UP LATE the next morning.

He'd spent the whole night tossing and turning.

It might have rained during the night; as he lay there, the window shook in its frame, the wind still pounding against it. Strangest of all was the thought that he was lying in this city. As evening turned into night, every sign of life had somehow disappeared all at once—even the few lights that had shone here and there through the windows of the various buildings all blinked off. Drawing the curtains aside had revealed a pitch-black thoroughfare with every streetlamp turned off, lit only by the occasional set of headlights.

Yosŏp was the last one to eat breakfast, and the place was practically empty by the time he arrived. He had a bowl of soup and finished off his meal with a glass of Sindŏk Spring Water. He was coming out into the second-floor lobby when the professor waved at him from a corner armchair.

"Reverend! Over here!"

The professor began speaking in an animated voice as soon as Yosŏp sat down beside him.

"I'm going to meet my family!"

"When?"

"In about half an hour or so. The guide came and told me a minute ago while I was eating. I think other people are meeting their families, too—the scheduled activities for this morning have been canceled."

"Why, that's wonderful! Who's coming? Have they told you?"

"Mother . . . my mother, she's still . . . alive." Suddenly overwhelmed, the professor's voice cracked and tears started streaming down his face. He took out a handkerchief and wiped his eyes and his forehead, all the way up across his bald head. He glanced at his wristwatch.

"Reverend, please. Please stay with me. I'm too nervous to handle this alone."

"I'd be happy to, seeing as nothing's planned for this morning, but . . . do you think they'll allow it?"

"Oh, don't worry about that. I can be pretty stubborn myself. I just can't see my family alone, surrounded by *them*."

All Back and Soprano were coming in through the lobby and sweeping the room with their eyes. Soprano reached them first, her fat body shaking.

"Well, well, so you've been here all along—we went all the way up to your room to look for you!" she said, her tone overly dramatic.

All Back joined them and, without sitting down, raised his arm to point in the direction of the dining hall.

"Let's get a move on. Everyone's waiting."

"Your mother, your older brother, and sisters, too, have come. Remember, this is all made possible because you have visited the Motherland."

Despite the insistence of the two guides, the professor looked only at Reverend Ryu.

"Come, Reverend, let's go."

"Oh, has your family come as well, Reverend? Only the involved party is allowed in."

The professor shook his head at All Back and spoke firmly.

"I will not go alone. Reverend Ryu is the minister of our church, and I need him with me as my witness."

"Your witness?"

"When I go back, you see, I'm going to need someone to testify before the congregation that I really did meet my family."

"Huh. You *are* stubborn, aren't you?"

All Back glanced over at Soprano, and she moved away through the chairs, her swift, agile gait rather unbecoming for such a big person. As if he had no other choice, All Back took a seat next to Yosŏp.

"You live in New York, do you not, Reverend?"

"Yes . . ."

"But you, Professor, you live on the West Coast in a place called See-something, correct?"

"Seattle. What does that have to do with anything?" the professor retorted, frowning to feign ill humor. In response, All Back turned to face Yosŏp.

"The professor lives in the West, so he can't possibly attend your church in New York, can he? All I'm saying is that it doesn't make any sense."

Yosŏp decided he had no alternative but to humor the professor.

"I often give sermons out west. Ministers at different Korean churches throughout America often visit each other's parishes to give sermons, so . . ."

"I see."

"The point is that I can't go to meet my family all by myself. Besides, I need someone to take pictures for us."

Soprano ran back just in time to cut off the problematic conversation. Wiping the nape of her neck with a handkerchief, she spoke loudly enough for everyone to hear.

"Comrade Supervisor says that it is no problem. He also says, however, that no other visitors aside from Reverend Ryu are allowed."

And so Reverend Ryu ended up with a role all his own in the professor's dramatic family reunion. All Back and Soprano led the professor and the minister to one of the many rooms that faced the dining hall windows. As they approached the door, the professor began to lose his composure—his eyes were bloodshot, and he kept glancing backwards like a frightened child to make sure that Yosŏp was still with him. Soprano was the first to open the door and enter the room. Flinging her arms out, she cried, "Now, here is your mother!"

Holding the camera tightly in his hands, Yosŏp stood directly behind the professor. Suddenly, the professor leaped into the room, momentarily oblivious of Yosŏp's presence, and dashed over to embrace a tiny figure.

"Mother . . ."

The tangle of mother and son was embraced once more by the outstretched arms of a second man and woman. Together with the guides,

Reverend Ryu stood out of their way and watched the reunion from the doorway. The family members hugged each other and pawed the air. On one hand, it was a rather ridiculous sight to behold; on the other, it was a scene that tore at the heart of the coldest onlooker. Like the first drops of sweet rain to fall on a land long parched by drought, tears began rolling down the old grandmother's wrinkled cheek. The professor bent down at the waist and buried himself in his old mother's tiny, shriveled bosom, wailing and crying out loud. It was only after a long time that he straightened himself up and really looked at the old lady. He held her face in both of his hands.

"Mother . . . your face . . . let me . . . your face . . . "

"Oh, oh, you're our second, aren't you? You've grown so old."

"And Father?"

"Your grandfather and grandmother passed away right after the war— it's been over ten years since your father died."

"I'm your older brother. And this, here, this is your younger sister."

The professor turned towards them, and the three siblings embraced. Yosŏp took several pictures during these first embraces, but then, unable to hold back his own tears any longer, he stole out of the room. Soprano was standing outside the door, her eyes red, blowing her nose over and over again into a handkerchief.

"This . . . this is the tragedy of our people."

Yosŏp walked back to the lobby, still holding the camera—he hadn't had a chance to give it back. All the visitors were apparently off meeting their families; the place was quiet except for a few unrelated guests who seemed to be holding consultations. Fatty approached Yosŏp.

"May we offer you a cup of tea?" he inquired courteously.

Fatty, who turned out to be "Comrade Supervisor," and Soprano ignored the coffee shop in the lobby and led Yosŏp to the escalator instead, taking him to a bar on the second floor that was divided into separate compartments. Inside one of them was a large couch. While Soprano was off fetching a hostess, Fatty addressed Yosŏp.

"I'm not sure whether or not it is my place to say this, but we do feel kind of bad that you seem so unwilling to open up to us. Our sole aim is to help you reconcile and form a new relationship with the Motherland you left behind."

Yosŏp replied honestly, "I really do appreciate that, but what do you mean when you say that I'm not opening up to you?"

Fatty gave a gentle laugh.

"Reverend, is there any chance that your hometown might be in Hwanghae Province?"

"Well, that's . . . "

As Yosŏp hesitated, Soprano came in behind him.

"Reverend Ryu, don't you want to meet your family?" she said.

Yosŏp inadvertently let out a long, relieved sigh.

"To be honest with you, my real hometown is . . . Sinch'ŏn."

"Ah . . . is that so?"

The two guides' expressions became tense. Silence reigned until the hostess finally came in. She put down three cups of ginseng tea on the table and left. The supervisor took out a cigarette, lit it, and went on in a low voice:

"We knew all along. Your older brother is Ryu Yohan, isn't he?"

"Yes, yes that's right. How did you . . . "

"How could we possibly forget *that* name?"

Yosŏp hung his head, momentarily immersed in thought. Soprano, now speaking as an alto, butted into the conversation.

"And why didn't you bring your brother with you?"

Yosŏp, interlacing his fingers, hung his head even farther down.

"My brother passed away three days before I left America," he mumbled. Looking up, he added, "I beg your forgiveness. I've come . . . instead. As a Protestant minister, I admit that my ideas may be different from yours. All the same, I know that my brother was a sinner."

Fatty the Supervisor inhaled deeply and exhaled a gust of cigarette smoke.

"I myself am from North P'yŏngan Province, so I'm not very well acquainted with the affairs of your region. The whole purpose of this game we're playing now is to heal old scars, wouldn't you say?"

"Please tell us about your family, Reverend," said Soprano, her voice still soft. Reaching into the inner pocket of his jacket, Yosŏp handed over the list of names he'd written down. Fatty the Supervisor took it.

"Why, you've come all prepared. If you had given this to us right away, you could have met your family this morning."

Looking at the list together with the supervisor, Yosŏp tried to explain. "This is my sister-in-law, and this here is my uncle, on my mother's side. I've no idea whether or not he's still alive. And this, this is my nephew. He'd be around fifty years old by now."

"Ryu Tanyŏl? I believe he's already been located and confirmed . . . "

The supervisor turned to Soprano, who took a notebook from her handbag and checked inside.

"Yes, that's right. We've already contacted the city authority of Sariwŏn about Ryu Tanyŏl."

"And who did you say these female names belonged to?"

Yosŏp pointed at the names one by one, explaining, "Those are all my nieces. Every one of them would be over fifty years old by now. Those names right there, underneath—those are my older sisters."

"Both of them?"

"Yes. They were already married back then."

"Don't worry. We've identified your nephew, so we should have all the other information, in detail, by sometime this afternoon."

Fatty handed the piece of paper to Soprano, giving her a look that she acknowledged with a nod. Bowing, she disappeared behind the compartment. When the two men were left alone, the supervisor closed his eyes gently for a moment, seemingly deep in thought.

"During the war, over the short month and a half the American Imperialist invaders occupied the northern districts of our Republic, they committed the most horrible atrocities. It wasn't just the foreign powers; landowners whose holdings had been impounded, Japanese collaborators, racketeers, and deserters all did their part, becoming the paws of America, acting as their accomplices. Throughout the course of the war, however, our Great Leader instructed us to leave the family members of the criminals and reactionaries in peace—we were not even to question them—as long as they had no prior criminal records and had not been active participants in the issue at hand. The principles we are adhering to during the promotion of this 'Homeland Visit' project are similar—Koreans from abroad who are visiting the Motherland, if repentant, are not to be asked about their pasts."

Recalling his own experiences with Yohan, especially over the past few years, Yosŏp couldn't help but interject, "But . . . the wound, it must still *be* there. It always was with our family."

The supervisor nodded.

"It will heal eventually. At least, between us, it will heal. It is the foreign powers that are ultimately to blame for all of this—let's just leave it at that."

❖ ❖ ❖

Around three o'clock that afternoon, the Homeland Visitors were in the middle of touring the Students' and Children's Palace. As the group quietly made its way through a room in which an accordion practice session was in full swing, All Back approached Reverend Ryu and pulled him gently by the sleeve.

"You need to come with us. Your nephew has arrived."

Yosŏp followed him outside to find a sedan waiting. They got in the car.

"Reverend, you should know that the Party is giving your case a great deal of special consideration. Look how quickly we were able to locate him."

Yosŏp felt more bewildered than excited.

"Thank you," he replied.

Back at the hotel, Yosŏp was led to a small banquet room on the second floor. All Back opened the door and Yosŏp entered the room, looking about unsteadily. Fatty the Supervisor was sitting in the room, his back to the window, and a man wearing a flaccid orange suit with a red necktie sat sandwiched between two other men in gray, short-sleeved people's uniforms. Right away, Yosŏp could tell that the one in the orange suit was his man. The supervisor introduced them, pointing at the suit.

"This is Comrade Ryu Tanyŏl. This gentleman here is Mr. Ryu Yosŏp."

Yosŏp walked over to the banquet table and took one of the empty seats across from his nephew.

"Your father's name—is it Ryu Yohan?"

"Yes, that's right. You're my uncle, aren't you?"

Before he even realized what he was doing, Yosŏp found himself halfway up out of his chair, reaching out for his nephew. His nephew, in turn, did the same and grabbed his hands. Luckily, the table between them made a full embrace impossible. Wanting to control himself, Yosŏp did his best to stifle the burning sensation he felt behind his eyes. His nephew's face crumbled, and the younger man let go of his uncle's hands, covering his eyes with his arm. He began to sob. Waiting for an end to this outburst from a nephew whose face he would never have recognized, Yosŏp dabbed at his eyes.

"Stop, please stop . . ."

Yosŏp was the first to sit back down—Daniel went on crying a little longer before he finally took a deep breath, inhaling through his nose, and sat down facing his uncle. Brushing his already graying hair to the side a few times, the younger man made a visible effort to control his emotions. Yosŏp asked after his sister-in-law first.

"Your mother, is she . . . still alive?"

"Yes, she lives with me in Sariwŏn."

"And she's in good health?"

"She was doing quite well up until last year, but this year she hasn't been so good."

Yosŏp made his way through the rest of his family members, one by one. Tanyŏl's two sisters, Yosŏp's nieces, were both dead. They had died young, during the hard years that followed the end of the war. Yosŏp's own sisters, who had been married and raising their own families, were also gone. They had passed away even earlier, around the beginning of the war.

Daniel added, "Ah, you didn't know. Only one uncle-in-law survived. He said it was the American Imperialist scum that killed both aunts."

"What about Uncle Some? Is he still alive?"

"Yes, Grandfather Some is doing fine. Even now he comes every so often to visit Mother."

The supervisor, who'd been watching them all along, cut into their conversation. "It seems to me that you've covered most of the things you were curious about. Come now, let's take a moment to all say hello to one another. These two comrades have come from the Sariwŏn City Authority. They are responsible for bringing Comrade Ryu to us."

The two men in people's uniforms stood up and took turns shaking Reverend Ryu's hand. One of them spoke.

"Comrade Ryu Tanyŏl is a very devoted Party member."

"Yes, I must say I was quite surprised myself. We are told that he is in charge of the Cooperative Farm," added Fatty the Supervisor, nodding.

Yosŏp felt unable, as yet, to break the news about Yohan to his nephew.

Yohan had simply taken it for granted that his wife and children had all died long ago, and now it turned out that they were not only alive, but Party members, too! For the first time, Yosŏp was feeling rather shocked. It was Fatty who got up first.

"Well now, we should let you two have some time alone, shouldn't we? You probably will not be allowed to spend the night together tonight, but we *are* arranging something quite special for you, Reverend."

Falling in beside Yosŏp as they all walked out of the room, All Back said, "Why don't the two of you go up to your room? Tomorrow there will be another family reunion—for now, you two can have dinner together before you call it a day."

Yosŏp led the way back up to his room. Offering a seat to his nephew, who looked rather lost, he went over to his bag and took out some photographs. After first showing him a picture of Yohan alone, Yosŏp handed his nephew a photograph of Yohan with his second wife, as well as a family picture that included Samyŏl and Pillip.

"That's your father. I guess you wouldn't be able to remember his face— you were just a little baby."

Yosŏp's nephew took the pictures and, after a quick glance, burst into tears once more.

"Daniel, your father passed away three days before I left to come here."

Although the younger man continued to cry, the news of his father's passing didn't seem to make much of an impression. Yosŏp sat down at the head of the bed, waiting for some sort of a reaction. Abruptly, his nephew slammed the photographs down on the table, shouting,

"My name is Ryu Tanyŏl, not Daniel! And how dare you show up now, searching for your family! Do you have any idea how hard it's been for us, just to live from day to day?"

Yosŏp got up and walked over to the window. He stood there for a long while, looking out at the sky. He felt the room behind him grow silent and knew that his nephew had regained some measure of control.

"I don't know if you know this, but our family has been Christian for generations. You, too, were christened as a baby. Your father was a presbyter, and I've become a Protestant minister. A lot of the things we believed in conflicted with the ideology of the People's Republic."

"No, no, it's not the religion that bothers me—that's just a relic of the dark days, all that superstition and such. I don't even care whether you were reactionaries or outright criminals—but, killing people? Why did you kill people?"

"People hated and killed each other back then. Now even those who survived are dying, leaving this world one by one. Unless we find a way to forgive one another, none of us will ever be able to see each other again."

Yosŏp went and sat down in a chair facing his nephew, taking the younger man's hands in his own. The nephew didn't pull away, and the uncle continued.

"Your father thought you were all dead. I can't tell you how relieved I am to see you alive and well like this, to know that you've made a life for yourself as a part of this society, even joining the Party."

His nephew hung his head once more and burst into tears yet again.

"You have no idea, no idea how much I had to suffer to become a Party member."

◆ ◆ ◆

The next morning, when Yosŏp went down to the dining hall for breakfast, he found All Back waiting to take him back up to the second floor. There, in the same compartment, the supervisor was waiting for them.

"You met your nephew yesterday—that must have been wonderful."

"It was a bit awkward. It would have been better if we'd had a chance to spend the night together and talk more about the rest of our family."

The supervisor nodded.

"We've considered that as well. Today we will be arranging an exclusive event for you, Reverend. We're also looking into the possibility of giving you a chance to see your family again. Perhaps even spend the night with them."

Standing beside the supervisor, All Back interjected, "Today, you visit your hometown, Reverend."

"My home . . . Sinch'ŏn?" Reverend Ryu Yosŏp found himself stammering.

All Back went on, "It won't take more than an hour or so to get there—we now have a highway that runs all the way across Hwanghae Province down to Kaesŏng."

"We had a reason for wanting to see you . . . it was decided that we really must tell you something. For the sake of the solidarity of our people, there is one thing you must be sure to keep in mind, one thing you need to understand. The fundamental reason we are divided is the influence of foreign powers. Imperialist Japan and Imperialist America have made us this way."

The supervisor held out his hand for a handshake.

"Go and see for yourself how your hometown has changed, Reverend. We'll see each other again later."

Yosŏp wandered back down into the dining hall and looked around. He spotted the professor between the oval tables that held the morning's breakfast. Yosŏp went over and sat down across from him.

"How was yesterday's family reunion?"

"I looked for you afterwards, but they said you were meeting your family as well."

"Yes, they located my nephew. I heard about my other relatives, too."

"That's wonderful. I feel a little . . . different, now," said the professor, smiling awkwardly. "Now that I've met my mother and my older brother, this whole place is starting to feel rather cozy and comfortable. It's so much better here than in America—everything there is so different, so alien."

Glancing around, the professor lowered his voice. "Reverend, it seems the communists, too, can be quite humane, eh?"

"Well, of course . . . all men are children of God."

As the members of the group finished up their breakfast and began heading back to their rooms, Yosŏp turned to the professor.

"It looks like I'm going to be visiting my hometown today."

"Is that so? My, my, that certainly is special treatment."

The two men didn't discuss it any further. Yosŏp didn't want to get into any details, particularly concerning his brother, with anyone who wasn't his flesh and blood.

They already had a car ready, so Yosŏp simply packed a shirt and some toiletries in a small bag and headed out. September had arrived, but the weather outside, away from the air-conditioning, was still rather hot and humid. The only person waiting in the car was the chauffeur. Yosŏp climbed into the back seat, and All Back got in the front. Once they passed the outskirts of the city, the view consisted of nothing but mile upon mile of vegetable fields, dotted here and there along the edges with clusters of adobe-brick tenement houses. Soon they were entering a four-lane cement highway.

The highway was practically empty, with only the occasional freight car rattling by. They stopped at a checkpoint on the provincial boundary, and All Back rolled down his window to display some sort of travel permit. Writing something down in his records, the guard let them pass. With no road signs in sight there was no way to know exactly where they were, but after an hour or so of driving the car veered onto a side road. It was a narrow dirt road flanked on either side by fields of sorghum. The car stirred up little dust; the dirt was tightly packed. Not long afterwards a paved road appeared, followed by a street lined with houses and buildings.

"Can you tell where we are?" the guide asked, turning around to look at Yosŏp. Yosŏp looked out the window and concentrated. The fields went on and on, but as the outline of a mountain off in the distance gradually came into view, he realized it looked quite familiar—it was a shape he recalled, albeit vaguely.

"Ah, that looks like Kkonme . . . " he mumbled to himself, remembering the long-forgotten names of the mountains around his hometown—Mount Uryŏng, Mount Hwa. Now that he was thinking about it, he realized that the roads themselves were nearly the same as they had been, too, although the buildings and houses were different. He spotted several men and women standing together on the side of the street. All Back motioned towards them.

"Stop over there."

Following the guide's instructions, the chauffeur pulled the car over in front of the small group. As they climbed out of the car, one of the men, who had gray hair and wore short-sleeved working clothes, approached Yosŏp. The guide introduced them.

"Reverend, this is the Party Secretary of Sinch'ŏn County."

Assuming the title would be equivalent to that of mayor, Yosŏp made a deep, courteous bow. The man took Yosŏp by the hands, saying, "You've had a long, arduous journey."

All Back turned towards the old man who stood behind the party secretary.

"This is the Comrade Director of the museum."

The whole company began walking, stepping on each other's heels as they followed a narrow side path. Eventually they reached a brick wall set with a large gate of vertical bars. Next to the gate was a sign, a square, wooden board that read, "Sinch'ŏn Museum." Inside the gate, a spacious paved yard was occupied by a couple of parked buses. The museum was a two-story building that looked like a typical Korean school: a front door placed directly in the middle of the façade with straight rows of windows stretching out to the right and left. A pine tree and a tall poplar each shaded a side of the door. Walking into the building, one was presented a view of the staircase that led up to the second floor and a set of hallways on either side that led away to the opposite ends of the building. A quote from Chairman Kim was posted on the wall facing the front door. A woman in *hanbok* who'd been following quietly behind the director of the museum came forward and bowed to Yosŏp, holding a thin stick with both hands.

"How do you do? I am the guide who will be helping you with your tour."

Reverend Ryu responded with a nod. "Thank you."

The female guide held up her pointer, indicating the chairman's quote, and began to read aloud, "At a certain point in history, Engels identified the British Army as being the 'most bestial' of all armies. During World War II, the German fascists surpassed their cruelty. It was said that the human brain could not imagine any atrocity more cruel or more terrifying than those committed by the villain known as Hitler. However, here in Chosŏn, the Yankees actually managed to surpass Hitler and his rogues."

With that, the woman turned to the right and employed her pointer once more to explain the nuances of a chart on the wall at the entryway to the exhibition room. The figures she rattled off didn't really register with Yosŏp but he did hear phrases such as "destruction and burning of private residences," "destruction of public buildings and irrigation systems," "destruction of various mechanical instruments and facilities," "destruction of various means of transportation," not to mention "looting cattle," "destruction and looting of farm tools," and "destruction of farmland."

Gradually, the guide's voice grew louder and higher.

"During the Motherland Liberation War, the American Imperialist invaders committed the atrocity of manslaughter on a scale so grand as to be unprecedented in the entire history of Chosŏn, thus revealing to the world its bestial nature as a twentieth-century cannibal. The massacre that took place in Sinch'ŏn, as ordered by Harrison the Vampire, then acting commander of the Americans soldiers stationed in Sinch'ŏn, surpassed by far the bloody horrors of Hitler's World War II concentration camps. The American Imperialist invaders ordered that anything that lived and moved in Sinch'ŏn be buried under ashes, and over a period of fifty-two days they slaughtered 35,383 innocent people—one quarter of Sinch'ŏn's entire population—in the most cruel and vicious ways. This fiendish atrocity shall never be forgiven, not in a thousand years."

Most of the exhibits were made up of photographs, but posters and foreign newspaper clippings from the time period were also pasted up all over the place. A separate group of men and women appeared to be in the middle of their own tour—every now and then a young man could be heard explaining the different exhibits. The strident intonation of Yosŏp's female guide reached its peak as they reached a box-like display inside a wood-panel compartment on the cement floor. Thinking it was just a heap of miscellaneous objects placed atop a box, Yosŏp moved forward to get a closer look. It was a pile of shoes. The first to catch his eye was a pair of women's white *komusin*.* One of the pair was severed in half, right through the center, and completely discolored—it was now a dirty yellow. A crumpled pair of dress shoes, several shoe heels with rusty nails sticking out of them, tiny children's black *komusin*, a single bedraggled black tennis shoe with a broken shoestring, countless telephone lines all tangled into a ring the size of a bracelet, and thick metal wires—their owners no longer existed, and seeing so many empty shoes, shoes that were once worn, made the absence of the dead that much more conspicuous. A cool breeze blew in through the screen in the open window but Yosŏp felt a sudden burst of sweat cover the back of his neck. He fancied that he could hear his heart murmur, I know. . . . They must have dug these things out of the pit. All of a sudden, he thought he heard the faint sound of a violin.

> Endlessly long, hot summer days,
> always you bloomed so gorgeously.
> Beautiful maids, maids pure and true,
> once smiled and played, welcoming you.

---

* *Komusin*: traditional Korean shoes made of rubber.

As Yosŏp trailed along behind the female guide, the other tour group was in the process of moving on to the next room. A couple of the stragglers in the group casually glanced back in his direction. In that fleeting instant Yosŏp saw clearly Uncle Sunnam, wearing the shabby, pale green people's uniform buttoned all the way up to his chin. As if that weren't enough, the other man turned his head and grinned at Yosŏp over Sunnam's shoulder— it was Ichiro Illang, his head shaved clean as it had always been. I can't believe they followed me all the way out here. As soon as the tail of this group disappeared into the next room, Yosŏp began to wonder whether all the tourists in the group might not be dead.

Trying to catch up to them, Yosŏp quickened his pace, making his way towards the next exhibition room. All Back, who'd been following close behind, pulled him lightly by the sleeve.

"Reverend, we aren't through with this room yet."

Yosŏp turned back and saw the female guide staring at him blankly, her pointer still held up in midair. The county's party secretary and the director of the museum both stood quite still, their hands clasped behind their backs. With a foolish look on his face, Reverend Ryu turned again towards the entrance of the room that the other visitors had disappeared into. He asked the museum guide, "Those people in front of us—where did they come from?"

Bewildered, she asked him back, "Why? Did you see someone you know?"

"Well, no, it's not that, just . . . there definitely *was* a big tour group in front of us, right?"

Listening to their exchange, the director of the museum cut in.

"People from all over the country organize group tours to come visit our museum."

Only then was Yosŏp convinced that they had actually been real people, visible to others as well as himself. He realized that the war was not yet over in this place. His tongue felt dry. He was thirsty, out of breath, and, above all, anxious. He wanted to find someplace to hide in, to run away to.

"On October 18, the day that followed the beginning of their occupation, the fiendish American Imperialist murderers enacted the mass slaughter that they had been planning for so long. Locking up approximately nine hundred citizens, including some three hundred women and children, in an air-raid shelter in Sinch'ŏn, they covered the whole area in gasoline and burned them all to death. When we are through here, we will go visit the site of this atrocity. On the nineteenth and the twenty-third, in a trench situated near the air-raid shelter, the Americans killed no less than six hundred people, some of whom were buried alive and others who were, once more, set on fire. In this way, the number of people murdered in the air-raid shelter and in the trench alone amount to approximately 1,530."

The exhibits in the next room were largely made up of so-called murder weapons. They had, most likely, been found in the nearby fields and mountains. There were rusty swords, broken M-1 bayonets and pistols, machine guns, M-1 rifles with only the barrels intact, carbines, and helmets full of holes from all the rust. The bayonets were discolored, and the dark red rust on the concave part of the blade made them look stained with blood.

In yet another room, the female guide showed Yosŏp the bust of a young boy who had refused to disown the Party and paid for it with his own life. There were also photographs of a reservoir where, the guide claimed, people had been drowned en masse, as well as a hot-spring resort where countless women had been raped before they were thrown into a pond and blown up with grenades. Workers at the Sinch'ŏn Rice-processing Factory had been tied to oxcarts and pulled from both sides, tearing their bodies apart. The walls were packed from top to bottom with photographs of dead bodies.

By the time they came back out the front door where the tour had started, Yosŏp's shirt was soaked through with sweat. The museum director spoke to Yosŏp: "The air-raid shelter is over there, still exactly the same as it was then. We'll see that first before we move on to the site of the massacre in Wŏnamni. Then we'll be done."

The blazing sun beat down on the concrete of the museum's front yard— Reverend Ryu Yosŏp felt as if the heat were sucking up all the moisture in his brain and heart. What different colors he and his brother Yohan must have used as each of them painted their own picture of home, of the carnage. These people have constructed yet a different vision of their own, Yosŏp thought to himself, but it all stems from the same nightmare, the one we created together.

Crossing the street, they walked up to a small mound covered by a flower bed. Facing the building was a green tract of land, somewhat elevated from the rest of the ground, which was topped by a square, chimneylike structure. The guide identified it as an air shaft that connected with the underground air-raid shelter.

"The beasts poured gasoline through this hole. This air-raid shelter was initially built during the Japanese occupation, but it was also used as Sinch'ŏn's main shelter during the Korean War. Shall we go in?"

A single lightbulb hung at the bottom of the steep staircase. The inside of the structure was completely sealed in with concrete. The ceiling was covered in a thick layer of soot and what had once been a latticed wooden pillar in the passageway was now a vertical heap of charcoal. Here and there, the decaying cement wall had crumbled away. "This is the place where nine hundred innocent people were shut up. They all burned to death," whispered the museum director to Yosŏp from behind. "Look over there, in front of the ventilator. Fingernail traces."

Yosŏp saw the marks in the wall. The scratches looked as if they'd been made with a knife or a piece of glass. He spotted clumps of synthetic fibers that looked like clots of burnt hair.

It grew hotter and hotter outside as noon drew near. Despite the fact that Sinch'ŏn was supposedly quite a large county, not one person was out on the deserted street. It was a busy time of year for farmers—perhaps that was why. As they recrossed the street to return to the car, something fluttered through the air, riding a whisper of a breeze. Trembling, it wavered up and down, finally falling to the ground after sticking for a moment to the side of a building as it slithered its way down. Yosŏp stopped for a moment to take a look. Judging from the big and small letters, it was probably a page out of some newsletter or magazine. That was all, nothing more. The blinding sunlight reached about halfway down the main street of the town; the square cement buildings, the painted blue window frames, and the glass windowpanes, too, were all divided into light and shadow as if pieces had been cut away. In the perfect silence, only certain sections could be seen distinctly, as in a dream, and when a man happened to come into view, walking slowly into an alleyway up ahead, his movements appeared two dimensional, like a figure moving across the monitor of an old video game console.

The site of the Wŏnamni massacre was located on a thickly wooded hillside. Two storage buildings remained standing, one above and one below the slope; the exhibition itself was in a separate, newly built structure.

Displayed inside were various photographs and remains. Visitors were filing through, lined up two abreast, making their way up and down the steps and listening to their guides' comments. The buildings had once been used, as Yosŏp well knew, as warehouses for storing fruit. According to the guide, they were later used to store gunpowder during the war. There were bullet holes here and there, but the walls, charred by some past fire, had been left largely untouched.

"'The mothers will be too content if we allow them to stay with their children,' said the brutes. 'Tear them apart at once, and lock them up separately! Let the mothers go mad with worry, calling for their little ones, and let the children die crying for their mothers,' declared the beasts. Brandishing their swords and guns, the murderers tore the children from the bosoms of their mothers, who fought desperately to keep them. They locked the babes up in a different storage building. The heartrending cries of the children calling for their mothers and the pitiable wailing of the mothers asking for their children—it was all too much. Hungry for blood, the fiendish monsters poured gasoline and straw over the heads of the surviving women and children and set them on fire, and then, as if they hadn't already done enough, they threw in grenades. In these two storage buildings alone, 910 innocents, including 400 women and 102 children, were slaughtered in cold blood."

Yosŏp looked at the pamphlet he had been given at the entrance. It had fuzzy photographs of the crime scene and some written material. Included was a witness account:

> When I opened the storage door, I found layers and layers of the children's dead bodies in a heap right up against the door. It was obvious that they'd all been trying desperately to get out. Some had frozen to death, others had died of starvation, and still more had been burnt to a crisp. Most of their fingernails were broken off and clotted with blood—it was plain to see that they had done everything they possibly could to try to escape their agony, up until the very last moment.

On the hill to the right of the storage building were two burial mounds, one for the 400 women and another for the 102 children, each as high as that of a royal tomb. Two stones had been erected, one on each side, and a line of people were queued up to pay their respects.

❧ ❧ ❧

By the time they returned to the county hall back in town it was way past one in the afternoon. Of everyone in the group, Yosŏp was the most exhausted. Their lunch was already laid out and waiting for them in the dining hall, a treat from the party secretary. All five sat down together at the table: their host, the director of the museum, All Back, Reverend Ryu Yosŏp, and the female museum guide. Yosŏp used a cool, wet towel to wipe the back of his neck and around his eyes, then gulped down a glass of Sindŏk Spring Water. All Back, the guide from the capital, spoke first.

"You must be hungry. It must be quite tiring for you to visit so many places."

Feeling a bit dazed, Yosŏp just sat there. For some reason, nobody else seemed to feel like talking. Without even a cursory smile, the party secretary raised his hands, palms up.

"I know it's not much, but let us eat."

There were two bottles of white wine on the table and, without a word, the party secretary opened one of the bottles and held it out to Yosŏp.

"I don't really drink. Besides, it's only lunchtime," said Yosŏp quietly.

"Come, just take a glass—you don't have to drink it. We had this brought out especially for this occasion."

The museum director seemed determined, so Yosŏp had no choice but to accept a glass. As soon as it was filled, the director thrust his own glass right under the party secretary's nose.

"Here, here, fill it to the brim, now."

Showing no emotion of any kind, the party secretary filled up the director's glass and offered the same to the guide, too. The rice was white rice and the soup was fish soup. There was also fried pork, greens, vegetable pancakes, *toenjang tchigae*, lettuce, and sand anchovies, all tasty. Everyone ate and finished their drinks in silence. The female guide bowed good-bye and returned to the museum. The rest of the company moved to the party secretary's office for a cup of tea. The museum director seemed to be feeling the effects of the wine. He said, "I really can't go on doing this; it's infuriating. He's party secretary, so he acts all grave and dignified, stroking his beard, and I'm like a python in a dry pond, circling round and round repeating the same old story, always about dead people."

"Good heavens, man, if you're drunk just go on home and take a nap. An old man should have a sense of shame!"

As the party secretary grumbled and turned away from the director, All Back asked the director, "Are the two of you friends from the same hometown, sir?"

"We're more than just friends—we've been through everything together, ever since we were children. We know why they call man the most evil creature in the world, don't we?"

Shooting the director a sidelong look of disapproval in lieu of a response, the party secretary walked out of his office. Suddenly, the director of the museum turned to Yosŏp and implored, "This year I turned seventy years old—not a day less! To have survived this long, it's a miracle, don't you think? All these people here now, but less than two in ten are really *from* here, you know?"

"There was a lot of shifting after the war," retorted the guide halfheartedly.

But the old man was getting worked up now.

"They were punished by Heaven, you see, 'cause they did it to each other. All the rice paddies and vegetable fields, they were all completely ruined, choked with weeds like some sort of haunted house."

Trying to help the director understand the situation, All Back said indirectly, "This is the Reverend's hometown, as well."

As the guide's words sank in, the director staggered up from his seat, glaring at Yosŏp.

"And you're a minister? You believe in Jesus?"

With that, the old man cleared his throat and spat on the floor. Stalking out, he added, "I don't drink with big-nosed bastards!"

❧ ❧ ❧

There are always witnesses.

The female guide returned and informed All Back that all necessary preparations were complete. The latter stood up and asked Reverend Ryu Yosŏp to come to the reception room. Without an inkling as to what was going on, Yosŏp did as he was told. The room was spacious, with sofas lined up along the walls and a long, low table in front of each seat. The center of the room was empty except for a silk carpet embroidered with magnolias. Judging from the white screen that hung on the right wall, the space must have been designed to hold different kinds of meetings. Already in the room, sitting across from the screen, were a man, four women, and the party secretary. As Yosŏp walked in, they all got up and applauded. The female guide introduced them.

"The comrades here are all survivors who witnessed the tragic events we were discussing earlier. They are gathered here today to share the full truth with you."

At first the "witnesses" seemed a bit nervous; they all began their stories rather cautiously. As they went on, however, their anger and sorrow gradually increased and, as if possessed, their voices grew louder—some even shed tears. Still, Yosŏp knew only too well that their testimonials were all fabrications. He himself had been there, in that same place at that same time. True, the tragic events themselves had probably taken place. A nightmare is real, but how light, how colorless the words that must be used to convey it after one wakes up! Words that had been repeated hundreds, even thousands of times, over and over again—they fluttered in the air, distorted and charred like the pages of a burnt book. Their original typeface, the messages they were once meant to convey, had long since turned to ash.

Their words flitted past, like short sentences typed out on a keyboard, typing away Yosŏp's past and future. They all said "the American troops," but Yosŏp knew for a fact that the troops had simply been passing through. They were never stationed in Sinch'ŏn; they were in a rush to get further north. Both Yosŏp and his brother Yohan knew for a fact that during those forty-five days, before the arrival of the U.S. troops and after their departure, most of the military strength in the area had consisted of the security forces and the Youth Corps—all Korean.

❖ ❖ ❖

Kim Myŏngja. Currently employed in sales at Pyongyang Department Store. Eight years old at time of incident. First-grade student at local elementary school. Father was supervisor of People's Military Committee. Father was tortured, covered in gasoline, and set ablaze. Wriggling and twitching, he howled like a beast, flopped to the ground, and was consumed by the flames like a piece of cloth. Myŏngja was one of six children. Missed chance to retreat north due to road blockage. Family members left behind in village were taken to enemy campsite, where large bonfire was burning. Drunken, they beat her mother and tore off her clothes. Calling the children "red brats," they picked them at random and threw them into the fire. Mothers who tried to jump in the fire to save their children were shot. For one week Myŏngja was locked in a warehouse designated for children. They were given no water. The younger children cried from hunger. The infants' cries soon grew weak. It was December, dark and cold. The children were so starved that roundworms in their stomachs crawled up into their mouths. The famished children chewed them up. Mothers, ready to face the last, screamed for water. The enemy brought buckets filled with sewer water. The children's tongues ripped and bled from licking the spilt water with their tongues. Mothers fed children with urine they'd collected. American soldiers came and checked the girls' faces with flashlights, shouting, "Sexy, sexy." Big Sister was dragged away. A female teacher from the elementary school was dragged away. They did not return. Harrison decided mothers and children would enjoy being together. He gave orders to separate them and let them die of worry, crying for each other. Mothers and children were torn apart and locked up in different warehouses. Children cried, crawling around on the concrete floor, asking for mothers. Their knees and elbows were scraped, bleeding. Children continued to cry for water. Guards brought bucketfuls of gasoline. Laughed as children dipped their shoes in gasoline and drank out of them, writhing in pain afterwards. Set inside of warehouse on fire. Children who did not burn died of suffocation. Many children died by the air shaft when the monsters threw in grenades. That night, climbing on top of the children gathered by the wall, Myŏngja got up and out of the air shaft, made a narrow escape, and survived.

❧ ❧ ❧

Chu Ch'angwŏn. Currently a farmworker. Brought up as orphan. Five years old at time of incident. Shoved his face into a palm-sized hole in the wall. Miraculously rescued but crippled from grenade splinters.

❧ ❧ ❧

Ch'oe Kyŏngnyo. They stripped her mother naked and dragged her around by a wire they pierced through her nose because her husband was in the army.

❖ ❖ ❖

Oh Ŭnsun. Ten years old at time of incident. Currently employed as guide at the Sinch'ŏn Museum, exposing imperialist America's crimes to the world. Father was Party member. Also member of Mount Kuwŏl guerrillas. Family was unable to retreat. Family went to mountain in search of father. Mother was caught while foraging in village for food. Ŭnsun was locked up in landlord's storage house. Unexpectedly ran into her father. Reunion between father and daughter was not allowed. Father was tortured in front of small daughter. Daughter fainted. They buried the father alive in a dugout. Ŭnsun crawled out. Approximately twenty of Ŭnsun's close relatives were killed.

❖ ❖ ❖

Cho Sunwŏn. Ten years old at time of incident. Father was Committee Chairman of Party Cell. Witnessed father being beaten to death with clubs by large crowd. Final interrogation was held on November 1 according to lunar calendar. Nine o'clock that night they came with something wrapped in white cloth. It was live ammunition. Eighty-two women and children were dragged through landlord's front yard to execution site. Were stood on hillside and shot. Sunwŏn's six-year-old baby brother was shot first. Bullet went through his abdomen. He survived. Muttering that he was a tough one, they used bayonets. Sunwŏn suppressed the urge to scream. He bit his lips. Sunwŏn was hit by four bullets. All his younger siblings, including the baby on his mother's back, were shot and killed. They sorted out the live ones from the dead and stabbed or beat them to death. At dawn, Cho Sunwŏn crawled out from under a pile of corpses. A ghost rose up from among the corpses. The ghost untied the telephone cords that bound Sunwŏn. The ghost of the woman who used to live next door. Cho Sunwŏn climbed up the mountain, dragging along another boy who wasn't dead yet.

❖ ❖ ❖

Yu Maemul. Currently acting Chair of Women's League in Sinch'ŏn. They committed all sorts of atrocities to extract information concerning the hiding place of People's Guerrilla Corps. Snatched three-year-old Ŭnja from mother's breast and interrogated mother by dipping child in swamp. Later threw child into swamp. When the mother protested, they struck her head with a club. She died on the spot. Took Yu Maemul hostage while roaming around in search of Guerilla Corps. Thinking she was dead they discarded her on an icy road. Because of the resulting frostbite, Maemul spent the following fifteen years in different hospitals. Lost six toes.

❖ ❖ ❖

Ri Inhwa. Nine years old at time of incident. Father was Committee Chairman of District Party Cell. Four men in village, including Inhwa's father, were dragged by wire pierced through their noses. When father refused to respond to interrogation, they trampled her younger brother to death. Inhwa hid underneath the wooden floor.

❖ ❖ ❖

Ah, finally they're all through with their stories. But no, it's not over yet, Yosŏp thought.

Yosŏp came out of the county hall and waited for the car that would take him back to the hotel. He stood under the dangling fruits and wide leaves of a fragrant sycamore tree. In the old days, on days like today, Big Brother Yohan and he had played war, using sticks for swords and wearing crowns made out of these huge sycamore leaves. Yosŏp took out his pocket Bible and thumbed through it. He turned to Ephesians:

> For he is our peace; in his flesh he has made both groups into one and has broken down the dividing wall that is, the hostility between us. He has abolished the law with its commandments and ordinances, that he might create in himself one new humanity in place of the two, thus making peace, and might reconcile both groups to God in one body through the cross, thus putting to death that hostility through it. So he came and proclaimed peace to you who were far off and peace to those who were near;

for through him both of us have access in one Spirit to the Father.

Yosŏp felt tears welling up in his eyes. In the hazy distance, he spotted the approaching vehicle. Sitting in the passenger seat was the guide—he'd left earlier to fetch the car. Another man sat in the back seat. He opened the door for Yosŏp then scooted further in. It was his nephew, Daniel, whom he had parted with yesterday. When Yosŏp got in, Ryu Tanyŏl addressed him in a tone much more courteous than before.

"Comrade Assistant Chief has asked me to spend some time with you, Uncle."

Realizing for the first time that All Back must be the Assistant Chief, Yosŏp showed his appreciation by bowing his head.

"Thank you for your consideration."

"Well, there was an order from above—we're going to let you take it easy today. You may go to your hometown with your nephew. The inns here aren't suitable, so I'll take you to the guesthouse."

The car raced along a tree-lined avenue that sliced through the rice paddies. Scores of young men and women in shabby working clothes were marching along the lane. Each one was armed. They looked like some sort of farm village army reserve. They made their way through the field, slowly, without a single look towards the speeding car.

5
A Pure Spirit
CLARIFICATION BEFORE RECONCILIATION

THE GUESTHOUSE WAS BUILT in the style of an old-fashioned inn. Immediately inside the front door was a large hall for receptions and conferences. Farther in, there was a small dining hall and a kitchen. Beside the reception hall was a corridor, and at its end was a common room. The bedrooms were all lined up along the left side of the corridor. On the right side, a series of glass doors looked out onto a backyard. The room assigned to Yosŏp and his nephew Tanyŏl was the VIP suite—it included a parlor, a study, and a bedroom. The Assistant Chief, All Back, had a different room at the far end of the corridor. After supper Yosŏp and Tanyŏl went out together to take a stroll around the guesthouse. It was surrounded by trees with broad leaves, providing an abundance of cool shade; farther off was a forest of pine trees. Uncle and nephew walked side by side along the narrow path that wound through the forest. The cool evening breeze was quite pleasant, and though it was still fairly light out, the crickets had already begun to cry. The path was a gravel one so they were accompanied by the crunching sound of their steps.

"Your mother . . . does she still have her faith?"

Yosŏp asked the question without turning to his nephew, looking straight ahead, and Tanyŏl kept his gaze fixed on the ground as he answered.

"My mother doesn't talk about the past."

"Not even about your father?"

"No."

"Then how do you know so much about him?"

Silent, Tanyŏl just kept on walking. Yosŏp was thinking that here, now, they could finally throw caution to the wind; they were outside, and no one was around to listen in but the pine trees.

"You, you know your father's name, and you seem to know about his past—"

"*Everybody* knows about his past. I heard about it constantly, all through my childhood. Grandfather Some told me a little bit, too."

"Does he still live in the same village?"

"Yes. He's a guard at the farm library now. He's helped our family enormously. It's only because of his pull that I was able to join the party at all."

Tanyŏl stopped abruptly in his tracks and turned to face Yosŏp, staring him straight in the face.

"Think about it. Do you have any idea what it was like for us? No one in the village would speak to us. Children at school didn't want to have anything to do with me. All we could do was go to the Cooperative Farm, do what work was allotted us and get our food rations. That was my life, my whole life, until I turned fifteen. Then, thanks to Grandfather, I was able to move to Some. And now, now that I've barely managed to inch my way out from under the shadow of the crimes committed by the man who was my father—now you're here, trying to uncover the past. I mean, if you'd only just leave us alone, we might finally be living a quiet life."

"There is an old saying that goes 'Start by plucking a hair, end by killing a man.' It is also said, 'Two hands must meet to make a sound.' The atrocities that happened here weren't carried out by strangers—it was us, the people who'd once lived together harmoniously in the same village."

"They say it was the superstitious freaks who did it."

"No, it was Satan who did it."

"Come now, what sort of a ghost is that?"

Ryu Yosŏp replied, "It is the black thing that lives in the heart of every man."

At the end of the pine tree forest appeared a levee that was as tall as a man; a set of cement steps led up to the top. They walked up the steps. The first thing to greet their eyes was the vista of a wide, open field. The sun was just coming down over the field; it was a gorgeous sunset—breathtaking. The chirping of birds, magpies, maybe, could be heard from afar along the early autumn breeze as it blew across the grass. Yosŏp finally felt as though he had truly arrived; this was the hometown of his childhood. He sat down quietly on the grass atop the levee. Below him was a reservoir. The surface of the water, calm under the setting sun, rippled now and again when a fish would jump up in a flash of blinding white before it disappeared again. Each ripple was audible, and the glossy surface was momentarily broken by a series of concentric rings.

"Come, sit with me for a moment."

Hesitant, Tanyŏl sat down beside his uncle.

"Do you know why I came here?"

"Well, I—"

"I've come here to cleanse us all of the crimes that were committed by people like your father and me."

His nephew's hollow face, tanned and expressionless, became slightly distorted as a cynical smile began to form on his lips.

"Father was a reactionary. He can never be forgiven, not in a thousand years. How could such a crime ever be cleansed, especially now that he is no longer in this world?"

Yosŏp reached into the inner pocket of his jacket. He fumbled for the little leather pouch, drew it out, and untied the leather string. He reached in and took out the sliver of bone that had belonged to his brother. Cupped in his palm, the yellow-tinted bone looked just as much like a *tojang* as the first time he'd seen it.

"Your father was cremated before I left to come here. This piece of bone is his, part of his remains. In a way, your father has come home with me."

Tanyŏl craned his neck, staring at Yosŏp's palm.

"Well, go on. Touch it," said Yosŏp.

His nephew held out his hand. Tanyŏl's trembling thumb and forefinger touched the bone, held it for a moment, and then leapt back to his side. The younger man began to sob, his face buried between his legs. Waiting for this wave of emotion to die down, Yosŏp put the bone back into the pouch and placed the pouch back in his inner pocket. Tanyŏl wiped his face with both hands, sniffed a couple of times, and picked himself up from the grass.

"I am a Party member. Reactionaries like us are forever indebted to our Honorable Leader, who has embraced us into the great bosom of our Republic. I have been assigned the task of spending time with you, Uncle, in order to convey the sincere hopes of the Party that you will help lead the mission of unification for our nation."

"Yes, yes, right, that's right, and I thank you for it," said Reverend Ryu Yosŏp, patting his nephew on the back.

They passed back through the pine forest once more and returned to the guesthouse. The guide was waiting for them at the front gate.

"Your bath is ready. You must be tired. Take a bath and get some sleep."

A couple of bathrobes and bath towels had been placed neatly on the bed. Taking off his clothes, Yosŏp turned to his nephew.

"Tanyŏl, go ahead and get undressed—we can bathe together."

"You can go first, if you like."

"I'd like you to help me scrub my back."

The bathroom at the guesthouse was a cozy size, about five *p'yŏng,** and the round, tiled tub had a separate faucet. A small stool made of wooden boards stood in the middle of the floor. The heavy smell of sulfur seeped out of the pipes, and the water looked slightly yellow. Without a word the two men got into the tub and sat there with their eyes closed. Climbing out of the tub, Yosŏp sat down with his back to his nephew. Tanyŏl splashed some water on his uncle's back and began to scrub it for him with a wet towel. When his nephew's hand touched his back, without letting him see what he was doing, Yosŏp lowered his head for a moment and said a prayer.

❖ ❖ ❖

Thirsty, Yosŏp woke up in the middle of the night.

The sound of snoring filled the room. In the bed next to him, Tanyŏl was fast asleep. Fumbling, Yosŏp opened the door and walked out into the pitch-black living room. Groping along the wall, he managed to turn the light switch, but there was no response—the light was out. He thought he

* *P'yŏng*: a unit of measurement equal to about 3.3 square meters.

remembered hearing that the power was cut off in the countryside after midnight in order to conserve electricity. He decided to give up on the light. Feeling around on the table for the water bottle, he found it and took several deep gulps. He was sitting down on the sofa, intending to stay for just a moment, when two men suddenly materialized out of nowhere and sat down as well, facing him. It didn't even surprise him anymore. One was Yohan, elderly with his white hair, and the other was the same middle-aged Uncle Sunnam.

How—are you two going to leave now? You're on such good terms with each other.

The phantom of Big Brother Yohan, wearing his traditional Korean shroud, nodded.

That's right. But before that, we thought we'd come by and clarify a few things.

Uncle Sunnam, still wearing the people's uniform with the buttons all the way up to his chin, smiled. His eyes half-closed, he said, Now that I'm through with all this, now that I've left it all behind, it doesn't really seem that horrible anymore. We do need to talk about it though, to be fair and honest. Besides, you have to finish any unfinished business before you leave if you don't want to get stuck wandering around in this world.

❖ ❖ ❖

The first few months following liberation, everyone fell into a mindless frenzy of activity. We visited our town and traveled to Haeju and then on to Pyongyang to set up the Committee for the Preparation of Korean Independence, and we Christians were the first out of the five northern provinces to put their ideas into action. But then the trouble started—the Communists decided to change our title to the People's Committee. I was twenty-one at the time, and I'd long been a member of the Christian Youth Association, so it was only natural for me to go on and become a member of the Democratic Party. In Haeju, the right-wing raided the headquarters of the Provincial People's Committee and killed three people. There were demonstrations in the streets—all this not even a month after liberation. After that the left-wing peacekeeping troops took over all the law enforcement agencies. By then any Japanese collaborators who'd been exposed had long since disappeared—when autumn came, all those people who participated in the Committee for the Preparation of Korean Independence, all the landlords and businessmen, not to mention the presbyters of the various churches, they all began crossing the border down into the South.

That November, scores of students and Christians died in Sinŭiju, protesting against the Communist Party and Soviet authority. When we got back home, the Provincial People's Committee for our area had already been founded—the state of the town was just ridiculous. Everyone and his grandmother, all the servants and good-for-nothings and vagabonds, the ones who felt they'd been treated badly in their own towns and villages, they were all sticking together. Naturally, we cut ties with this so-called People's Committee and formed our own group, centered around the church.

I went to Sanjŏnghyŏn Church in Pyongyang with our father. You see, there'd been a proclamation regarding the reconstruction of the Church, made by the Protestant ministers who were imprisoned for seven, eight years during the Occupation for refusing to comply with the Japanese enforcement of daily worship at their heathen Shinto shrines. The proclamation declared that all pastors and presbyters who'd submitted to the Japanese now had to repent before God. After two months' suspension from their posts, they would have to confess and publicly acknowledge that Shinto worship goes against the teachings of Christ. This proclamation, however, was greeted by a significant backlash from the very people it referred to. These folks claimed that they, too, had been persecuted by the Japs, often ending up in prison and, when their churches were dissolved, they strove to quietly maintain their faith underground. They insisted that their lot had been no less difficult—after all, they had forced themselves to endure humiliation at the hands of the Japanese so that they might continue to watch over all the Christians in hiding. That winter, at Changt'aehyŏn Church in Pyongyang, we organized an alliance of all the churches in the five northern provinces. It was not long after the Sinŭiju Incident, and we ultimately resolved to unite as one and fight against the Communists.

On March 1, the year after liberation, everything finally came to a head. We, the Christians, would soon become the mortal enemies of the Communists. With the arrival of the new year, the Joint Presbytery of the North had begun working to make preparations to celebrate the anniversary of the March First Independence Movement—our celebrations were to be based around our churches. Representatives from the Korean Independence Party and the Anticommunist Youth Corps had been visiting us from South Korea, helping to plan a nationwide uprising. We decided to hold a united prayer meeting, so our county, too, dispatched messengers to Pyongyang and Haeju. In the end, Christians from three counties: Ŭnnyul, Sinch'ŏn, and Chaeryŏng, made plans to meet at the Sŏbu Church in Chaeryŏng to celebrate Independence Day together. Some time earlier, Presbyter Cho Mansik had voiced his opposition to the Russian trusteeship of North Korea, a plan that'd been proposed at the Moscow Conference. As a result, Cho was placed under arrest at the Koryŏ Hotel in Pyongyang. We didn't really know what was right—whether we should oppose this trusteeship or support it—we just knew that it was opposed by the South but supported by the North, and that our churches were unanimously against it.

The maintenance of law and order had been left to the Red Guards, which was composed of the various peacekeeping troops, the Women's League, and the Democratic Youth League. They were all run by the provisional people's committees. They'd impounded everything the Japanese left behind—ammunition, pistols, shotguns—and they knew they had the upper hand. All the same, we were determined to resist. Together with the young men from the Bible class I held in the back room of our Kwangmyŏng Church, we ran off leaflets on a mimeograph machine. At the time, I didn't really understand what they said, but I assume it was along the same lines as the ministers' sermons—"We must stop the state's persecution of the Church," "We are against the Communists," "We are against the Russian military." Hwanghae Province was full of leaflets and posters back then.

On the morning of March 1, Independence Day, we put everything aside and set off to the gathering at Sŏbu Church in Chaeryŏng, traveling in groups of three and five. Since the boys in the peacekeeping troops would have their eyes peeled all night long, many of us had gone earlier— they got to the church a couple days early and waited. Older presbyters, like our father, started their journey in the predawn darkness. Thousands of people were at Sŏbu Church by the time we began. Inside the chapel, people had to go up and sit on the platforms, and the aisles were absolutely packed—outside, the yard was teeming with people squatting or standing. The Christian Youth guarded the gate, armed with clubs and picks. No one dared to try coming in—they just watched us from a distance. Well, actually, a couple of Party members *had* managed to make their way in, but that was before we got there; they were already sitting in the chapel. The place was full of familiar faces, especially for those of us from the same villages. We knew all about each other's family situations, everything, down to the littlest details, like who'd been beaten up by whom and who teased whom when we were kids.

Later on we would hear all about the big riots in Pyongyang, but in that moment, we all thought that the world was full of Christians, that it was just a handful of Communists making all the trouble. The minister told us that we Christians were the ones who had actually brought about the March First Movement and won our country's independence and that our new mission was to make our nation, liberated by the grace of God, into a Christian country. He told us that the Communists were heathen trash, ignorant atheists who knew nothing of the fierce punishment that would rain down upon them from heaven, idiots who simply did anything the Soviet Union told them to do. Suddenly, out of nowhere, we heard someone shout, "Enough!" and then stones came whizzing through the air in every direction, shattering all the church windows. Clubs in hand we rushed out to head them off, but the Leftist youths were already fighting at the gates, forcing their way in. Some bastard let a couple of shots ring into the air.

Sangho cracked his skull that day, and I ended up writhing in the dirt, my shoulder struck by someone's club. Our minister was dragged off by the police and the presbyters of the Joint Presbytery in Chaeryŏng, including Father, were arrested. Sangho and I hid at a fellow Christian's house until late that night, and even after we returned to Sinch'ŏn, we couldn't go home. We hid in a dugout for the next ten days.

There was a huge uproar in Pyongyang. The provisional People's Committee had sent a directive out to all the churches, saying that the celebration of the March First Movement was not to be observed in an exclusive manner by churchgoers and that churches would have to participate in government functions. The churches claimed that this was discrimination against Protestants and that we should be free to hold

Independence Day memorial services in whatever manner we chose. The battle of wills between church and state lasted a week. When the morning of March 26 dawned, around sixty well-known religious activists had been rounded up by the peacekeeping troops. By ten o'clock that morning, ten thousand Christians were gathered together at Changt'aehyŏn Church, the church that spearheaded the March First Movement activities. The church was seized by armed patrolmen. That day's sermon had taught us to continue on in the spirit of the March First Movement. We were told that we must never allow Chosŏn to fall under the trusteeship of other nations, that we must never settle for anything less than true autonomy, true sovereign independence. When the sermon was over, some five thousand churchgoers prostrated themselves on the spot, clasping their hands and praying aloud, completely united. They say that the sound of their weeping and wailing reached up into the heavens. In the middle of this prayer, armed police officers burst into the chapel and hauled away the minister, shoving him into their car. Churchgoers took to the streets in protest, waving crosses and the national flag. Weaving their way through the streets, they sang "Onward, Christian Soldiers" with all their might. That was when more Christians, those who hadn't been able to make it to church earlier, joined the crowd. Together they returned to the church to spend the night fasting and praying.

At that point, yet another incident occurred—this time, though, it was something that no one had really expected. In the middle of a memorial ceremony station hosted by the People's Committee at the Pyongyang train, somebody threw a hand grenade onto the platform where the key staff of the People's Committee and the representatives of the Soviet military administration were seated side by side. A Soviet officer grabbed the grenade and threw it away—his arm was blown off. Several days later, a second bomb exploded, this time at the residence of the commander of the Soviet Army. And then, within a fortnight, there was a third explosion in the house of the People's Committee's puppet, Kang Ryanguk, a minister who ran a Leftist organization called the Christian League. Kang lost his oldest son.

All these insurrections were the work of the Christian Youth. Of course, they were helped by young men from the South, members of the Anticommunist Youth Corps and the Korean Independence Party. If the

Communists had Marx's *Das Kapital*, we had our Bibles. We'd become the Lord's crusaders; they were the minions of Satan. It was a conflict that had begun long before, in the generation of our grandfathers, when the people of Chosŏn got their first taste of enlightenment.

Despite all this, though, people living in the same villages still couldn't quite bring themselves to rise up against one another. You know how weak Chosŏn people can be when it comes to having a shared history with someone—we've got a soft spot for that kind of kinship. You just can't look somebody like that in the face and be cruel and heartless. But then, you see, something happened, something we could never have imagined, something completely unheard of. What, you ask? They tried to take away our land, the land that'd been handed down to us from generation to generation. It was the beginning of what they called the "land reform." And you know, even then, if it had been total strangers or some foreign bastards who showed up and tried to rob us of our land at gunpoint, well, then we might have just cried our hearts out, been mortified at our own helplessness, and given in—but that wasn't how it happened. It was our friends, the kids we grew up with, the ones we'd known from babyhood until we got old enough to grow pubic hair, swimming naked together and fishing in the river—people we'd shared broth with, sometimes sleeping under the same roof after we worked side by side in the same fields and mountains—these very same sons of bitches started showing up, completely poker-faced, telling us to just hand over our land.

❖   ❖   ❖

All right, you've had your say. Now it's my turn. It was around the twenty-fifth, I think, when the Soviet Liberation Army marched into Hwanghae Province. The Soviet political officer came with his advance troops, and he met with Chosŏn representatives from all those community organizations—it was all in compliance with decisions that had been made in Pyongyang. So was changing the name of the Hwanghae branch of the Committee for the Preparation of Korean Independence to the Hwanghae Province People's Political Committee. Then they just went ahead and appointed a Christian presbyter as the chairman of the committee. Except for a few Leftists, all the members were either landowners or other rich folk with lots of influence. I'd just gotten home from Ŭnnyul, so I went to look up Mr. Kang and see some old friends, the ones I used to read the bulletin with.

All sorts of organizations were springing up back then in Hwanghae Province, like weeds that grow like crazy after a heavy rain. I remember the Hwanghae Province Regional Committee of the Chosŏn Communist Party had a pretty motley crew back then, from former tenant farmers to men who'd been schooled in Seoul or Japan, who had book learning and knew all their -isms. And then there were the ones who, as we used to say, were just "whatever-ists," the ones who just joined because they thought it looked good. Those "security forces," as they called themselves, and the "peacekeeping troops"—they were all good-for-nothings who used to hang around town, and those were the groups some of the young Christians ended up joining. The Christians and the Committee for the Preparation of Korean Independence were basically one and the same, too. It was different in Hamgyŏng Province, they say, but that's how it was in P'yŏngan Province and Hwanghae Province. We—the young men—we were far from content. The way we saw it, the bastards who'd lived so well through the occupation, fawning all over the Japs—they were still the same ones who were getting the higher positions, even after liberation and still ordered us to do this and that. Things were in a sorry state.

To tell the plain truth, your father, Presbyter Ryu Indŏk, and your grandfather, Reverend Ryu Samsŏng—they came into their land by working as agents for the Japanese Oriental Development Company, managing the contracts of tenant farmers. Practically everyone who attended Kwangmyŏng Church, in fact, lived quite comfortably, and most of them had at least a plot of land to their name, small or large. As for the churchgoers who lived in town, they were all restaurant owners, pharmacy owners, schoolteachers, millers—all pretty loaded, really. And the members of the so-called Committee for the Preparation of Korean Independence, they were the same kind of people. The only thing different about them was that they called themselves the Nationalist Camp. Anyway, we stood firm. Land reform had to be implemented using blind confiscation and blind distribution. That's when the Nationalist Camp flared up in a rage and refused to compromise. They said the very notion of abolishing the landownership system was unpatriotic. They wanted to employ the three-to-seven system, with thirty percent going to the landowners and seventy to the tenants, provided that all farming expenses were handled by the tenants—but it all amounted to nothing in the end. You see, even under the Japanese occupation, everyone argued over these exact same issues. You know what I say? Show me a Christian leader who didn't come from a family of landowners.

I'm not pretending that the Left didn't have its problems, too. Being Communist was our claim to fame, but there were so many inner factions that a country bumpkin like me could never keep them all straight. There was a domestic group that kept running to Seoul to find out which way the wind was blowing, a separate group from China, and a group of comrades with weird names who'd come with the Soviet army—but the number of partisans who, weapon in hand, actually fought against the Japanese, well, that was so small that none of them could even find the time to *visit* the simple folks in the countryside.

Still, after the Committee for Preparation became the People's Committee, things did get a bit better for us. When he returned from his visit to Pyongyang in mid-October, Mr. Kang told us what had happened at the Enthusiasts' Rally of the Five Northwestern Provinces held by the Chosŏn Communist Party. He told us that General Kim said our newly liberated country would be weakened by any internal strife and that we all had to do our best to work together with the conscientious national capitalists. The General said we shouldn't assume that every last person who'd worked under the Japanese occupation was a Japanese front man—he said the real battle ahead of us was against the landlords, against the true Japanese spies who were masquerading as members of our Party. Two days after the Enthusiasts' Rally came the Pyongyang People's Rally, and that's where we found out that the Protestants were claiming we'd only been liberated by "the grace of God." Following that, the Honorable General made his first ever public appearance. In order to build a democratic Chosŏn, he told us, those with money needed to provide money, those with knowledge, knowledge, those with strength, strength, and so on and so forth, so that the entire race could finally unite as one and create a truly autonomous, independent nation. But then, in Pyongyang, the Protestants formed the Chosŏn Democratic Party and grown men like your father, Presbyter Ryu, youths like Yohan and Sangho, and all kinds of riffraff like the trash who raided our office—they all actually became official Democratic Party members. Up until that point, we'd just put up with it all, doing whatever you young ones told us to do. Everyone told us to just bear with it for the sake of national unity. It was real easy to tell a Leftist from a Rightist back then, even from far off, you know, just looking at their clothes and build. I mean, we'd all been underfed as children, and we still had no money for clothes, so we just looked wretched all around.

Actually, you, Yohan, you put it quite well. Both sides were in the wrong at Sinŭiju. Whenever times get confusing, you know, all the sleazy con men come out of the woodwork. A lot of the Communists, all they did was offer lip service, and since Sinŭiju is a border city it was full of people who'd made their living by kissing Japanese Imperialist ass. There were a ton of you churchgoers, too—they don't call Sinŭiju the Jerusalem of Chosŏn for nothing. There never were a lot of tenants in that area, just lots of traders and landed farmers. Everyone was pretty well-to-do, so there were plenty of schools, lots of students. Anyway, those who claimed to be Communists may have made the blunders, shooting their guns like that, but you churchgoers have got to admit—you did egg them on.

You guys may have had no idea what anti-trusteeship and pro-trusteeship was all about, but we studied it systematically—we knew it through and through. You know and the whole world knows that America and Russia are both just full of big noses. Their official goal was eliminating the "temporary military measure" of the thirty-eighth parallel and supporting Chosŏn's bid for independence, but the truth is, what they really wanted was to gobble up the entire peninsula—neither one was willing to settle for half. Trying to reduce Russia's influence to a fourth of what it was, the Americans tried siding with China and England. Russia, though—Russia maintained confidence in the people of her former colony and changed the proposition at the Moscow Conference to help establish the Chosŏn Provisional Democratic Government. They said officially that Chosŏn should be an independent nation. It was all or nothing for a while, but then the Americans and Russians decided to compromise, at least for the time being. Depending on how we did, we could always use the foreign powers to unify our country three years down the line. You people keep wanting things to be either good or evil, but our philosophy is that reality is what matters most. You chose to be idealistic and went for anti-trusteeship, but we were pro-trusteeship. The American military government based in South Korea assessed the situation and decided to begin by securing the South. Pretty soon their propaganda was everywhere, claiming that Russia was for the trusteeship while America was against it. By then, even the anti-Japanese faction was divided about trusteeship. I still remember what the insider documents used to say in those days:

"We must commit ourselves to the class struggle ever more forcefully. All known Rightists are pro-Japanese, landowners, capitalists and puppets controlled by America, other enemies of the People, and reactionaries in the South. A democratic base must be established in the North in order to demolish the foreign powers and other enemies of the class. All arable land and forests in the possession of Japanese and Chosŏn landowners, traitors of the people, must be nationalized. With the introduction of land reform, the tenant system must be abolished and the land freely distributed to farmers.

In January, the farmer's off-season, each district received instructions to select a representative for the farmers and send him to Pyongyang. The notice said that the class principle had to be observed in the selection, too. Each district chose, as they understood they should, from the tenants, servants, and daily laborers, and those representatives were sent up to the central government. Illang was selected to be Ch'ansaemgol's representative, so he went on up to Pyongyang. When the provisional People's Committee was first formed, I, too, went up to the central government to attend training sessions on founding local Party cells. The issue we all thought about most was class struggle. And then the Independence Day incident broke out. Our political position on the issue was simple.

Democratic social reform in the North had to be carried out under conditions of violent class struggle. The disintegrated landowner class and the Japanese collaborators, the remnants of the bourgeoisie and bureaucrats, the institution of the Church and a number of specific Protestant ministers who had long been on intimate terms with foreign missionaries and were none other than the harbingers of American invasion were identified as the reactionary powerhouses of the country. These categories often overlapped, and the most readily identifiable common element was Christianity.

You know, in the old days, if you went to the marketplace and entered a pottery shop, you'd probably have seen a malformed pot or two. The irregularities happen after the lump of clay has been formed into a pot, probably from some mistake in the drying process. Anyway, in the end, what you've got was a defective pot. These pots, they were never thrown away—they just got sold for half the price. The nicely shaped, well-made pots cost several times more. Really rich folk would even buy ceramics that had colored glazes and elaborate designs. The defective pots were for the poor. Placed in a sunny spot in a three-room, straw-thatched hut, they would be used to keep soy sauce or kimchi, food you saved to eat during the long winter days. You know, even when a poor family somehow moved on up in the world, they always held on to those ugly pots, passing them down as family heirlooms.

You see, the poor people and needy farmers of Chosŏn—they were the ugly pots, bashed in by the Japanese. To hold them up, to display them as something precious—that's been the position of our class. You people, you people just want to smash them to bits and be rid of them.

❖ ❖ ❖

At first we had no idea what was happening to our village. We were still hiding out in the mud dugout because of what happened at Sŏbu Church in Chaeryŏng. Myŏngsŏn and her younger sister, Chinsŏn, would take turns bringing us food. One day, Myŏngsŏn came and told us someone wanted to meet us. It turned out to be Pongsu, the oldest son of the man who owned the rice mill in town. He'd graduated from a commercial high school in Pyongyang, where he ran a huge general store that bought and sold local products. Then, during the Japanese occupation, he moved back home. He'd been there in his hometown when the country was liberated. He was known for being generous with his money, and the man could definitely hold his liquor—on the other hand I guess some might have called him a libertine or a womanizer. Sangho and I knew him from when we were kids. He moved up to Pyongyang right after he graduated from elementary school, but he always came down for vacations. We were never really that close, but when we joined the Democratic Party and formed the Youth Corps after liberation, he became a leader among the young men in town. When Myŏngsŏn brought us his message, he was already on the run—he'd had a hand in the raiding and burning of the People's Committee office.

We'd just assumed he'd run to Pyongyang or Haeju. Sangho and I left the dugout and made our way to the funeral house on the outskirts of the village. It was an open shed on the hillside where they stored the funeral bier, near the three-way fork in the main road. As we groped our way along in the dark, we heard someone clearing his throat.

Is that you, Pongsu?

Yeah, come on up.

It was so dark inside the funeral house that we couldn't see a thing. Pongsu struck a match and lit a candle. It was a pathetic stump of a candle stuck to a wooden shelf. Wearing a suit and standing next to a packed knapsack, Pongsu turned to us.

I hear you guys went to Chaeryŏng and raised hell—that right? If we're going to establish a nation of God, we're going to have to chase out every last Commie bastard.

The boys from the peacekeeping troops are swarming all over the place out there, red in the eyes, saying they're gonna get you! What the hell are you doing here?

Pongsu responded to my frantic question by laughing out loud.

What do you mean "get me"? Haven't you heard the talk? We turned Pyongyang inside out!

We heard there were bombs going off all over the place.

You heard right. We got quite a lot of help from the South—they sent friends. I'm actually on my way down to South Korea right now—I'll be crossing the thirty-eighth parallel. Anyway, that's part of the reason I asked to see you—we need the Christian Youth to organize, underground. We'll be sending up some more men.

It'll be quieting down soon. When it does, the men we already have in Sinch'ŏn, Chaeryŏng, and Ŭnnyul alone will make quite a force, Sangho said.

Once again, Pongsu laughed.

You kids still have no idea what's gong on out there in the real world, do you? No way is it ever going to quiet down. They've just declared that they're going to start enforcing this land reform business. North Korea is like a beehive someone poked with a stick. Anyone who lived well under Japanese rule, anyone who had land—anyone at all—is now being considered a reactionary.

Pongsu glanced at his watch and got to his feet, hoisting the knapsac onto his back.

Got to go. Don't forget what I said. When the men come up from the South, they'll be sent to you.

Suddenly, in the darkness outside the funeral house, a sharp whistle cut through the air. Pongsu hurriedly blew the candle out and climbed down. Following him, we spotted two men waiting at the bottom of the hill. Pongsu ran down before us and exchanged a few words with them. He introduced us:

These men are our fellow soldiers from the South. Say hello.

Sangho and I shook hands with the two men, but it was impossible to make out their faces in the dark. The one shaking my hand spoke.

I'm from Hwanghae Province, too.

Pongsu and the two young men disappeared into the darkness. As dawn broke over the hills, Sangho and I boldly went down into the village, strutting along with a derring-do kind of bravado. Nothing seemed to be out of the ordinary. At the mouth of the village we ran into a neighbor, taking his cow to pasture as usual. When we bowed to him, he spoke first.

Your father, he's back home now, isn't he?

Has he been away?

Oh, I guess you didn't know—he was taken to town, to the police station.

That's when Sangho and I finally grasped that something awful must have happened in the village while we were away. The first person I saw when I got to our front yard was Mother at the well.

Mother, has something happened to us, to our family?

Oh Lord, something, something indeed.

She grabbed hold of me and her eyes began to well up.

Where's Father gone to?

The neighbors just went and carried him back from town.

In accordance with the Land Reform Order, issued nationwide on March 5, our father had officially become a personage who merited "close surveillance." At the Farmers' Rally, held three days later on March 8 in Sinch'ŏn, he was identified as a reactionary. There were about a dozen big landowners in Namuribŏl, Chaeryŏng, and our area, Ŏruribŏl, but most of them had fled South after the formation of the thirty-eighth parallel.

Those who remained owned about ten thousand *p'yŏng** each, including rice paddies, fields, and orchards. When the Land Reform Order was first issued, only those who possessed more than fifteen thousand *p'yŏng*† were to have their land confiscated, but very little time passed before the order was broadened to include any and all land tilled by tenant farmers. The land that had been left behind by the Japanese was, of course, the property of the state, and any land in a given village tainted by the slightest trace of Japanese collaboration was also unconditionally confiscated. Among the old-time landowners who had chosen to stay, hoping to weather the storm, those with over fifteen thousand *p'yŏng* were branded as reactionaries and banished to a distance of one hundred *ri*‡ from their former homes. While confiscating land that had belonged to landlords and distributing it to tenants might have seemed logical, confiscating the land of one independent farmer to give to another independent farmer in the name of fair distribution ended up turning the entire population into tenants of the state. "Blind confiscation" and "blind distribution," they called it, but the twelve thousand *p'yŏng* of rice paddies that had once belonged to our family was cut down to five thousand overnight. Seven thousand had been farmed by tenants, they declared, and besides, they were unhappy with the fact that Father had worked as a clerk for the Oriental Development Company. At least at that point they couldn't yet openly persecute him for being a presbyter at the church—compared to what they did to Sangho's family, we were getting off easy. They hung a sign that read "Wicked Landowner" around Sangho's father's neck and dragged him around town. Then they tried him before a kangaroo court and locked him up. Their excuse was that he had been uncooperative about following the Land Reform Order. Our father had agreed to limit his claims to the land the government parceled out to us and obediently stamped his *tojang* on the document. He was released. When I entered the room, Father was lying on the floor, huddled under a blanket. His hair looked like a magpie nest, and the rims of his eyes were bruised to a dark blue. His lips, too, were cracked and black.

---

* Ten thousand *p'yŏng*: approximately eight acres.
† Fifteen thousand *p'yŏng*: approximately twelve acres.
‡ One hundred *ri*: approximately twenty-four miles.

Father, who's done this to you? Who hurt you?

Father just pulled up the blanket and closed his eyes.

Ah, you were someplace safe. Pray, I say, and sing a hymn.

I wasn't exactly in the mood to gather my hands together for a prayer, but father's request was so subdued that I ended up doing exactly that, together with Mother.

Almighty God, give me the courage to fight fearlessly against distress and persecution. No matter how fiercely the hordes of Satan come down upon us, help me at least to die as a martyr of our Lord. God teaches us that those who are persecuted and wronged for His sake should rejoice, for they will be rewarded in Heaven. We know that some of us suffer already—not just from jeers and whippings—some of us have been bound and thrown into jail, some us have been stoned, knifed, and sawed to death while still others were forced to crawl, clothed in sheepskin and goatskin, starved and mistreated. Oh, if we live, help us to live for Thee, Our Lord, and if we die, help us to die for Thee, our Lord.

Finished with the prayer, I sang the hymn "The Way My Savior Leads Me" two times in a row. Later, our mother gave me the details of what happened. I found out that Illang had been in charge. I also learned the names of all the men who had taken Illang's orders. Most of them were former tenants of ours, but some had been tenants for Sangho's or Pongsu's families. There were about fifty households in our village at the time—the entire population, including the womenfolk, numbered around two hundred. Out of this two hundred, the total number of official Party members back then was, at most, around five or so. The fact that Illang was appointed chairman of the local Farm Village Committee and put in charge of the land distribution was ridiculous enough to make the cows laugh. We didn't even find out what that good-for-nothing's surname actually was until some time after the liberation—and even then, everyone in the village just called him by his Japanese name: Ichiro. No one really knew for sure when it was that Ichiro first showed up in Ch'ansaemgol and started living in our midst. He was somewhere around forty at the time, but none of us knew his exact age, either.

Our home, Ch'ansaemgol, with its large expanses of rice paddies, vegetable fields, and orchards, was known throughout the area as a wealthy farming village. Three or four families owned a significant amount of land, and more than half of us were independent farmers who made a comfortable living. The rest were tenants. Nobody really had any special need for servants, especially since the tenants would come by and help out their landlords during the busy seasons. Of course the bigger landowners, like Father, would usually have a couple of men and women workers all year round, but these were usually former tenants who moved in as house servants. That was how Uncle Sunnam, too, came to live with us and work in our orchards, remember?

Eventually a group of independent farmers chipped in and hired Ichiro as a kind of village servant. In the summer, he'd do things like fix the broken stepping stones in front of the village, manage the village mill, and take care of the community compost heap. During the busy farming seasons he'd go from house to house and help out with the farmwork. His wages were paid to him in rice. Sometimes he'd even draw water from the well for the families that were really short-handed. Anyway, do you remember all the dugouts that used to be at the mouth of the orchard, next to the mill and near the funeral house? You know, those mud cellars where we used to keep the saplings. Ichiro made one of them deeper and covered it up with straw mats. That was where he lived for a while, at least, at first.

No one in the village used the polite form of speech to Ichiro, but he would use the high honorific form to all the married men, regardless of whether they were older or younger than himself—he only spoke the low form of speech to young children. The children, in turn, spoke it right back to him, as if he was one of them. . . . To think that man laid his hands on Father—if that's not an example of the world turning completely upside down, I don't know what is.

Within six months of the liberation, Ichiro suddenly became "Comrade Pak Illang." His attitude had already started changing in the fall of that year, but no one dared quarrel with him about his new manner of speaking. Putting their personal feelings aside, even the adults in the village started to use the polite form of speech when addressing him. A few years before liberation Ichiro had moved out of his dugout and into the village *sarang*, where he spent his time weaving straw mats and mesh nets. Then one day, he simply disappeared. He showed up a few months later, when winter was nearly over.

According to Mother, on the day he took our father, Ichiro just walked right into our house, bold as you please, wearing his people's uniform and an armband that said "Rural Village Committee Chairman." He was accompanied by some boys from the Democratic Youth League. He called out for Father. When Father came out and asked what was going on, Ichiro whipped out a piece of paper and waved it in his face. "The Land Reform Order has come down from the provisional People's Committee," he said, "and I am here to execute it." He asked Father if he was willing to donate his land for fair distribution or if he'd rather subject himself to blind confiscation. Assuming that the bastard was illiterate, Father said his vision was too weak to read the document and asked Ichiro to read it aloud. Ichiro held it up and began to read it slowly. Father yelled at him to stop, snatched the paper away from him, and tore it to pieces. In that same instant, lights burst before his eyes—you see, Ichiro punched him right in the face. Father collapsed to the ground, cradling his face in both hands. Mother saw it all with her own two eyes. She leapt on Ichiro and grabbed him by the throat.

"You ungrateful beast! How dare you lay your hands on him!"

Slowly, Ichiro twisted Mother's wrist. Then, all at once, he thrust her away. While she was down on the ground, he went into the main room without taking his shoes off and ransacked the chest of drawers with his gang, searching for the title to our land. He found it. Then, Mother said, he concluded with his new catchphrase.

Comrades, arrest this enemy of the People.

❖　❖　❖

I, too, know a little bit about Brother Illang.

As I told you before, I went to night classes for a while before I left your orchard to go and work at the mines in Ŭnnyul. In those days, I used to go to the village *sarang* to practice writing or to read leaflets all by myself. That was back when Brother Illang was still Ichiro. In the winter, the young ones in the village like your brother Yohan and some of the older men were constantly in and out of the *sarang*. They would always stay late into the night, so we never really had a chance to share the thoughts that lay deep within our hearts. Because he'd spent his entire life serving others, Ichiro hardly ever opened his mouth. You remember, don't you? And the man always shaved his head. He might have let it go for a month or two, but just as it started to get a little bushy he'd go into town on a market day and have it shaved clean with a pair of hair clippers.

It was after the autumn harvest that I finally became friends with Brother Ichiro. I, too, decided to start spending my nights in the village *sarang*. You see, no matter how bland or boring a guy seems, if you start sleeping together in the same room every night you're bound to develop a sense of kinship. There were plenty of branches to be pruned off the trees in the orchard, so we had more than enough firewood. We stuffed the furnace full of them, and by the time we entered the room the floor was always boiling hot. We cooked peas and steamed sweet potatoes together. Every now and then you boys would bring us some *tongch'imi*, and then we'd take a bite of sweet potato and wash it down with *tongch'imi* juice that still had bits of ice floating in it. We'd pick out the crunchy slices of radish that floated in the *tongch'imi* bowl and chew them up. I saw that Brother Ichiro was in the habit of sleeping without a blanket—without any covering of any kind, actually. The floor might have been warm enough, but the room could get quite chilly, especially at dawn. I asked him, Brother, why don't you cover yourself with a blanket when you sleep?

I've never had anything to cover myself with . . .

I was so dumbfounded that I asked him again, You mean you've never slept with a blanket, not even when you were a child?

That's right. There aren't any blankets up in the mountains. The first time I ever saw one was after I came down into the village.

That's when I realized he had lived in the mountains, in the slash-and-burn fields, ever since he was a child. I tried asking him a different question.

Brother, doesn't it make you angry when little children talk to you in low form?

They are all the precious offspring of my masters—why would I be angry?

Brother, I'm five years younger than you—please, don't use honorifics when you speak to me—plain form is enough.

Brother Ichiro simply smiled in response and didn't say a word. Living together in the village *sarang* for four seasons, we became as close as if we were real brothers. I found out that Ichiro was born in Sanp'an. He'd lived with his parents and his grandmother in a nearby hill village; they all worked at an eatery for laborers. The name "Ichiro" was given to him by a Japanese foreman. His father was working as a logger when he was crushed to death under a log, and then his mother left to make money. She never came back. Eventually, he and his grandmother moved to the slash-and-burn fields, scraping together a living by working other people's land. All they could grow was millet and potatoes, and since they were working as a kind of tenant family they had to give up half of what little they harvested to their landlord. When he turned eighteen, Ichiro found a woman, got married, and even managed to stake out a little slash-and-burn field for himself by burning off the slope of a hill. Then, as luck would have it, the government began to crack down on the slash-and-burn fields, and Ichiro was sent to prison. By the time he got back to his home after serving his ten-month term in Haeju, the whole place had been burnt to cinders and, thanks to a wide-scale evacuation, everyone had scattered to heaven knows where. His grandmother had died, and his young wife had disappeared. After that, he just drifted from one construction site to another until he ended up along the Chaeryŏng River. Eventually, just like my family, he floated on over to Ch'ansaemgol in search of rice paddies to work.

When we were liberated from the Japanese, the first thing I did was search out Brother Ichiro. Like I said before, I learned all about Communism during my time in the mines, so when we formed the Hwanghae Province Regional Committee, I told Mr. Kang about Comrade Pak Illang. While you Jesus freaks were organizing your Chosŏn Democratic Party, we were busy too, forming our Communist Party. We set up a security office at the police station in town, held the People's Committee meetings in the county hall, and started giving lessons at the community center. In Ch'ansaemgol, Ichiro the village servant, two other household servants, and Uncle Chungson were the first to join the party. They were all recommended by me, you know.

In three months, from October to January, Comrade Pak Illang learned to read and write. He left Ch'ansaemgol and went to work as a guard at the county hall. Day in and day out, he memorized the *han'gŭl* alphabet that Mr. Kang had written out for him with a brush. A man from Pyongyang who'd served in the China's Eighth Route Army showed us how to apply layers and layers of pork fat onto a wooden board and paste a thick laminated sheet of paper lacquered with bean oil on top of it—if you do that, you can write on the board with a stick, then lift the oiled paper to erase it. He told us that was how they studied during field operations. Ichiro, the same Ichiro you all thought was a brainless half-wit, the same Ichiro you talked down to—just think about it for a second—that same Ichiro learned to read and write. He learned to write his own name. Pak Illang. If that's not what the liberation was all about, I don't know what is. Comrade Pak Illang, who used to carry firewood and work like a cow while you people ate white rice, slept under warm blankets, learned at schools, sat in churches, read Bibles, prayed and sang hymns—well, he learned too, and now he could read and write words like *land reform.*

Because I helped to organize the Red Guards with members of the Democratic Youth League and the Women's League, I was put in charge of security. I ended up going with Brother Illang when he went up to Pyongyang to take his training course. We got on the train in Sariwŏn. I had a little spending money, so I bought some soft drinks and boiled eggs. Brother Illang ate an entire case of eggs in one sitting. I think I had three or so myself. Back then I hadn't yet broken ties with the idea of the family system, so I still called him "brother." I said to him, Brother, you're eating way too much—you'll give yourself indigestion.

He told me he'd had a couple of eggs before, at the village feasts, but he'd had to eat them so sparingly—he'd just always wanted to eat them to his heart's content. There are ten eggs in one case, you know.

At the training session in Pyongyang, they knew there was no way any talk about Bolshevism or the writings of Marx and Lenin would ever make any sense to us. We'd all just barely finished learning *han'gŭl*, and the only use we ever had for books until then was to roll cigarettes or wipe our asses—big, complicated words were still a bit beyond us. But you see, the way the Japanese had oppressed us, the way the Japanese collaborators and the landowners had, step by step, ruined our lives—that was easy to understand. Especially when it was explained to us in simple, easy words, like a children's story:

"Comrades, open your hands and look down at your ten fingers. Seven of your ten fingers are tenants who don't have an inch of their own land and poor farmers who do have a bit of land but have to work as tenants, too. The three fingers that are left are the Japanese companies and the pro-Japanese landowners. Now, let's say that all the farmland in the country equals ten. Those three fingers own eight out of that ten. And that's only counting the rice paddies and the fields, since the rest of the land and the forests belonged to the Japanese. To prove that we are truly free, that we have completely driven out the Japanese, the People need to take back their land. Comrades, what is feudalism? Feudalism is a system where the king dishes out land to a handful of subjects who are willing to guard him, with the lower-ranking officials and the *yangban** class controlling the common people and forcing them to work as tenants. When our king surrendered to the Japanese, our nation became a Japanese colony, and the emperor of Japan and the Japanese governor-general took his place. Soon after that, the *yangban* became Japanese collaborators, which made the life of the common people even worse than before. Comrades who owned no land and had no education worked their fingers to the bone, living as servants or dirt-poor farmhands for generations on end, but they were given nothing, nothing in return for their hard labor. Comrades, from now on, starting the moment you go back home, you must take back what is yours. No matter what, land should belong to those who farm it. When you go back, comrades, will you be able to tell the village elders and the gentle, honorable landlords to give back your land? They will shout, eyes glaring, angry that you dare to be so impertinent. If you feel frightened at the thought of this, you will be a slave to feudalism forever. Never forget that these are the enemies who sucked the blood of your ancestors, enemies of the People who must be overthrown. Come now, everyone, can you do it? Louder! Ah, naturally, in a small village you are bound to have emotional ties—there will be familiar faces and fond memories around every bend—if, however, you do not sever these ties, cutting them as with a knife, you will never be truly free."

With simple words like these they taught us the foundation on which the reactionaries had built their lives was that of the feudalistic tenant system. In order to maintain feudalistic power in the rural areas, the landowners were sure to oppose any form of democratic reform. And yet, obviously, the land belonged to those who tilled it, those who had been tilling it for generations. The land that used to belong to the Japanese organizations, the land that belonged to those who worked for the Japanese or for the

* *Yangban*: formerly the upper class of Korean society; the nobility or aristocrats.

political organizations that were in place under Japanese rule, the land of those traitors of the People who fled their hometowns upon the nation's liberation, any land over fifteen thousand *p'yŏng* owned by Korean landlords, any land, regardless of size, that had been used for tenant farming, and any land over fifteen thousand *p'yŏng* that was owned by the churches, temples, or other religious organizations—these were all subject to confiscation. Blind confiscation and blind distribution, that was the principle. We were fully prepared to deal with any resistance from those determined to hold fast to the old order.

❖ ❖ ❖

The big landowners and those who had openly collaborated with the Japanese all fled, crossing down into the South. The ones who lagged behind, lingering too long in the North—they were mostly Christians. They felt that they hadn't done anything they needed to be ashamed of, and they'd been told they would be free to worship in whatever way they chose.

After all, the ministers and presbyters were still busy trying to establish a nation of God by bringing the Chosŏn Democratic Party to life, regardless of the cost. In response to the Land Reform Order, the Christian Youth and churchgoers throughout the North launched various counteractive campaigns. Within a week of the order's issuance the citizens and students of Hamhŭng held a large demonstration. The result? Six dead, thirty-three wounded, and over two thousand arrested. More demonstrations followed, in our district, in Changyŏn, and in Unnyul.

The campaign against the Supreme People's Assembly representative election, which was to be held on November 3 of that year, became the last public movement to be organized by the Christians. It just so happened that the day was a Sunday, and the Joint Presbytery of the Five Provinces of the North held a meeting. They adopted a strong stance against what they saw as the state's general persecution of the Church. Sunday being a sacred day, there was to be no participation in any kind of public event whatsoever except for church services. All throughout the nation, ministers and churchgoers gathered in their churches and prepared to become martyrs. They refused to participate in the general elections.

We gathered together at Kwangmyŏng Church. Sunnam ordered the place surrounded, and the men who used to be our servants and the boys from the peacekeeping troops did exactly that. Sunnam entered the church all alone. The number of believers had gradually decreased in the months following liberation, so only a few dozen people were in the church that day. All the so-called churchgoers from before—those who used to welcome their minister's home visits—they were now reluctant to openly attend church services since the beginning of the land reform movement, afraid they might fall into the Party's bad graces. Unarmed, Sunnam sauntered into the church, his step firm as he took off the work cap he always wore. At the time, our church was run by a preacher named Mr. Kim, someone my father had recruited from the Pyongyang seminary. Mr. Kim was about the same age as Sunnam. Sunnam was in the habit of visiting the church every now and then, but he always addressed the new preacher as "Comrade Kim," never "Preacher Kim."

Comrade Kim, isn't today's service over yet?

On the preacher's behalf, my father looked up and replied, We're in the middle of a prayer meeting. Would you like to join us?

You know very well, sir, that today is election day.

Well, you see, our prayers are not yet finished.

Oho, and to whom do you pray so ardently, sir?

Isn't it obvious? Where do you think we are? This is God's sacred temple.

Obviously biting his tongue, Sunnam swept his eyes over the inside of the church, all the way from the top of the ceiling down to the pews. He mumbled, And just where is this God of yours? If He exists, why can't you show Him to me?

Springing up from his seat, Father pointed at Sunnam and shouted, How dare you! How dare you show such disrespect! This is a holy house of God—

Calm down, sir. Let's just call a spade a spade, that's all I'm saying. My point is that I have no trouble seeing the masses that cry out for the sovereign power of the People, but I still can't seem to spot God anywhere.

You fool. Can you look into your own heart and see your conscience?

Sunnam's reply was immediate, as if he'd known for a long time that he would one day be asked this exact question.

Just as your heart is different from mine, each of our hearts is different from any other.

And with that, Sunnam turned around and left. We all stayed at the church, praying until well after midnight. At daybreak, Sunnam returned. Though he did not try to reenter the building, he did stand at the gate and call out to us in a resounding voice, his tone soft, This is the last time. I promise not to come anywhere near this village again. It's just that Sunday is over now, and we've left the County Committee office open until dawn, just for you. Come and vote. I will be forced to report the names of those who abstain from performing their civic duty.

That son of a . . .

Clenching my fists, I began to rise from my seat when Father pulled me back down.

Come, come, we must protect the church. We must survive.

Quite a few of the people who stayed at the prayer meeting all through the night went to the county office and voted that morning. On the following day, our preacher was arrested and taken to Haeju before any of us even realized what was happening. A sizeable number of religious workers throughout the country were taken into custody that day. Still, even then, the church continued to be guarded by the true believers, and, above all, the services we held in private homes through individual house calls continued to be quite popular. You see, those home services also doubled as our information network.

❖ ❖ ❖

A door opened. Tanyŏl's voice floated out of the dark.

"Uncle, are you out there?"

Sitting on the sofa, Yosŏp turned towards his nephew.

"I'm over here. Why did you get up? You ought to sleep."

By the time he turned back around, the phantoms were gone. Tanyŏl fumbled with the curtain and drew it aside. The sky outside was turning pearly gray with the break of dawn. Tanyŏl came over and sat down across from his uncle.

"It looks like you had some trouble sleeping."

"I was thirsty, so I got up for some water."

His voice still drenched in sleep, Tanyŏl mumbled, "I saw my father in a dream . . . for the first time in my entire life."

"Oh yeah? How was it?"

"His face wasn't very frightening, really. He was dressed in white."

"Did he say anything?"

"No. He just watched me."

Yosŏp walked over to the window and listened to the birds twittering. The world was waking up again. Tanyŏl came up and stood by him, looking out the window. The day was still not quite light. Quietly, as if to himself, Tanyŏl spoke.

"To tell you the truth . . . I shouldn't say this, but . . . "

Yosŏp waited patiently for his nephew to continue. Tanyŏl's voice faded into silence even as he said the words.

"Mother prays, every now and again. She has ever since I was a little boy."

"What kind of prayer?"

"Father's hands—she said that he stained them with blood, right after she gave birth to me. She said she had to pray for forgiveness."

"Stained with blood, yes. But . . . "

Reverend Ryu Yosŏp let out a long sigh and added, "There's no such thing as a soul beyond redemption."

6

God, Too, Has Sinned

PARTING THE CLOTH

IT WAS ALREADY AFTER ELEVEN when Yosŏp and his party finally finished breakfast and left the guest house at the hot springs. The Assistant Chief was the only guide to accompany them, and the car and chauffeur were the same ones that had driven them out of Pyongyang. Although the day before had been hot and humid, today's skies were thick with low-hanging clouds. The clouds weren't exactly black—they were closer to gray, really, and they were just floating around, clumped together. It didn't look like the kind of sky that would be content to sprinkle a light shower; once the first drop actually fell, it would probably pour incessantly throughout the entire day.

"I wonder if we'll finally get some rain today. This heat is just too much. I can't stand it," said the Assistant Chief, looking up at the sky as they drove away.

"The radio forecast said it'll start raining sometime this afternoon or evening," offered the chauffeur.

"Ah, it'll be cooling down, then."

They drove slowly along the dirt road they had traversed the previous day, only picking up speed when they reached the paved highway that connected Pyongyang and Kaesŏng.

"Well, did you relatives enjoy your time together last night?"

The Assistant Chief turned to look around from the passenger seat as he swept one hand back across his neatly combed hair. Yosŏp was watching the buildings. They looked like factories of some kind, and they were whizzing by on the other side of the empty, white cement road. Reading a sign that sat against the side of a hill, he realized it was a pig farm.

"Well, ah, I suppose it's the kind of meeting that's bound to be a bit awkward, for both sides."

The guide's comments finally registering, Yosŏp nodded hastily.

"I wanted to thank you for yesterday. This young fellow and I've become quite close now—isn't that right?"

Reverend Ryu turned to look at his nephew, who lowered his head and grinned shyly.

"Comrade Ryu, does your uncle strike you as someone you've seen before somewhere? They say that's how it feels when you're reunited with a long-lost family member."

Tanyŏl glanced sideways at Yosŏp's profile for a second.

"Well, I wouldn't really know, sir—I've never seen my own father."

"Ah, is that so?"

In an attempt to return the guide's friendly overtures, Yosŏp tried to do his part to keep the conversation afloat.

"I didn't see it when we first met, but as I spend more time with him I've begun to recognize how much he takes after his father and grandfather."

"Ah. Yes. Well, in any case . . . we are now on our way to see your sister-in-law, Reverend. How much time do you think you'll need for the reunion?"

"Hmm . . . "

Yosŏp decided to answer him with a question of his own.

"It's been almost fifty years—how could a single day be enough?"

The Assistant Chief turned back to face the front of the car for a moment, apparently giving the issue some thought. He twisted around in his seat once more to address Yosŏp.

"All right. Two days. What do you say?"

"Thank you, thank you very much. But . . . would it be possible to spend the first day with my nephew's family and the second visiting my uncle?"

"Your uncle . . . was there an uncle?"

The Assistant Chief–cum–tour guide hastily reached for his notebook.

It had a blue vinyl cover, and he kept it in his inner jacket pocket—he was constantly checking it to verify this or that. Skimming over a page that was covered in names, running over them with the tip of his ballpoint pen, he came to a stop.

"Well, well, here it is."

He looked up from the book for a moment, turned back and asked, "But this address here, this is Sinch'ŏn, isn't it?"

"Yes, that's right."

Facing the front once more, the guide muttered, "Huh, that means we'll have to go all the way back. Let me see . . . we'll send your request up and wait until tomorrow morning to find out whether or not it's been approved."

In less than half an hour they were in Sariwŏn, the second largest city in Hwanghae Province. There were high-rise apartment buildings and even two of those department stores—the ones that deal exclusively with foreign shoppers. A sign with red letters spelling out "Rice Cakes" whizzed by outside the car window. A small crowd was gathered out in front of a fish shop. Office workers and laborers were out on their lunch breaks, and so the city center was nearly as crowded as Pyongyang had been. Amazed, Reverend Ryu turned his head this way and that, taking in the sights.

"Actually, hang on—could we stop at a store somewhere?"

"What do you need to buy?"

"I can't visit my sister-in-law empty-handed, can I?"

At that, the Assistant Chief turned to the chauffeur.

"Over there, at the corner of that intersection. See the store for foreigners?"

The car pulled to a stop, and the Assistant Chief led the way inside, Yosŏp and Tanyŏl following directly on his heels, side by side.

"But Uncle, you're on vacation—why are you spending money?"

"It's all right, don't worry about it. Now, what's something your mother might like?"

"She likes curly noodles a lot."

"Curly noodles?"

"You know, those bone-dry noodles."

Yosŏp finally caught on.

"Ahh, you mean *ramen*."

There was a surprisingly large number of customers in the store; each cashier had several people waiting in line. Most of the goods for sale had been made in Japan and China. The whole place was basically an arena for circulating foreign currency. Following his nephew's advice, Yosŏp bought a box of Japanese ramen. He also bought some clothes for his nephew's children and a dress from Singapore for his sister-in-law. For his nephew, he bought a thermos and an electronic wristwatch. Then, remembering that he might be visiting his uncle, he decided to get several cartons of cigarettes, too. He started to put the Japanese cigarettes into a bag with the rest of the gifts, then stopped to take two of the cartons out and pack them separately in a vinyl bag—he would give them to the guide and the chauffeur. Just like that, he'd spent several hundred dollars in the blink of an eye. As he got ready to pay, random people around him came rushing up to rummage through his purchases, apparently for the sake of pure entertainment. Yosŏp felt a little flustered. He thought of the huge selections in the gargantuan New York shopping malls with their labyrinthine aisles, of all the times he had wandered around, quite lost, searching for the right exit. In stark contrast, this place was so simple and rudimentary that it seemed almost unreal.

They left the store and went on to make a stop at the city hall to meet the party agent who had brought Tanyŏl to the hotel in Pyongyang two days earlier. The Assistant Chief held his hand out to Yosŏp for a handshake.

"I'll be saying good-bye here, Reverend, for the time being. We don't know yet whether you'll be able to make it to your uncle's tomorrow, but, well, it should be all right."

"I'm hoping for the best. Are you returning to Pyongyang?"

"No, I'm staying here tonight. If the order to do so comes down tomorrow, we may be going back to Sinch'ŏn together. The Sariwŏn City Authority will be assigning a guide to take care of you today."

The new guide, his hair also combed neatly back, was wearing a short-sleeved people's uniform. His complexion was dark and sunburnt, but he looked younger than Tanyŏl, whose hair was already half white. They changed cars and climbed into a Russian jeep, a vehicle often used by the local government offices. They left the city and drove into the suburbs. The road was, of course, unpaved, and the car jolted back and forth. A cool breeze blew in through the open windows and, following a series of tiny smudges that began to spread across the windshield, a shower of respectably sized raindrops began to fall to the ground.

"Ah, rain. Now the heat is really over," murmured the guide in the front seat to no one in particular.

"I hope it doesn't rain too much. The crops need sunny weather to ripen properly, don't they?"

"Well, we still need some rain for the greens. Vegetable farming is important, too."

Along either side of the road, fields of corn rippled gently in the wind. Past the cornfields, one could make out rice paddies. They were just starting to turn a ripe golden brown. The corn leaves, waving back and forth in the falling rain, looked positively delighted. As they entered the village, a line of low houses with tile roofs came into view. Every one of them had a waist-high wooden fence out front, painted white. Each household was growing beans, their vines creeping up the fences. Housewives peered out at them over their fences and beans. By the time they reached Tanyŏl's house and got out of the car, some of the more curious neighbors had actually come out into the street, despite the drizzle. The Sariwŏn guide told them politely to go and mind their own business, but the small crowd stayed where it was, staring at Yosŏp and his suit and tie from every angle. Tanyŏl led the way, opening the latch on the fence and walking into the front yard. Reverend Ryu Yosŏp and the guide followed. From the front yard, they could smell some sort of frying and sautéing going on in the house. A tall, lanky boy in his teens suddenly appeared around the corner.

"Hey, hey, get over here—your granduncle's arrived."

Tanyŏl waved the boy over.

"Uncle, this is my oldest."

"Oh, I see."

The boy bobbed his head at him, and Yosŏp grabbed both his hands, holding and shaking them as he examined his face. Tanyŏl looked around again.

"Where's your sister run off to? And your mother?"

"Big Sister's gone out to the field, 'cause it's raining. Mother's cooking in the kitchen, and Grandmother's inside."

Apparently having heard the voices clamoring outside, an old woman opened the sliding door to what was probably her room, which had a tiny wooden veranda attached to it. Yosŏp studied her features carefully.

She was awfully wrinkled, and her front teeth were now missing, but the narrow chin and the creased eyelids—they were familiar.

"Sister-in-law, it's me. It's Yosŏp."

"What's that? Why, I can't . . . am I dreaming or awake? You sure you're my little brother-in-law?"

"Yes, Sister-in-law, yes I am. I've come alone."

The two reached out for each other simultaneously and, as their fingers interlaced, the sister-in-law let a few of her tears fall onto her brother-in-law's hands.

❖ ❖ ❖

The family feast, the first of its kind in a long, long while, lasted well into the evening. The actual family members consisted of Tanyŏl's family of four, Yosŏp and his sister-in-law. Also in attendance, however, were the guide and the director of the Management Committee of the Sariwŏn Cooperative Farm, who was also a Party member. Most likely, the people from the farm had lent a hand in getting the food ready. Finding the unfamiliar spices and salty seasoning unpalatable, Yosŏp put down his spoon after a few half-hearted tries. His sister-in-law kept clucking her tongue, worried.

"This—well, *toenjang tchigae* was always Brother-in-law's favorite, but we just can't get good *toenjang* these days. You just can't find it any more, not even in the countryside."

"Ah, come now, he's traveled all the way from America! I'm sure he's not interested in *toenjang tchigae* . . ."

At the words of the committee director, the guide spoke up, his tone all-knowing.

"Oh no, you see, that's exactly it—all the more reason why he must be hungry for the flavor of his own people. It's just too bad that *koch'ujang** and *toenjang* are all factory-made these days. They don't have that special homemade taste anymore."

It was only after evening had turned into night that the visitors finally excused themselves, leaving the family members to themselves at last.

* *Koch'ujang:* spicy Korean staple seasoning and side dish made of thick soy paste mixed with cayenne pepper.

The house consisted of three rooms: two bedrooms with a living room in between, the way it used to be in the old days. The living room had a heated floor and doubled as both anteroom and guest room. Tanyŏl seemed to be quite satisfied with his present life as a supervisor at the farm, saying that the housing conditions were much better in the countryside than in the cities, and that food, at least, was plentiful. The main bedroom was offered to Yosŏp, he being the honored guest, but Yosŏp categorically refused and insisted on sleeping in the living room. He and his sister-in-law settled down, readying themselves to try catching up on all the impossibly overdue news and stories. As the night deepened the rain shower turned into a veritable downpour, and Yosŏp could hear the water running down through the gutters along the eaves. Someone must have put a bucket underneath the spout; the water made quite a racket as it gushed into the overflowing container.

"I hear their father passed away."

Not without difficulty, Yosŏp's sister-in-law finally opened her mouth after the rest of the family had retired for the night. He could sense that she wanted to ask more about her husband. It seemed that Tanyŏl, who'd returned two days earlier from their first meeting in Pyongyang, had already told his mother what little he knew.

"That's right. He passed away quite suddenly, three days before I left America to come here."

"Was he sick?"

"No, not really. He was pretty healthy. He passed away in his sleep. The church took care of his funeral. Ah, yes—please, don't be upset by this, but Big Brother remarried after we went down South, after he'd spent a great deal of time alone. She was gentle, and she had a good heart—the match was made by our fellow churchgoers. Big Brother had two sons, Samyŏl and Pillip, from that marriage."

"I see. So that man lived to die a natural death. If he'd only taken us with him—then, at least, I could have tried to forget. I spent ten years of my life living as a sinner, back in Ch'ansaemgol."

"Sister-in-law, come, let us leave that in the past."

"Do you have any idea how many people Ryu Yohan killed? Just the ones I know of—and you can be sure that wasn't all—number no less than ten in our village alone."

Yosŏp remained silent for a moment before he opened his mouth again.

"I remember."

"What happened to Father-in-law and Mother-in-law?"

"Father did very well down South. His business was a success, and he even built a church before he passed away. Mother passed away a year before Big Brother immigrated to the States, so we buried her with Father."

"They tell me you've become a minister?"

"Yes, I have a parish in America."

His sister-in-law bowed her head for a moment. Then, in a small voice she said, "Would you say a prayer and read from the Bible for me?"

"Even now . . . you still believe in God?"

She glanced quickly in the direction of the bedroom. Her voice hushed, she replied, "There are times when I still pray . . . once in a while, when I think of my father."

"What kind of . . . what do you say . . . in your prayers?"

Shifting to correct her posture, she smoothed her white hair neatly back with both hands and said, very calmly, "I've thought about it all my life. I mean, why is it that men hate each other so much when everything in this world has been created to make us better? Even the Japanese couldn't have had so much hate. I was left here, alone, as a sinner. . . . I lost all my daughters because I couldn't feed them properly, and trying to go on with that one over there, the only one I have left, well, I couldn't help but think . . . God, too, has sinned."

It suddenly occurred to Yosŏp that his brother's hatred had stayed with him until the day he died. The thought made his heart pound. Was it fear that had kept Big Brother's hatred alive? Was it terror that the people who'd been tortured, punished horribly like the victims of the inquisitors back in the churches of the Middle Ages—terror that they might come back to life? Having spat out the most blasphemous words possible for a Christian to say, Yosŏp's sister-in-law sighed heavily.

"God, too, has sinned, that's what I used to think. He looked down on this blazing hell, and he remained silent. Lately, though, I've started thinking about it differently. It's been a long time since I last read the Bible—I've forgotten almost all of it. But Job, Job I remember. My father used to tell me all the Bible stories when I was a small child, as if they were fairy tales.

God and the devil had a bet, I remember, to see if Job could hang on to his faith. There comes a time, too, after he becomes a leper, when even Job feels bitter against God. They say suffering is something that man is born with. The people your brother killed—well, they all had souls. They weren't Satan. Ryu Yohan wasn't Satan, either. His faith was twisted, that's all. I know now. I know that God is innocent."

"Sister-in-law, what is it that you want from me?"

"I want nothing. Peace on earth, glory in heaven—that's what's on my mind. Even if the world is filled with sin, we human beings should just try to get rid of it a little at a time as we live our lives."

"Sister-in-law, let me say a prayer."

At his words, Yosŏp saw her slowly clasp her hands together and lower her head. Doing the same, he drew a deep breath and began.

"Our Father in Heaven, I have returned to my home. Father and Mother and Big Brother Yohan, one by one, have left me—they have gone on to the next world. Though our family left this place together, I have returned alone. Here is my sister-in-law, Thy faithful daughter. Daniel, who was named after one chosen by God, is here also, living with his own family. Those of us who left this place lived our lives without hope, believing that those we left behind had all passed away, and yet here they are, alive and well. I have seen with my own eyes that this land, too, is still a home for souls Thou hast not forsaken—I know this now. Please, Lord, help us to not resent the suffering we caused each other in days long past. Help us to forgive one another. Accept my sister-in-law's faith, faith as precious and as fragile as a flower bud in midwinter. Help it to grow. Forgive my family for all their sins. Though I, too, am a great sinner with no redeeming qualities, I pray. In the name of our Lord, Jesus Christ. Amen."

As Yosŏp finished his prayer, he just barely heard a faint amen come from his sister-in-law, her head still hanging low. Yosŏp reached into the inside pocket of his jacket and took out his Bible, turning to the page he had in mind. It was the beginning of the confrontation between God and Satan over Job.

> Then Satan answered the LORD, "Does Job fear God for nothing? Have you not put a fence around him and his house and all that he has on every side? You have blessed

the work of his hands, and his possessions have incre:
in the land. But stretch out your hand now and touc
that he has, and he will curse you to your face." The Lᴏ
said to Satan, "Very well, all that he has is in your pov
only do not stretch out your hand against him!"

Yosŏp skipped ahead to the scene where Job, after he has lost everything, protests against his fate:

He has cast me into the mire, and I have become like dust and ashes. I cry to you and you do not answer me; I stand, and you merely look at me. You have turned cruel to me; with the might of your hand you persecute me. You lift me on the wind, you make me ride on it, and you toss me about in the roar of the storm. I know that you will bring me to death, and to the house appointed for all living.

Yosŏp closed the Bible and turned to his sister-in-law.

"Here we are shown that God keeps a different godlike being near him, a being that acts as an enemy to human beings. God is presented with the temptation to make a wager by this enemy. This shows us that God, though he is omniscient and omnipotent, can also possess inner conflict. This is not a blasphemy—it simply means that the recognition of God as the perfect being that he is can only come to us when, and only when, a human being's belief in him is absolute. In this mire of sin, a human being is born anew only when he truly repents before God, the perfect being."

Yosŏp finished his brief sermon. The faintest of smiles hovered around his sister-in-law's face as she whispered to herself, "I knew it all along. . . ."

She addressed him once more.

"Both the oppressors and the oppressed have suffered because of the test. Brother-in-law, do you know why I couldn't go on believing in the same way I used to?"

"No. Why?"

"Well, what that thing, that so-called husband—what he left behind was not his family."

"What was it, then? What did he leave behind?"

"Guilt. What else? It was because of guilt that I couldn't bring my faith back to life."

Only then did Yosŏp remember the pouch in his pocket. He brought it out, just as he had done with Tanyŏl. Untying the string, he took out the tiny bone.

"This is Brother Yohan. After he was cremated, I kept this to bring here with me."

He held out the little sliver of bone to his sister-in-law. She stared at it for a moment before reaching for it, picking it up with her thumb and forefinger. The tips of her fingers trembled slightly. She examined it closely, holding it right up to her eyes, then suddenly clutched it with both hands and hung down her head—unlike his nephew, however, she didn't cry.

"Why did you bring this here?"

"It just happened that way."

Yosŏp decided not to tell her about seeing his brother's phantom. Instead, he said, "I may pass through Ch'ansaem tomorrow. I'm thinking about burying it there."

His sister-in-law was still holding the bone in her hands.

"Who asked him to come back like this, in this awful form?"

At the end of a long silence, she handed the thing back to Yosŏp. He took it quietly, putting it back in the pouch and fastening the string tightly. His sister-in-law said, "At least he's back, thanks to you, even if it is like this. Now that that spirit full of sin has come home, the souls who have been waiting to greet him will cleanse him. Uncle Sunnam, Uncle Ichiro, Pak Myŏngsŏn's sisters Chinsŏn, Yŏngsŏn, Insŏn, and Tŏksŏn, Uncle Chungsŏn's wife, the lady teacher at the elementary school, and well, the people from those things they did in that warehouse—"

To stop the flow of words spilling out from his sister-in-law, Reverend Ryu raised his voice.

"Enough!"

For a long moment, the two sat together in silence. Unable to get up and leave without seeming awkward and abrupt, Yosŏp remained seated, listening to the pattering of the incessant rain. At length, his sister-in-law whispered, "There's no God of Israel, no God of Chosŏn. God . . . God is simply God."

She looked at Yosŏp.

"You're a minister, so you should know . . . do you think I, too, can go to heaven?" she asked.

Yosŏp answered, "Observe the law of the nation. And pray, even if it's all by yourself."

7
The Birth of a New Life
WHO LIVES IN THIS WORLD?

◆

IN THE MIDST OF A DARKNESS that could have belonged either to the depths of night or the morning hours just before dawn, Yosŏp felt sleep slowly falling away—a vague, faraway sound reached his ears. It was still raining; he could hear the water as it fell endlessly from the rainspout.

Hey, hey, wake up.

With a start, Yosŏp looked around. Where am I? Ah, right. This is Daniel's house. His family must be asleep now in their bedroom, and Sister-in-law is probably sound asleep in the next room. I see it's still raining.

Yosŏp. Wake up, I say.

The sound was coming from the head of his bed. Slowly he sat up and looked behind him. Big Brother Yohan's phantom had come to call yet again.

Big Brother . . . you're back again. How long do you mean to follow me around?

Until you let me go.

Where's Uncle Sunnam gone? Has he left you to yourself?

They'll all find their way back eventually.

So. What brings you here today?

Listen, you have to bury me in Ch'ansaemgol.

Then you'll leave—without any lingering regrets?

Yes, I'll follow my friends, go wherever it is they've gone. I'm so relieved to see that Daniel is here.

Daniel hates you, Brother.

That can't be helped. Everybody here hates me. But you know, it's a brand-new world for those who've been reborn.

Well, the thing that inspires all the hate shouldn't follow them into that new world, should it? You need to cleanse yourself and leave.

I told you, that's why my friends are waiting to take me with them.

Then, in the blink of an eye, the phantom disappeared. Yosŏp lay down again to the endless sound of rain.

❖   ❖   ❖

The rain stopped the next morning, but the sky remained murky. Everyone was up early, making a fuss over setting the breakfast table just as they had over dinner the night before. Yosŏp saw his sister-in-law open the side gate along the hedge fence and walk into the front yard. She held a hoe and a bunch of flowers in one hand. From the doorway of the living room where he'd been sitting, Yosŏp called out to her.

"Where did you go so early in the morning?"

"To pick some flowers . . . no flowers in the neighborhood. I've been all the way to that hill over there."

"What kind of flowers are they?"

"Ah, this, these are . . . what-do-you-call-them . . . Siberian chrysanthemums."

She held up the bundle, revealing a cluster of yellow pistils nestled inside the white petals, and came up into the room. Using a pair of scissors, she trimmed the stems evenly. Then she walked over to the kitchen and said to her daughter-in-law, "What, don't we have a bottle or something? Fill one with water for me."

Tanyŏl's wife handed her a soda bottle filled with water, and the old lady put one stem at a time, each at a different height, into the mouth of the bottle. When she was through, she sat back and gazed at her handiwork. Walking into the main bedroom, she called out to Yosŏp.

"Come in here."

Yosŏp entered the room and was slightly taken aback. The dining table had been pushed up against the wardrobe, and although the rice and soup and other side dishes weren't arranged in any ceremonial fashion, they were obviously set for a purpose other than that of a regular family meal. Yosŏp's sister-in-law placed the flower bottle carefully at the head of the table. Bewildered, Yosŏp asked her, "What's all this?"

"I know it's not the old way, but these days this is how people around here make do."

"But who is this *chesa** for?"

"Who else? Who but that poor ghost? It's for the man who died so far from home."

While they were talking, Tanyŏl, his wife, and their children had entered the room, all washed up and dressed neatly. Yosŏp had performed memorial services often enough, but this was his first time at a traditional *chesa* for one's ancestors, especially in a Christian household. He just sat there with his mouth shut, feeling awkward. His sister-in-law looked at her son.

"What are you gawking at? Come on now, bow," she chided.

At a silent sign from Tanyŏl, the family of four got to their feet and lined up, single file. They bowed towards the head of the table, one half bow followed by two full bows. Then, like well-behaved children, they all sat down quietly along the wall. They sat like that for a long while, silent, their heads lowered. Again, it was his sister-in-law who broke the silence.

"Go ahead and pray," she blurted out. "You, Brother-in-law, you don't live here—you're not from here, so it shouldn't matter if you pray."

"Mother . . ." Tanyŏl began, raising his voice, but his mother stopped him.

"I say it shouldn't matter. Besides, a ghost won't understand if you don't speak his language, no?"

"What's all this talk about ghosts in front of the children?"

Turning to her grumbling son, the mother spoke freely.

"They live inside you, inside me—they're everywhere. Come, say your prayer."

Yosŏp hesitated for a moment but ultimately reached into his inner pocket for his Bible.

---

* *Chesa*: traditional Korean ceremony performed in honor of one's ancestors.

"This is a book, so . . . instead of saying a prayer I'll just read a passage from the Bible."

As he began to thumb through it, a random passage caught his eye.

"What have you done? Listen; your brother's blood is crying out to me from the ground! And now you are cursed from the ground, which has opened its mouth to receive your brother's blood from your hand. When you till the ground, it will no longer yield to you its strength; you will be a fugitive and a wanderer on the earth."

Cain said to the LORD, "My punishment is more than I can bear."

Yosŏp flipped to a different page and continued to read out loud.

While they were eating, Jesus took a loaf of bread, and after blessing it he broke it, gave it to the disciples, and said, "Take, eat; this is my body." Then he took a cup, and after giving thanks he gave it to them, saying, "Drink from it, all of you; for this is my blood of the covenant, which is poured out for many for the forgiveness of sins. I tell you, I will never again drink of this fruit of the vine until that day when I drink it new with you in my Father's kingdom."

Yosŏp closed the Bible and returned it to his pocket. No one spoke until his sister-in-law said to her daughter-in-law, "Now, now, hurry up and bring in the breakfast. The children will be late for school."

They brought in the rice and soup, and everyone ate in silence. As soon as the children had said their good-byes and left, Yosŏp's sister-in-law asked him to come to her room. Once there, she took out a small bundle from her chest of drawers and pushed it towards him, saying, "Take it with you."

"What . . . is it?"

Instead of answering, the old lady began untying the bundle. Inside was a pair of worn-out underwear, discolored to a darkish yellow, full of holes where the stitches had come undone and blackened all over with large stains.

"It belongs to him. Burn it, and put it together with his bone when you bury it in Ch'ansaemgol. I used it to wrap Tanyŏl when he was born."

Yosŏp took the bundle in silence and tied it back up. He packed it in the small bag he had brought, with his own underwear and toiletries.

The jeep didn't arrive until after ten o'clock, carrying the guide from the City Authority. Tanyŏl, his wife, and Yosŏp's sister-in-law bid Yosŏp farewell from the hedge fence. Tanyŏl and his wife were the first to say good-bye and bow.

"Uncle, come and visit your fatherland often from now on. Don't forget the warm consideration the Party has given you, and always, the unification of our nation."

"Yes, yes, I understand. Take good care of your mother and write to me at the address I gave you. Be sure to contact me if your mother happens to fall ill—I'll send you money or medicine."

With that, Yosŏp turned back to his sister-in-law.

"Sister-in-law, stay in good health. Next time I come, I'll bring my wife, too."

Her voice breaking as she held back her tears, Sister-in-law replied, "Well, see if you can bring his children, too—the ones born over there. One was Samuel, right? And . . . I forgot the other's name."

"One's called Samyŏl and the other Pillip."

"Yes, that's right. The world is theirs now. It's time for us to move on—please, bury it without fail."

Yosŏp said good-bye once more and went to get in the jeep. His sister-in-law stood in front of the hedge fence for a long, long time, long after the car had driven away, disappearing around the corner at the end of the alleyway.

❖ ❖ ❖

The first big snowfall hasn't come yet, but the hill behind the village is covered in a thin blanket of white. The ground has frozen over and thawed out so many times that you can hear the crunch of ice breaking. There isn't a dog to be heard in the entire village. Ever since the start of autumn, those young men—the ones who've been hanging around here, claiming to be guarding the bend in the road—all this time, they've probably been gobbling up all the dogs they can get their hands on. For months now, people haven't been going out. Already there are over thirty empty houses, and these days if you go out into the alley after dark you feel like a pair of bony hands will jump out of one of those empty doorways and grab you by the nape of the neck.

Gunshots start ringing out as evening draws closer, and voices ring out from every direction, calling and searching for one another. I listen to my husband's warnings and never set foot outside after dark. Father-in-law, my husband, and now little Brother-in-law, too—nobody really comes home too often anymore. Judging from the eerie silence in the main quarter of the house, it seems like they've left again. I light the fire to heat the floors and go into the bedroom to lie down and warm my back. I'm so sleepy. Since the start of winter life has become much better than before the war—we have as much rice as we could possibly want and the children can nibble away to their hearts' content. My husband even brought home a sewing machine and radio from somewhere. My two daughters are only one year apart—they've filled their tummies with white rice for dinner and they're asleep beside me, sprawled out across the floor. My belly is so big, all the way up to my sternum, so big I can't even turn over in bed anymore. I'm expecting—any day now, but there's no sign yet.

In the dead of night I'm startled out of sleep by gunfire—a lot of gunfire, coming from somewhere very close by. I am thirsty. It takes me forever to get out of bed and actually stand up. I have to drag my body towards the wall and brace myself against it with one hand, placing the other on my knees to slowly raise myself up. Taking one little step at a time, both hands on the wall, I make my way towards the door. Opening it I come out onto the little wooden veranda. It would be so nice if someone could be here, someone ready to fetch me a glass of water every time I rustle around in bed. Slowly, I crouch down onto the veranda, stretching one foot out, feeling around for my shoes. A sudden, thrusting pain shoots through my lower abdomen. Oh, God. This is it. Frightened, I crawl back to the bedroom. Just barely managing to close the door behind me, I stretch myself out on the warm floor. The pain disappears for a while, but then it's back; it's spreading through my entire body. The intervals between the attacks are growing shorter and shorter.

I hear footsteps coming through the front yard. Ah, that sound. The sound I won't be able to forget for another fifty years. I hear my husband, his voice crisp as he calls from the front door.

Hey, hurry up. We have to go.

I can't even respond. I moan. He bursts through the door.

What's the matter? Are you sick?

Clicking his tongue, he takes off his army boots in the darkness and puts his gun down, resting it in the corner before he enters the bedroom. He snaps his lighter open and kindles the kerosene lamp with the flame. The room lights up. My entire body is already soaked—my face covered in beads of sweat.

I . . . I think the baby's coming.

Huh, what timing.

Oh God, oh . . . it's killing me.

What on earth am I supposed to do? You dying in childbirth is not the issue right now—they'll kill me if they find me here. Not just me, either—they'll kill us all. They'll probably skin us alive.

I clench my teeth. The baby is coming. Gasping, I beg him, please, just . . . help with the baby . . . I'm dying. Just do what you did before.

Oh, shit . . . what the fuck . . . .

Looking around frantically, he reaches over and violently pulls open the clothes chest. Clothes spill out everywhere. Grabbing one of the garments, he delivers the baby with it. I can hear it crying. He starts yelling, suddenly excited, Look! It's a *koch'u*,* a pepper! It's a boy!

He goes out to the kitchen and brings back a wooden basin full of hot water. I think he's washing the baby. He lays our first son down beside me and goes out onto the veranda to have a cigarette. Faint gunshots ring out in the distance. Shots are being fired nearby, too—rat-a-tat-tat—like the sound of a billet cracking in a fire. He rushes back into the room to turn out the lamp. The sound of his harsh breathing fills the silent room.

You stay here. I'm going to Sister's house. I'll check to see if we can leave the baby with her.

I can't say a thing. What is there to say? I have given birth to a son! What more can I possibly hope for? I hear his footsteps crossing the front yard and gradually fading away, off into the distance. As the silence grows, I suddenly realize that he's gone. He's gone, gone to someplace far away, and he's never coming back.

---

* *Koch'u:* a commonly used colloquial word for "penis,"—it also means "pepper."

8

Requiem
JUDGMENT

THEY HEADED FOR DOWNTOWN Sariwŏn to meet up
with the guide from Pyongyang once more. He was waiting for them at the
city hall.

"Well, Reverend, you certainly are a lucky man. Permission for your
second visit has been granted from above."

Reverend Ryu Yosŏp clasped his two hands together and bowed
politely.

"I thank you."

All Back must have been rushed that morning—his hair was looking a
tad bushy, and he kept trying to comb it back with his hand.

"So, what was it like to see your family again?"

Once again, Yosŏp bowed to the guide.

"I was truly surprised. My older brother's family—well, as you can
imagine, we always thought of them as the ones who were left behind—
and yet they're all doing so well. My sister-in-law even seems to be in good
health."

The guide's response was surprisingly terse.

"They were not directly involved. The present and the future, that's
what's important to us."

Hastily changing the subject, All Back opened up his notebook.

"I see here that your uncle, your mother's brother—his name is An Sŏngman. Is that correct?"

An. Sŏng. Man. Yosŏp had to repeat the name several times, muttering to himself, before he could nod his agreement.

"Yes, that's right."

It was correct all right, but just as the proper name of his own mother still felt unfamiliar, his uncle's full name sounded like that of a total stranger. To Yosŏp, his uncle would always be Uncle Some. The guide looked up.

"I am told he is known to be a very fine man indeed."

Uncle Some was a common farmer. The younger brother of Yosŏp's mother, he, too, was the son of a minister. As such, he'd been baptized as an infant. In his youth, Uncle Some had left his home and gone off to Haeju, where he stayed all the way through middle school. Upon graduation, he came straight back home and started farming his father's land. Yosŏp's maternal grandfather had been deeply disappointed by the fact that his son did not go on to join a seminary. Yohan had always believed that Uncle Some might still be alive, even after he had given up hope and begun thinking that all the other relatives left behind were surely dead. That was why Yohan had told Yosŏp to go to Uncle Some in order to find out where the rest of their family had been buried. It was difficult for Yosŏp to picture what his uncle's face might look like in old age. There'd been certain features in his sister-in-law's old face that had pretty much matched his expectations, but Yosŏp had a hard time even remembering what his uncle had looked like as a young man. What little he did remember from his childhood was that his uncle was a quiet man and that when he visited his grandparents during the school holidays his uncle would simply stand behind Grandmother, grinning. With his nimble hands, Uncle Some used to make all sorts of toys for Yosŏp, using nothing more than a block of wood and a kitchen knife, or maybe a scythe. Once, he made Yosŏp a boat with royal gold sails to float in and out of Usanp'o Port. After the war broke out, though, Uncle Some never, not even once, came to Yosŏp's house. Every now and then, though, Yosŏp's mother would mention running into her brother somewhere in town. Yosŏp remembered most clearly the years that came after liberation, and by then his maternal grandfather had already passed away. Meanwhile, there'd been no news at all about his maternal grandmother. Everyone simply assumed she would be living in Some with her son, the aptly named Uncle Some.

"It is my understanding that your uncle used to be the managing director of his Cooperative Farm. I hear the people there still think very highly of him," the guide continued, getting into the car.

Whenever the conversation turned to the topic of her family, Yohan and Yosŏp's mother would always take a moment to brag about her younger brother. According to her, even as a child he'd been a grown-up. He was so thoughtful and openhearted that their father had wanted him to become a minister. "And to think he's turned into such an ox of a man!" she used to say, lamenting the loss.

It was right around lunchtime when the group entered Sinch'ŏn once more, just as it had been on their first visit. This time, though, the car drove straight through the downtown area, racing north for a good fifteen *ri** or so until they reached the wide open fields of Ŏruri. Soon after that they found themselves at the base of a low mountain—a largish hill, really—that rose gently up from the middle of the fields. They were in Some. A Cooperative Farm village with the mountain at its center, the place was completely surrounded by rice paddies. The paddies were already beginning to turn gold and, with just the right amount of clouds up in the sky, the breeze, too, was agreeably cool.

The Some Farm was somewhat larger than Tanyŏl's village. Single-story houses and cement brick duplexes lined the streets. Most of them appeared to be empty, probably because it was harvest season and the majority of the villagers were out in the fields. What looked like some sort of community center but turned out to be the farm office was situated in the center of town, along with a library and a public nursery. Grass lawns and rows of trees bordered either side of the concrete walkways, giving the whole scene a parklike look. Wooden benches had been placed here and there, and when they got out of the car they spotted a couple of old men straddling one of the benches, playing *changgi*.† The managing director, a woman, came out of the office to meet them. She exchanged a few words with the Pyongyang guide, greeted Reverend Ryu, and took them over to

* Fifteen *ri:* approximately four miles.
† *Changgi:* Korean chess.

the elderly *changgi* players. One of them, his eyes meeting Yosŏp's instantly, slowly got to his feet. The woman introduced Yosŏp to the old man.

"Grandfather, your nephew has come to see you. This person right here is—"

Before she had a chance to finish, the old man broke in, a big smile lighting up his face.

"You're Yosŏp, aren't you! But why are you here alone?"

The voice and expression alone were more than enough for Yosŏp to know that this old man was, indeed, his uncle. Uncle Some's back was still straight, and his face didn't look any darker than it had in the old days. He had obviously begun balding, but he'd dealt with this by shaving the rest of his head to match—meanwhile, on the other end of his face he'd managed to grow himself quite a fine beard.

"Uncle! Have you been well?"

As Yosŏp bent at the waist to offer up a deep bow, his uncle grabbed him by the arms and drew him in for an embrace. Pulling away slightly, he looked into his nephew's face with reddened eyes.

"Your mother . . . ?"

"She passed away—long ago."

"And Yohan? Where does he live?"

"He also . . . he died a few days ago."

The old man blew his nose with a resounding honk and thumped his nephew on the back.

"Come, let's go home. The whole family's waiting for you."

Yosŏp looked around, trying to see if he could remember his maternal grandparents' old home, but nothing in his line of vision seemed familiar aside from the low mountain in the open fields. Walking along at his uncle's side, Yosŏp said, "Thank you, Uncle, for taking such good care of Tanyŏl and his family."

"Well, well, so you've seen your sister-in-law, have you?"

"Yes, sir. I stayed with them last night."

"She's been through a lot over the years. I hear you're a minister now, is that right?"

When his nephew answered to the affirmative, the old man nodded several times.

"How old are you now, Uncle?"

"Me? I'm eighty-five."

Uncle Some walked ahead, going to the front of a two-story duplex and pushing open a side gate attached to the low hedge fence, just like the one at Tanyŏl's house. The small front yard, which led into a vegetable garden, was filled with people. Uncle Some introduced his son, a man in his mid-forties who stood towards the front of the small crowd, as well as his daughter-in-law and grandchildren. Inside the house, someone had already set the table for lunch—just as it had been at Yosŏp's sister-in-law's. His uncle had always been an extremely quiet person by nature, and his entire family seemed to take after him. They must have felt rather awkward in the presence of Yosŏp, who was essentially a stranger; whenever their eyes met his they would simply respond with a broad, innocent smile. No one dared to actually speak throughout the entire meal.

That afternoon, Yosŏp followed his uncle to the Farm Management Office and took a look around the Farm Library where, he was told, his uncle worked part-time. Uncle Some briskly informed Yosŏp that the library held some three thousand volumes, many of which were donated by households belonging to the farm. The rest had been sent from different locations throughout the country. There was no bragging nor supplementary information—it was a far cry from the flowery explanations Yosŏp had gotten used to from the other guides.

In the evening, the managing director brought over some alcohol. Though Yosŏp declined initially, he eventually ended up accepting a few glasses, feeling somewhat obligated by the presence of his uncle. It had apparently been a while since Uncle Some had had any *soju*; the old man busied himself making up for lost time by putting back glass after glass. His face, looking so healthy and flushed, belied his age. His laughter grew more and more frequent.

"Let's move on up to the second floor!"

Picking up a pair of candles, Yosŏp's uncle walked out into the front yard. Without a clue as to what was going on, Yosŏp followed him out and discovered that a series of cement steps had been attached to the outer wall of the house. The door at the top of the staircase was thrown open to reveal a three-room apartment. It was identical to the one downstairs in terms of its layout—the second floor entryway was really the only difference. A single, faint thirty-watt bulb hung from the middle of the ceiling in the main room.

"Is this place yours, too?"

Uncle Some laughed.

"Ha, ha, so it would seem, at least for now. A family was supposed to move in, but they were reassigned at the last minute, so this little apartment is still vacant. It's cool here all through the summer, like one of those royal villas from the olden days."

With that, he put the candles down on a small, round wooden table that was marred by a number of scorch marks. He lit them.

"Why the candles? It's not even that dark yet."

"The lights go out after nine. Lately they've been going out even earlier—they have to send the electricity to the factories first, so there've been cuts out here in the rural communities—"

In the middle of his sentence, the lightbulb actually sputtered and blinked out. It seemed dark at first, but once their eyes began to adjust, the space around the table seemed brighter than ever.

"So. What was it that killed Yohan?" his uncle asked, out of nowhere.

"Well, I don't really know. He was quite healthy—he only started looking a little worn out these past few years . . . his sons left, you see, after his wife passed away. They moved to other cities and started their own families. He was living all by himself."

"How old were you then?"

"I'm sorry? When?"

"When do you think? During the war."

"Fourteen, I think. I'd just started middle school."

"Ah. So you saw it all."

Yosŏp had a pretty good idea of what his uncle was trying to say.

"This and that. Just pieces, really . . . but I remember."

"Those people, you know, on both sides—I knew them very well."

Yosŏp decided to go ahead and ask his uncle the question that had been on his mind for so long.

"Uncle, why didn't you become a minister? Grandfather was a minister and, as I understand it, he always hoped you would go on to join a seminary."

His uncle smiled.

"I went to middle school in Haeju and, well, something happened while I was there. It just so happened that my teacher and I were living in the same boardinghouse, and one night he was taken away by the Japanese police. He spent a couple of years in prison before he was released, and when he finally did get out he was sick and ailing from God only knows what. He passed away. There was this one thing he would always tell us in class—regardless of one's cause, one should always treat those close to him as well as humanly possible. He told us we should always be good to our neighbors and the family members we see every day. He said that we should always work for the food we ate, that the only alternative to working your share was laying traps to take the share of others, and that was the worst sin of all. I may not have become a minister, but I *have* done my best to live my life according to his teachings."

Yosŏp wasn't about to be put off that easily.

"What about faith? You were a baptized Christian, weren't you?"

"I still am. I'm also a Party member. After the war, when I started working on the farm, I joined the Party."

"Is that even possible?"

"I might not have become a Party member if the massacre that took place that winter had never happened. That's what made me decide to stay here, as a repentant Christian."

"They slaughtered us Christians, too."

"Well, as you people put it, they weren't believers, were they?"

Finding himself at a loss for words, Yosŏp hung his head. The candle flames flickered violently in the wind that blew in through the open window. Yosŏp made up his mind to tell another person, for the first time, about the ghosts he'd been encountering.

"My dead brother, Yohan . . . he keeps on showing up. The people he killed, too, have been appearing before me. They speak to me."

"Me, too."

"You mean you see these phantoms, too?"

"At first they simply showed themselves, but then, at twilight, as I walked the cow home from the fields, I would see lines of the dead walking along the levee across the way. Sometimes when the weather was bad, I would see spirit fires over Some. Now, though, when they appear, they speak to me. I haven't seen your brother yet."

"What do you do when they come?"

"I just watch them. I just sit there and gaze at them."

"You don't pray?"

"You aren't supposed to pray at times like those. You look at them when they appear, and you hear them out when they speak to you. Maybe the world is about to change—they've been showing up quite often lately. Do you have any idea why that might be?"

"Is it because we have guilty consciences?"

Closing his eyes, Uncle Some bowed his head. For a long while he stayed that way, simply murmuring to himself. Instead of pressing him for an answer, Yosŏp waited. At length, his uncle lifted his head.

"I suppose the time is ripe for them now, for the people who were there. They're ready now, I think. So . . . they appear before us as part of their redemption."

"But you and I, we weren't to blame, were we?"

Suddenly slamming his thick palm down on the table, Uncle Some shouted, "Show me one soul who wasn't to blame!"

Looking down at the candle stumps, neither man had anything to say. After a long silence Uncle Some got to his feet, grunting with the effort.

"We have a bed ready for you in the room over there. Go on and get some sleep."

"Yes, Uncle. What about you?"

"I'll take the other room."

Crossing the anteroom, his uncle made his way towards the main bedroom. Yosŏp turned towards his retreating back.

"Was that praying, what you did a little while ago?"

His uncle turned around and smiled, just as he had when they were first reunited.

"I pray everyday."

"What do you say when you pray?"

"I pray for us all, for our salvation."

Disappearing into his room, Uncle Some closed the door behind him.

❧ ❧ ❧

My day-to-day life wasn't changed much by the liberation. I worked hard to feed my family with my two cows and five thousand *p'yŏng* of rice paddies. I continued going to church every Sunday, just as I had before. Even with the onset of land reform, my life stayed pretty much the same—I was an independent farmer, so I kept my land and continued to work it. The taxes were hard at first, but later on that stabilized as the system was put into order, and everything became pretty much fair and square as far as I was concerned.

I kept thinking that the church and the Party were both being driven by youths, young boys who were just brimming over with spirit and passion. I still remember the fight on election day. Doesn't it say in the Bible that that which belongs to Caesar will go to Caesar? They could have voted as they returned home from the Sunday service, or the state could have given them the chance to vote without compromising their religious freedom by extending the election to the following morning . . . but you know, both the enforcement and the refusal, they were nothing but excuses. Anyway, the fact that the poor were being given land to live on so they wouldn't have to go hungry—that was a wonderful thing no matter what, especially when you think of the deeds of Jesus Christ. Following that line of reasoning, it was only natural that land belonging to the churches and temples ought to be distributed to the tenants, too.

Back then, I think, both sides were just very young. They needed to grow up enough to realize that things get quite complicated in the business of living, that a lot of things require mutual understanding and compromise. I mean, when you get right down to it, all business for us men on earth is based on material things—so we've just got to work hard and share the fruits of our labors with one another. Only when that is done righteously can we render our faith honorably to God. Within a generation of adopting a school of thought in the name of New Learning, be it Christianity or socialism, we all became such ardent followers that we forgot the way of life we'd led for so long.

At the time of liberation I was thirty-five, which was none too young, especially back then. It's true that the young men, younger than me and my peers, the ones who attended church for the five years leading up to the war, were a bunch of troublemakers. A great many of them crossed the thirty-eighth parallel down into the South, and most of the ones who stayed behind were from families that had some land. Still, they were more like children of the middle class—the really big landowners and rich families only hung around long enough to see which way the wind was blowing; they were gone within the first few months, packing up all their things and disappearing into the night. When the conflict between church and state began heating up, the young ones who'd gone down South started getting involved with politics, joining groups like the Korean Independence Party or the Youth Corps. Then they started frequenting the North again through the Democratic Party, which consisted mainly of Northern churchgoers.

I think the situation was more or less similar all throughout the North at that point, but resistance was especially severe in our area because we had so many Christians—not to mention the fact that we practically bordered Kyŏnggi Province, making us about as close to the South as you can get. I still remember a bunch of those incidents, from the time they threw grenades in that hall in Pyongyang during the March First anniversary celebrations, to all the bombs they started planting in the homes of prominent politicians. Before we knew it the whole thing had become a kind of holy war, and everyone was ready to become a martyr—the Christians for their sacred temples and the Communists for the People and their class struggle. The entire student body at the middle school in Ŭnnyul went on strike, and in Changyŏn, with the female students taking the lead, the Christian Youth made leaflets and distributed them all over town. They literally covered entire buildings with their posters—buildings like the Party Hall and the office of the People's Committee. Countless Christians were arrested and taken away. Again in Ŭnnyul, the students formed an association called the Green Circle and led a demonstration. Their leaders were dragged off to Haeju, and nobody could find out what had happened to them. Then, in Hwangju, a couple of Christian students got hold of a mimeograph machine and ran off all those leaflets. They distributed them in all the villages they could, going to different marketplaces, but they were rounded up too, by the police—caught in some church, printing more leaflets in the middle of the night. That was when all the mimeograph machines in all the churches were confiscated. We couldn't even print our weekly bulletins after that.

The biggest incident of all was probably that thing with the Unification Corps. The Christian Youth throughout Hwanghae Province were linked through the different churches, and Yohan and some of his friends were members, too. Later I found out that the Unification Corps had been planning to obtain arms through its link with the Anticommunist Youth Corps in the South. They were planning to take over the major Party offices in Hwanghae Province, including the one in Haeju. While all this was going on a group of young men who'd rioted in Sinŭiju were arrested and executed. That's when the boys in our village took to the Kuwŏl mountains. They ended up hiding out there until the war actually broke out. Even then, though, the people in our village still helped each other out, lending a hand during the busy harvest season or sharing a meal together in the fields, regardless of whether you were a Christian or a Party member—I myself had no quarrel with anyone.

Wait, actually, there was that one time. When the harvest season came to an end, there was always a kind of mobilization of joint effort by all the villagers—we took it for granted, really, never thinking to complain, since it was something we'd done all the time under the Japanese. The People's Committee of the Province passed a proclamation saying that any able-bodied man between eighteen and forty had to do twenty days' compulsory labor. Some people were sent to factories, some to mines, and others went to build dams.

I was sent to a steel mill in Hwangju. Together with the men who'd come from nearby counties, I was admitted to an old shanty on the factory grounds that had been built during the Japanese occupation. The place had an aisle right down the middle with wooden bunks lined up on either side. Our job at the site basically consisted of assisting the skilled workers. We would pick out the iron ore from the freight wagons, grind it in the mill, then carry it to the conveyor belt. At the end of a day of constant loading and carrying iron, your shoulders feel as if they're about to fall off and your hands get all torn up and scabbed. There was this man we reported to, one who wasn't part of the regular factory personnel. He was sent to supervise us by the municipal authority. Along with two other young foremen, this guy was in charge of controlling our living quarters, too. I waited until Saturday, and then I went to the work site across from our quarters to speak to him.

I've come to ask you a favor, sir.

The supervisor—he was probably four, maybe five years older than me—had a fairly mild expression.

What can I do for you?

Tomorrow is Sunday. I'm afraid I can't work on Sunday, sir.

Why not? Are you sick?

No, it's not that . . . it's just that it's Sunday, so I've got to go to church.

What? Church? Out here for compulsory labor, and you're telling me that you can't work because you've got to go to *church*, is that it?

Yes, sir. You see, Christians must observe the holy nature of Sundays.

The kind face of the supervisor began to twitch, ever so slightly. Looking completely dumbfounded, he turned to the young foreman sitting at the desk beside him and blurted out a strange laugh. The young fellow lifted his eyes to mine and, pointing his finger right at me, shouted, You there! If you disobey the compulsory labor order, you'll be reported and punished! You got that?

Calmly but with determination, I replied, It is my understanding that freedom of religion is guaranteed in Articles 3 and 5 of the twenty articles in the Party platform of our Republic. I work on the farm, and I pay my taxes without fail, and I've never done anything to harm another human being.

The supervisor heard me out with his mouth hanging open as if he just couldn't get over what was going on. Then, obviously doing his best to be patient, he fell back on his habitual smile.

You really can't expect such special treatment simply because you are Christian—to be excused from work when everybody else has to! You can always go to church after you go back home, when you're done with your term here.

I said no more. After dinner that night, back at our quarters, everyone climbed into bed for the night. Afraid I might fall asleep, I didn't even take off my clothes. I just lay in bed all decked out in my work gear, complete with smelly socks, and covered myself with the blanket, pretending to be asleep. Peeking out through half-lidded eyes, I waited for dawn to arrive. I'd been working all day, and my body felt like a thousand tons of soaked cotton, teetering on the verge of sinking down into a bottomless pit of slumber. All around me people kept snoring and talking in their sleep. Even the dim indoor lights were all turned off. I thought I'd go crazy trying to stay awake.

Finally, I could begin to make out the shape of the mountain ridge outside the window—daybreak was near. I got up quietly, just barely sticking my toes into my work boots, and crept out of the shed. I ran all fifteen *ri* to the church. It was an early morning service so there were less than ten people in the congregation, but the minister was there. I told them that I was a new employee at the steel mine. After the service I had lunch at the minister's house, and then we all went back to church, where I prayed some more and attended the evening service. It was ten at night by the time I returned to the mine, and the country folks who shared the same quarters with me were worried about what would happen. It's just lip service when they say they don't care about your religion! Now what are these people going to think of you? We live in a world where being Christian is the same thing as being a reactionary! If you keep behaving this way they'll send you to the mines at Aoji! What good is heaven if you're already dead? They went on and on, but I pretended not to hear them, and for the first time in many days, I fell into a deep, peaceful sleep.

On the following morning when I went out to work, the supervisor came looking for me. He was visibly angry as he demanded that I follow him into his office. Brusquely, he ordered me to sit down in front of his desk. He took out the roll book.

Comrade An Sŏngman, I see that you're from Sinch'ŏn. Your father is a minister, an independent farmer. You did vote during the last election. Comrade, do you understand why the institution of compulsory labor exists?

Yes. Its purpose is to expedite production because the factories that were running during the Japanese occupation, as well as all the factories that have been constructed since liberation, are currently not producing at full capacity.

Exactly. So you understand well enough. The fact remains, however, that any attempts to sabotage our efforts in the name of religion, as you did, will leave us with no alternative but to take the proper measures and report your actions to the authorities.

There's no need for that, sir. I am more than willing to work three extra days to complete my share of the compulsory labor and make up for the Sundays I spend at church.

No. No one gets special treatment here. Especially not for church. Many people are criticizing you for being a reactionary.

On the following Sunday, I again crept out of my quarters and spent the whole day at church, returning only after nightfall. Just as he had the week before, the supervisor summoned me to his office. Striking the desk with his fist, he bellowed, I've tried being patient with you, but I see you are completely unshakable. Have you no fear? You, comrade, are an example of the kind of garbage that is being produced in this new age. You are addicted to this so-called religion of yours, like an opium freak is to opium! Don't come to me crying tears of regret when your idiocy finally catches up to you!

It did occur to me that someone might pop up and drag me away on one of the last weekdays, but I didn't think I'd done anything wrong enough to put the entire nation in jeopardy, so I simply went on working as hard as I could. Nothing happened until the third and last Saturday, when the supervisor called for me again. He took me to a corner of the dining hall, ordered me some noodles, and, with the same gentle face he'd worn on the first day, spoke to me.

Comrade An, Sunday is coming up once again. Are you planning to break the rules a third time and leave without permission?

That's the thing . . . couldn't you just give me permission?

The man looked absolutely thunderstruck for a moment, but then he guffawed and slapped me across the shoulder.

Very well. You can set your heart at ease. You may go to church tomorrow.

Do you mean it?

I think a comrade like you must be a man of real faith. We've been keeping an eye on your attitude at work, and your behavior back in the barracks with your other comrades. We have reached the conclusion that you really are a man of integrity. Not only do you do all of your own work, you help others to finish their share. I also hear that back in your quarters you actually washed clothes for some of the men when they fell ill. Is that true?

It was nothing. Tomorrow is the last day of my official term, but I will have missed three days by then. I'll stay on and make up the work I missed on those days and go home after that.

So, on the last day, I was able to go to church openly, humming a hymn. When everyone else piled onto a truck to go home, I was the only one left behind, waiting for some new work to do. When they were all gone, the supervisor called me over.

You know, if you'd just give up that religion of yours you would be a model comrade, working for the good of the People. Don't bother staying the three extra days—just go home. I'll put in a good word for you with the County Authority.

Before the war broke out, as conflicts along the thirty-eighth parallel became more and more frequent, you could have cut the tension throughout Hwanghae Province with a knife. People couldn't even visit neighboring villages after dark unless they had an official permit. I think it was around then that young men started joining the Democratic Youth League—they started soliciting volunteers. It was also around then that I saved the life of Yohan's friend, Sangho.

❖ ❖ ❖

I took the cow and went to Pujŏngnae. There was always plenty of good grass there, all along the hillside by the stream. It was around the time Big Brother Yohan first went into hiding—he could no longer show his face freely.

After the Unification Corps incident, a sizeable number of the Christian Youth fled to the Kuwŏl mountains. At first Yohan did the same, hiding in a dugout covered over with branches and leaves in a ravine of the neighboring mountain. Every other day I would take him cooked rice or some rice cakes in a wicker basket. Then the war started. There was a rally in town—they said that the valiant People's Army had reclaimed Seoul and taken full control all the way down to Taejŏn, all in one breath. By then the general mobilization had begun, so each town had its share of draft-dodging youngsters and thirty-somethings who could only drop in to visit their homes in secret after dark.

I tied the cow up at the bank of the stream and sat down a short distance away from it to study the Bible. I was attending a middle school in town back then, but I'd already promised Father that I would enter the Pyongyang Seminary someday.

Hey, Yosŏp, I've been looking for you. I went all the way to your house.

Crossing the footpath between the rice paddies, Sunho was making his way up the stream bank. Although he didn't go to school, we still ran into each other quite regularly. The young men in town were pretty much gone, and with nothing but women and children making up the households that were left, Sunho and I had to go out and help with the field work. The only young, able-bodied people still in the village, both male and female, were those who'd joined the Democratic Youth League or become Party members. Despite the general mobilization order, farmers who were over thirty-five and had a lot of mouths to feed had also been allowed to remain at home. Sunho plopped down on the ground beside me.

Your brother—is he still in the mountains? he asked.

There was no one around besides us and the cow, preoccupied with grazing.

Why?

I have a letter to deliver. From my brother.

I tensed. Sunho's brother Sangho had fled to the Kuwŏl mountains with the young men who'd joined the Unification Corps. The worst thing that could happen to Yohan if he got caught would be getting packed off to the army, but Sangho's was a different case altogether. His father had been jailed for a week at the police station, where they interrogated him on the whereabouts of his son.

What kind of a letter is it?

Don't know. He just said I had to get it to your brother, without fail.

Give it to me. I'll deliver it.

I decided to just ask him point-blank.

Wait a minute . . . your brother's come home, hasn't he?

What are you talking about? How could he come home?

Oh yeah? Then where'd you get this letter?

Okay, well, this is just between you and me. Your brother and mine, they're both on the same side, right? Big Brother Sangho came down from the mountain last night . . . but it was just for a visit.

Without another word, I held out my hand. Sunho reached into the inner pocket of his *chŏgori* and pulled out a yellowish paper ribbon. It was the letter, folded into a thin strip and tied in the middle.

I'll go up the mountain tomorrow and give this to him.

As I put the letter away in my pocket, my throat began to tingle from trying to swallow the temptation to tell Sunho that Big Brother Yohan was not, in fact, up in the mountains. He was hiding at home under the wooden floor.

Your brother Yohan must be having a really hard time. My brother's with a group of people—he says the time just flies by.

Suddenly, with a deafening roar, a formation of airplanes appeared over the mountain ridge. Back then, each day at dawn airplanes of every imaginable shape and color would streak across the sky. They would fly every which way. Silver, black, green and sky blue, some with propellers, others without but with fuel tanks on their wings, and then some B-29s with long white streams of smoke trailing behind. Just by looking at them we could tell what their targets would be. The ones with propellers came to destroy smaller stations or military bases nearby, but the jets and B-29s were on their way to bomb Pyongyang. The ones that had just come over the ridge were jets, so they were making their way towards a big city somewhere. A formation of four flew away like two pairs of birds, followed by another set of pairs, which were followed again by another set—again and again, pairs of planes kept flying by. Sunho was looking up, trying to keep count. Suddenly he exclaimed, Wow, today there are too many to even count!

Yesterday was like that, too.

They say this war's gonna last a long, long time.

Sunho looked up at the sky again, a worried expression on his face.

Listen, I gotta go, he said. Be sure to deliver the letter.

When I got back home, I looked around to make sure no one was hanging out around the fence before I went into the kitchen. Once inside, I squatted down near the big *hangari** and quietly called out, Hey, Big Brother—come out for a second.

The *hangari* began to totter. Grabbing hold of it with both arms, I dragged it a short distance into the inner part of the kitchen. The hole it had been covering came into view, and then brother's hand was visible, too. We'd broken down the bottom part of the wall and covered it with the *hangari*. The hole was connected to the hideout underneath the floor, a space that had taken Father several days to dig out before brother finally came down from the mountain. I'd crawled down there myself—it was spacious enough for a couple of people to sit down. We'd covered the earth with a double layer of straw mats and put in some bedclothes and blankets. It could get a little dark, but during the day there was enough light to lie down on the ground and read a book.

There's no one outside, is there?

No. I have a letter for you.

What letter?

Don't know. Sunho's brother sent it.

Sangho? That idiot. He should be lying low.

Big Brother Yohan sat down on the edge of the kitchen stove. Taking the

---

* *Hangari*: an often large earthenware pot used to store food.

letter out of my pocket, I handed it to him. He untied it very calmly. It was knotted with a piece of string and had been folded extremely meticulously. The moment he finished reading it, Yohan hastily clasped his hands together and said a short prayer under his breath.

Thank you, Lord. Amen.

He was beaming as he finished his prayer.

What does it say? Did something good happen?

Huh? Ah . . . well, the hard times are over now. Our freedom crusaders have finally landed in Inch'ŏn.

I snatched the piece of paper from his hand as he waved it about.

I wanna see it, too!

Hey! Hey, we have to get rid of that! Hand it over right now!

The letter was short. I'm fairly certain that it was something along these lines:

> Yohan. I hope this letter finds you safe and well. Thanks to the grace of our Lord, we are doing fine. We have received word that the U.S. Army landed in Inch'ŏn this past September. The time has finally come for us to raid the Reds. When the Crusaders make their triumphant entry into Hwanghae Province, we will be the first to rise. Let us all make ready to rise up together. Hallelujah!

As I tried to read through it one more time, Yohan grabbed it. Taking a box of matches out of his pocket, he lit the letter on fire. We sat together without saying a word, watching the flame eat away at the piece of paper until nothing was left but a pile of ashes. Cautiously, I broke the silence.

Brother, Sunho said that his brother came down from the mountain for a visit.

What? That imbecile! This is no time for him to be running around like some sort of squirrel.

He turned to me.

Where's your sister-in-law run off to?

Don't know. She probably went next door. It looks like no one's home—

I wonder if they're all out in the fields. Look here, you, I need you to do something for me. Go to Sunho and tell him to meet me at seven o'clock tonight at the funeral house.

You're going to meet with Sangho?

Yeah. This little note isn't enough for me to know what's really going on. Make sure nobody knows what you're doing, got it?

Brother Yohan crawled back into his hole.

Come on, cover it up.

I moved the *hangari* back over the hole and came out of the kitchen. Sunho's house was located in the inner part of the village, way up on a hillside that was much higher than the main road. Surrounded by pines and oaks, his house commanded a clear view of all the roads that led into and through the village. The main wing of our house was the only one with a tiled roof, but Sunho's house was huge and had tiled roofs for both the main quarters and the separate wing. Even their storehouse had a galvanized roof. Their front yard, too, was at least three or four times bigger than ours.

When I finally got to Sunho's, the main gate was wide open, and a group of people were milling about the front yard. I sensed that something was up, but I wandered into the yard anyway. The first person I recognized was Ichiro. Ichiro and a bunch of men from the police station were up on the *maru* of the house with their shoes still on, busy checking every room—even the kitchen. Sunho's father, the presbyter, was crouched in the front yard, smoking tobacco from his long wooden pipe. Sunho stood next to him. Sunho's mother, his grandmother, and his aunt were all huddled together by the entryway; his younger brothers and nephews had apparently long since set themselves to the task of wailing up a storm. Seeing me enter the yard, Ichiro motioned for me to come over. Some time had passed since we young ones stopped using the low form of speech to him, all because he'd become the party chairman of the village.

You. Come over here.

Feeling like I'd been called on by a teacher at school, I quickened my pace and came to a stop directly in front of him.

What did you come here for?

Nothing, really, had changed except for the worker's cap that now sat atop Comrade Pak Illang's head, and yet, unlike before, a certain chill seemed to emanate from him these days.

I came to play with Sunho.

Your brother . . . where has he gone?

I felt my heart sink with a thud but tried to make my answer sound casual.

He said he was off to Haeju.

Where in Haeju?

I dunno, sir. He might have joined the army or gone to work in a factory. We haven't heard from him.

If he comes home, you be sure to tell him to come by the office, you hear?

Yes, sir. I will.

While we were talking, there was some sort of huge uproar inside the house. The reason became clear as two men from the police station dragged Sunho's brother out into the open living room.

You little bastard—thought we wouldn't find you if you hid in the attic, did you?

One of the men held Sangho by the neck and one arm while the other had grabbed his other arm and handful of his hair to drag him out. A third man jumped out of one of the bedrooms and began tying him up with a rope. When they stepped down into the front yard, the women of the family, screaming and wailing, threw themselves at the men. Quietly, I backed out of the place. I ran wildly down the main road. It had suddenly dawned on me that Big Brother would have to find a better hiding place before Sangho owned up to sending the letter. As soon as I got home I let everyone know what had happened, but Father decided it was safer for Yohan to stay hidden at home. From then on Big Brother no longer came out to sit in the kitchen during the day when it was quiet outside or to go next door for dinner like he once had—we just passed down food for him to eat. After that, he never came out from under the floor at all.

❖ ❖ ❖

I got to know Sunnam for a long, long time before that winter.

It was around the time I graduated from middle school in Haeju and came down to the country to work on the farm.

On market days, I would go into town to visit Mr. Kang, partly because it was great fun borrowing his books but mostly because I had so much respect for him. Somehow, Mr. Kang had arranged to use the Union storehouse to hold some night classes. He asked me to help him and I agreed to teach the beginning classes. That was how I first met Sunnam; he was one of my students in class. We were the same age, so we soon became friends. When I learned that he was living with his sister, working as a handyman, I began to take more of an interest. Sunnam was a man with a great deal of intelligence and passion, and he also read a lot of books he borrowed from Mr. Kang. After liberation I heard he'd joined the People's Peacekeeping Troops, but I was just a simple farmer in Some by then, so there was really no opportunity for us to get together. It was a full month after I returned home from serving my compulsory labor term that I finally saw him again. I was summoned up to the county hall, and when I arrived they guided me into an office. There I was greeted by the chief clerk, who'd apparently been waiting for me.

Ah, Comrade An, the reason we asked you to come by is none other than this: we were wondering if you would care to be in charge of the Christian League in Sinch'ŏn County.

Our church considered the Christian League, an organization established by the state, to be a bunch of heretics, just like the shrine worshipers during the Japanese occupation. I told the clerk exactly that.

We churchgoers consider members of the Christian League to be heretics, sir.

There's a war going on right now for the liberation of our nation. The churchgoers, too, ought to stand on the side of the People, don't you agree? What I mean is that you ought to believe in the God of Chosŏn, not the God of America.

I will give your offer some thought.

This position has been offered to you because you come so highly recommended from above for your earnestness and good nature. Think it over carefully.

Without actually giving them a yes or a no, I sat quietly for a while. Later, as I made my way out of the county hall, someone ran out after me. I couldn't place him right away, but his face was very familiar.

Sŏngman, it's me. It's Sunnam.

Delighted, he grabbed hold of my hands. Finally, I recognized him in spite of his changed appearance and shook his hand in return, overjoyed to see him again.

How long has it been? What's brought you here?

I told him the story about the League. He nodded.

First the country was divided; now the church is split in two as well. Anyway, do think it over carefully. Most of the reactionaries have left for the South, but there are still law-abiding Christians living among us in the People's Republic. Somebody has to protect their interests, don't you think?

I just listened to him. He continued.

Seoul was reclaimed the day before yesterday. Now that unification is right under our noses, we need people like you to help us transform the church into a national institution.

I went straight home after we parted ways, but my mind was so troubled that I couldn't get any sleep. I spent the night out in the front yard, praying out loud until dawn. Then, the following morning, I went back into town and found Sunnam. I agreed to accept the position as a committee member. The commissioner at the time was Reverend Kim Iktong of the Sinch'ŏn Church, the same man who'd organized the Christian People's General Rally and been branded a heretic by our church. There really wasn't much for the committee to do—our job was to meet once a week in a conference room that took up a corner of the Party Office and discuss religious matters or speak with Christians who'd been sent to us by the Party.

It was completely by chance that I happened to be there when Cho Sangho was brought in. Another presbyter among the committee members happened to mention the fact that Presbyter Cho's eldest son had been arrested. Having no idea that he was a close friend of Yohan, I went looking for Sangho with the vague hope that he might have some news about our family—his father had been Christian for a very long time and was close with my sister's father-in-law. When I entered the police station, everyone was quite friendly; they all knew me by then. When I said that I wanted to see Cho Sangho, however, the officer in charge frowned.

Oh, that little shit's a real problem.

Well, I don't know about that. Just because he's Christian and so has a different ideology hardly makes him a problem.

At that, the officer shook his head.

The Party wouldn't bother someone just because of his religion. This bastard's a reactionary spy who's been working with an underground network, hatching plots against us.

Even so, unless he's committed a grave crime, I'd like to try and talk to him. Isn't that the job you've entrusted us with?

He let out a long sigh, nodding in spite of himself.

We have no alternative at the moment. Unless he agrees to join the military . . .

The officer glanced at a clerk and soon, Cho Sangho was brought into the office. He cut a shabby figure indeed, shod in a pair of heelless *komusin*. I turned to the clerk.

Is there someplace quiet we can go?

The clerk shot a fierce, sidelong scowl at Sangho then led us to a room with "Investigations" written across the entrance. Opening the door for us, he growled, You shouldn't waste your time.

I entered the room and took a look around. One desk and three chairs, two chairs on either side of the door and one pushed back against the opposite wall. I took a chair and offered him one facing mine.

Here, take a seat.

His movements were docile as he went over to the chair and sat down.

I don't work for this police station, nor do I belong to the Party. I am a Christian, too.

I'm fully aware of that, sir.

Out of nowhere, he beamed as if he were overjoyed to see me. I was rather taken aback.

Are you saying you know who I am?

Yes, sir. I'm friends with Yohan.

I, too, was glad to hear that. Now that I was actively trying to place him, the lad did look vaguely familiar.

Is it true that you've joined the Unification Corps?

Some of my friends have, but not me. I was just hiding up in the mountains for a while, and then I came back home.

Why were you hiding?

Because the Church is against the war and I didn't want to join the army.

I see. Well, first and foremost we need to keep you alive, don't we? Tell them you'll join the army.

Hanging his head, Sangho lowered his voice.

It's too late now. The U.S. Army has landed in Incheon.

How can you be sure? I heard that the North has pushed all the way down to the Naktong River.

Well, now they're falling back.

I'll talk to them for you. Say nothing—just do exactly as I tell you.

After sending him back to the holding cell I went to speak with the police officer in charge, but before the man would speak to me he checked in with people at several different desks, deliberately taking as long as possible.

All right. If he wants to join the army, I'll turn him over to the Department of Military Mobilization—but keep in mind that we need you, Comrade, and one other person to guarantee his trustworthiness.

I'll have no problem doing it, but who else do you need?

Well, I'm afraid it will have to be a Party member.

It was then that I thought of Sunnam. I set out for his office at once. I explained the situation to him, got his signature, put down my name and my fingerprints, and brought it back to the police station. After that, though, no one really kept track of what actually happened to Sangho. The war was escalating too fast. Later on I learned, rather belatedly, that the recruits had been sent off to Sariwŏn in a truck. Thanks to the U.S. air strikes our vehicles could no longer move about during the day, so they only got started as twilight set in. Since headlights were banned, too, the truck was probably going about as fast as a bicycle. My guess is that Sangho simply jumped off the back of the truck as it made its way to Sariwŏn.

❖   ❖   ❖

A breeze blew in through the open window, and the bedroom door came ajar with a clunk. Yosŏp woke up, dazed from sleep.

Come out here for a minute.

Eh, eh . . . who's there?

Yosŏp squinted, peering through the darkness. He thought he could see something faint and whitish floating in through the crack of the open door. Fumbling in the dark, Yosŏp walked out of the bedroom. He had the feeling that someone was waiting in the pitch-black living room. As he came out of the room, he saw a row of milky white phantoms all clustered together. The one who'd called out to him was waiting by the door. As he

might have expected, it was Big Brother Yohan. The thing was murmuring,
This'll probably be the last time. All of us are gathered here together.

Yosŏp looked around at the line of phantoms standing along the wall.
More than a dozen of them, he thought. They looked like pieces of white
laundry hanging on a clothesline under an aging moon. They looked like
bleached pieces of darkness, slightly less drenched in black.

Sŏngman. You, too. Come out here.

Yosŏp turned around to look towards the voice and saw Uncle Sunnam
standing in front of Uncle Some's room. Just like Yosŏp, his uncle, too,
came stumbling out of his room. Without being told to do so, Uncle Some
came over to stand beside Yosŏp, staring at the phantoms lined up by the
wall. Uncle Sunnam opened his mouth again.

Before we take Yohan away we're going to free him—him and all the
people he killed. The things you do in life, the good and the bad, may be
dissolved when you die, but we should still go over what really happened
before we leave.

Yosŏp and his uncle, the two living men present, sat down towards
the upper end of the living room. Big Brother Yohan and Uncle Sunnam
seated themselves across the way, at the lower end, and the phantoms of
the villagers slowly slid down from their places along the wall and sat down
on the floor. The different genders of the ghosts were vaguely discernible,
but it was almost impossible to identify them exactly.

As in a dream, the scenes were completely out of sequence, impossible
to piece together, some of them shown in great detail while others whizzed
past.

❖ ❖ ❖

A river runs through wide fields. The area beyond the levee is thickly
wooded with willows and poplars. Over there, where Chosan Hill comes
into view—that's Chaeryŏng. Under the aging moon, the neighborhood is
pitch black. A man hurries home from the fields. Gasping loudly, he stops
briefly to catch his breath, exhaling deeply, and slows down for a moment.
Apparently in spite of himself, his steps quicken once more.

He's not taking the main road that leads into town—he turns down an
alley instead. Drawing closer to the Sŏbu Church, he walks further down
the alley. The path is packed on either side with straw-thatched huts and

shingle-roof houses. He stops in front of one of the wooden doors, looking at it for a moment before extending his hand to knock. The bell hanging on the door rings out, followed by the sound of someone coming out into the yard. The voice is cautious.

Is someone out there?

It's me. Ryu Yohan.

The door opens and Ryu Yohan steps into the yard. His host leads him to a room in the backyard. Inside the messy room filled with heaps of grain sacks, two men sit together on a straw mat. They get to their feet to greet the new arrival. At one end of the room a low oil lamp glows quietly, blinking in and out. Yohan enters, his host following closely behind. Yohan shakes hands with the two young men, then asks his host to sit down.

Presbyter, please accept my humble bow.

Come, there's no need—Presbyter Ryu Indŏk is also safe and well, I assume?

Yes, sir. We've left the church open as well.

It's truly amazing that you've all been able to escape discovery for so long. These two have also just come down from the mountain. How far have our Crusaders gotten?

The word is that they will be in Haeju by tomorrow at the latest.

Good, good. This is all made possible by the grace of our Father. Well, go ahead and chat—I'm going back out to keep an eye on things.

The host steps out and Yohan begins the district meeting with the two Christian Youth members. One is the youth group leader at Sŏbu Church, and the other is a deacon who's been shuttling back and forth between Anak and Sinch'ŏn, acting as a messenger.

It has been decided. This time, we will be the first to rise up and seize power, Yohan says.

The deacon nods.

Yes, we've also been informed. We got a message from Mount Kuwŏl.

Yohan continues, This coming October 13, Chaeryŏng and Sinch'ŏn will rise together. Mount Kuwŏl will come down to Anak, cutting off the path of retreat that leads to Hwangju and Sariwŏn.

And the weapons?

We must first raid the police box in the village and then the police station in town. Then we will take over the county hall.

It would be nice to have some guns.

Smiling at the youth group leader, Yohan replies, We have nothing but a few pistols—but remember, the area is completely empty. All the able-bodied boys have gone to the front. We can get by with picks and scythes if we have to.

❖ ❖ ❖

Dozens of young men line the top of the levee, lying on their stomachs. In their hands they are holding picks, scythes, and clubs. At the corner of a three-forked road stands a police box, its light shining brightly. Someone whispers, How many inside?

Just a couple. The night watch.

We have to cut the telephone lines first. Then we can just beat them to death.

They don't seem especially alert or tense as they get up and stroll across the street. The moment they get to the police box, they holler out in unison and rush inside. They fall on the two officers dozing at the desk, striking them with clubs and spearing them with their scythes. Moving into the back room, they kill a man who appears to have been taking a nap. They drag the limp bodies to the side, laying them side by side behind the desk, and break the locked storeroom door with a pick. Five rifles and some bullets. They arm themselves as well as they can. Cutting the telephone line, they turn out the lights and move back out into the street.

Thus armed, the young men make their way through the dark, moving towards the town. Without a moment's hesitation, they swarm the police station. There are about two hundred of them. The ones who have guns head for the main building. They seize all the officers on night duty and make them kneel along the floor. In less than ten minutes, the attack is over. Not a single shot is fired. Here, they find plenty of weapons: automatic firearms and even a few cases of dynamite.

The youth group leader is one of over a dozen leaders—eventually it is decided that the group will be put under the joint leadership of a young member of the Unification Corps who has just come down from Mount Kuwŏl and a man in his thirties who came up North from the South by passing through some island. Next, the group seizes the county hall and takes over the office of the Department of Political Defense and the office of the

Democratic Youth League and Women's League, both of which are located nearby. Having arrested several more officers on night duty, they dispatch armed guards to every large building and all the major streets, and place sentry posts along the outskirts of town. Those who have been captured are brought to the police station and locked up. The ones with familiar faces are executed first, before dawn. Going through the documents at the county hall, the group makes a list. Armed young men in groups of two and three go to arrest the Party members who live in town. News of their insurrection has spread far and wide through the night and by now the quick ones have already slipped out of town. Those who haven't yet fled are mostly in the lower ranks—regular Party members or members of the Democratic Youth League and Women's League: people the armed young men have had to deal with for some time now, stifling their antagonism day in and day out. Without a command post to take orders from or report back to, they begin to slaughter the people in the alleyways and in their front yards.

Huh, I guess the bastard got away.

All right, everybody out! Come on, now—the whole family!

See, they run away to save their own hides, but they leave their goddamn litters behind.

These are Reds, too. With Reds, you gotta dry up their seed.

The families are herded out into their yards. Simultaneously, the men load the rifles with a series of loud clicks. It's the first time in their lives to ever even hold such weapons. For one brief instant, they hesitate. Then they pull their triggers. A shot fired by one's own gun sounds no louder than the dry crack of a bamboo stick striking a wooden floor. In the darkness, people thud down to the ground before it even occurs to them to scream for help. Once they kill a handful of people, they feel like gods—they are all-powerful. At their next stop, there is no moment of hesitation.

We shouldn't waste our bullets on ones like these.

Anything they can get their hands on—an axe, a pick, a rake left lying around the yard—anything is good enough. When they run into a group of their own, dragging some Party members out into the street, they mock them.

Hey, hey now, what's this?

This bastard's a Party member, and this little thing here is a member of the Women's League.

Why bother dragging this trash around fully clothed?

Someone leaps on the woman and rips open the front of her *chŏgori.* The garment is torn in half. They yank her skirt down violently, revealing her underwear and naked thighs. Unable even to scream, she falls to her knees and begs for her life.

Though he's kept his mouth shut so far, the man who was captured with her protests, You call yourselves men?

Well, well, so the little son of Satan speaks, does he?

At once, they are all over him, beating him mercilessly with the butts of their rifles about the head and back. The man is sprawled out on the ground, soaked in blood, his legs twitching. Someone fires a couple of shots into his back. A bullet is used on the woman as well—in the beginning, there is no rape. Far from it. Many times, after a kill, the young men stand together in a circle to pray together. All throughout Chaeryŏng, the slaughter continues until daybreak.

❖ ❖ ❖

The U.S. Army has yet to arrive in Haeju. They've just passed Munsan and they're about to cross the Imjin River. The international dispute over the issue on the advance attacks just beyond the thirty-eighth parallel has come to an end, and now the Anticommunist Youth are the only ones infiltrating the seacoast.

The real front is located much farther down, but in order to prepare for the defense of Pyongyang a part of the People's Army stationed along the western front are beginning to retreat along the railways. They are about the size of a battalion. They run into a number of police officers and young members of the Democratic Youth League, unarmed and out of uniform. Hearing the news that Chaeryŏng has been seized by reactionaries, they stop their march north and begin to move southwest. The men are all from the regular army troops. They are hardened soldiers with a great deal of combat experience, not to mention superior firepower.

The People's Army divides their troops, sending an advance party on ahead to make a detour around the town of Chaeryŏng. They wait in ambush along the hillside by the road that leads to Sinch'ŏn. They intend to cut off the enemy's retreat. The plan of attack is to go in from all sides, besiege the town, and send in a heavily armed special unit with mortars to make a frontal assault. Those who escaped the Chaeryŏng County slaughter of the previous night take the lead, acting as guides. Unlike the day before, the Democratic Youth League and men from the police stations are now armed. The sentry post of young rebels who have barricaded the road quickly retreat back into town after firing some shots. The rebels posted in front of the county hall and the other buildings hold their ground for quite a while, shooting from behind piles of sandbags. Twenty minutes after first exchanging shots, as the siege begins to close in on all sides, the rebel line breaks. They flee, running for their lives through the smaller side streets. The rebels have been easily suppressed.

The People's Army takes care of business resolutely and ruthlessly. Wounded reactionary rebels are shot on the spot. Prisoners, after being sorted out by local Party members, are simply ordered to line up against a wall. They are executed all at once. The police officers and members of the Democratic Youth League who have come back into Chaeryŏng are able to calculate the approximate number of remaining rebels by questioning the prisoners and survivors in town. They muster military forces to ferret out the enemy. They go not only to the homes of known reactionaries but descend upon any and all Christian households. Just like before, entire families are executed in their homes. The troops secure command of the town for two days, waiting for a second party to join them. When the rear guard arrives, they continue their retreat in the direction of Hwangju. These three days and nights in Chaeryŏng plant the seeds for the further bloodshed that is to follow in the Mount Kuwŏl area.

❖ ❖ ❖

The uprising in Sinch'ŏn does not progress as quickly as the one in Chaeryŏng. It is only on the thirteenth that all the Christian Youth who had gone into hiding are finally contacted. Hundreds of people, however, are reached; the presbytery organizations of the church are still active. Resolving to delay the rebellion until the following day, those in charge of contacting the network of townships agree to meet in Hwasan on the night of the fourteenth.

In the Ch'ansaem funeral house Yohan meets the young men who have come out of hiding, including Cho Sangho, who has come down from Mount Kuwŏl. He accompanies them to the Hwasan ravine. Some of the young men from Mount Kuwŏl are armed with long-barreled rifles, standard issue for North Korean soldiers. Sangho has somehow managed to obtain a Japanese-style magazine rifle—he is wearing it. Yohan sticks a worn-out six-shot revolver into the waist of his trousers. It came into his possession while he was in hiding after the Unification Corps incident.

It is close to midnight when they finally reach the meeting place. The path is blocked by a large rock. Yohan picks up two stones and strikes them against each other several times. He waits for a moment and then someone responds, making the same sound from behind the rock. The person looks out at them, his head jutting out over the boulder. The area is surrounded by rocks, and the forest around them seems thicker because of the darkness. The head whispers, Who's there?

It's me. Ryu Yohan.

They walk around the rock and enter. There is a puddle on the other side and a large, open space. In spite of themselves, they are surprised. Judging from the voices chattering under their breath in the dark, there seems to be at least a few dozen men. The youth from the local church who was standing guard at the rock comes forward.

Yohan, we're in big trouble. We hear Chaeryŏng is in absolute pandemonium.

So. It really happened.

Someone calls out to Yohan from the back of the crowd.

Chairman Ryu—we're here, too.

It is the youth group leader and the young deacon Yohan had met in Chaeryŏng. They all have rifles slung over their shoulders and cartridge belts at their waists. Some are even equipped with hand grenades. A young man from Mount Kuwŏl who was at Chaeryŏng from Mount Kuwŏl and a man from the Youth Corps call Sangho aside to discuss something. All the young men from Sŏbu Church in Chaeryŏng start speaking to Yohan at the same time.

> The People's Army took over the whole town! My entire
> family was murdered!
> When did this happen?
> We just barely made it out of there!
> Are you the only survivors?

No way to know—we just scattered in every direction.

Sinch'ŏn must rise up—we can't just take this sitting down!

We're running out of time.

Sangho raises his voice, calling for everyone's attention, All right, all right. Let's put our heads together. If we don't act right away, Sinch'ŏn, too, will end up a whirlpool of blood. We have to secure public order before the Crusaders arrive. Anyone who wants to survive must fight.

We must rise at once! Tomorrow!

We have to take over the town first.

Once we've taken over, we need to eliminate anyone who shows the least sign of resistance.

Now, now, we just have to hold out for a couple more days. The Reds are retreating even now, and they're undermanned.

As soon as the sun sets tomorrow, we need to assemble our forces, one group in Namsan and another here in Hwasan, and mount a surprise attack.

It is agreed that they will take action the next night. They decide which buildings should be occupied. The first target is the police station, where they will be able to secure some more weapons. Next, they decide to organize a squad to take over the county hall, the office of the Democratic Youth League and Women's League, and the office of the Department of Defense. They plan to take over the entire town first and arrest any Reds, along with their families, that live in or near town—all before dawn. It is the only way to ensure their own safety. Yohan makes a suggestion.

When dawn breaks, we must be prepared to give our lives to God. We may have to make do without a hymn, but we must have a prayer. Now, let us pray.

They all lower their heads. Yohan begins his prayer in a low voice.

Our Father in Heaven, we have guarded our faith under the oppression of the Communists, the enemy of the Holy Ghost. Thou hast told us to wear the armor of God, to become strong so that we can fight against the scheming designs of the devil. Thou hast shown us that the battle we wage is not a battle of flesh and blood but a battle for sacred service and divine power, a battle against the rulers of the dark world, against Satan, that

, evil spirit. The only way we will win this war is to rely upon the power of God and to prepare ourselves with the weapons of God. The Crusaders of freedom are just around the corner, coming to liberate our brothers in faith, but the army of Satan continues to threaten us. Let Michael, the Archangel, come among us and grant us the wisdom and courage that was once bestowed upon Joshua and David.

The prayer complete, they all raise their heads. Each young man, like one enveloped by the flames of the Holy Ghost, burns with hatred and abhorrence—for Satan himself.

❖ ❖ ❖

The next day, we all went down into our respective villages and gathered up our peers, other men who'd been lying low. Then we heard that some of the men from the meeting we held the night before, the ones whose beliefs were well known in their villages, had been arrested by armed police officers and members of the Democratic Youth League later that same night. I was waiting at the funeral house, in hiding once more, when my brother Yosŏp came to tell me that Father, too, had taken refuge. I asked him where, and he said that he was in the same place I'd hidden before, under the wooden floor of our outer wing. I was relieved—I'd hidden there safely for three months. Yosŏp told me that Pak Illang had brought a bunch of men and combed through our house. Sangho joined us later on. He said that his father, Presbyter Cho, had been taken prisoner and that we needed to go rescue him immediately. We divided the party into detachments, joining forces with young men from all the villages in the area—Ch'ansaem, Palsan, Yongdaengi, Onjŏng, and Sansuri. We moved out towards Hwasan, avoiding the main roads by taking the paths that cut between the rice paddies and dry fields. There were quite a number of us, from all the neighborhoods around town except for Kyot'amni.

It wasn't until ten o'clock that we all managed to regroup in Hwasan. Christians from the lower township were in charge of the gathering in Namsan, and we heard quite a few had come together there as well. Initially, we numbered about three or four hundred total. Among those of us waiting in Hwasan were some who had fought in Chaeryŏng, so we had about sixty people with arms. All through the night more young men kept on coming to join us, and so our numbers kept increasing. Silently, we moved down into town. The men with firearms went first; those who had nothing but cudgels and farming equipment fell behind. We knew there wouldn't be many people at the police station or the county hall, so we weren't too scared. The two buildings faced each other, so we divided the party and attacked both simultaneously. By the time we got to the center of town, the Namsan group was coming in, too. The men guarding the police station couldn't put up much of a fight against a force our size. We passed through the front gates with no trouble at all and gunned down the man who'd been standing guard, running straight on into the building. We opened every door and shot anyone we found on the other side. Within ten minutes, we had the entire two-story police station under our control. After a few shots over at the county hall, it quieted down there, too.

We sent an armed party to the office of the Department of Political Defense and inspected the armory in the police station. Those of us who'd had nothing but clubs and scythes now had real weapons. That's when the group that was supposed to handle the Department of Political Defense sent for us—they needed us to hurry over there. Sangho and I rushed over to find them holding two prisoners. There had been six at first, but four had resisted during the attack, and were shot. The enemy had been interrogating the believers they had taken into custody. As soon as they received news about the uprising in Chaeryŏng, they'd started executing the prisoners. If only we had put our plan into action a day earlier, those men might have lived. We found about thirty bodies in a well in the backyard. The body of Sangho's father was there, too. It looked like the enemy had driven the prisoners into a well and thrown a hand grenade in after them. The division of the People's Army that had been in Chaeryŏng had already moved north, in the direction of Hwangju and Sariwŏn. The enemy we came across that day had been left behind—they were cut off from their army, completely isolated. They had taken care of the rebels, as they called us, but they hadn't had time to evacuate yet. After questioning the prisoners, we sensed that they had been planning to leave the next day.

We posted a crack team of armed men at each key point and set out to capture the Reds we knew best. If you were unable to find the one you'd been assigned, you were supposed to bring in their family members instead. We knew what had happened in Chaeryŏng, so we ordered the men not

to kill individual prisoners—we wanted them as hostages. Sangho was
grinding his teeth in rage, but he instantly understood the intentions of us
commanding officers. We arrested practically everyone who lived in town,
taking entire families into custody. We crammed them into the warehouse
at the police station and into the second floor of the county hall. Morning
arrived. Dividing our forces into smaller units, we began moving out into
all the different townships. If we were going to succeed in annihilating the
enemy, we had to take care of them separately—we couldn't give them the
chance to join forces.

❖   ❖   ❖

I probably woke up around six o'clock that morning, as usual. Hearing a
shot ring out in the distance, I jumped up and went out into the yard.
I could just make out a group of sturdy young men flocking in through
the alleyway. Back then nobody really had much of a front gate—just a
fence surrounding the house with wooden poles marking the entrance.
Half a dozen men entered my yard without betraying the slightest trace
of hesitation. I could see that one of them was a young fellow I knew well
from church.

What on earth do you think you're doing? And at this hour?

In response to my surprise, the young man pointed straight at me.

Arrest that heretic son of a bitch!

All the young men had their guns trained on me. A couple of them
pounced on me, beating me with the butts of their rifles. One of them
struck me on the head and I saw stars—all the strength drained out of my
body. Another smashed into my back, and I fell flat to the ground. Using an
electrical cord, they tied my hands behind my back. I came to my senses as
I was stumbling along, and I turned to the young man I'd recognized.

What have I done to justify this kind of treatment?

You accepted a post as a committee member of the Christian League.
For that, you deserve to die ten times over.

And that was how I ended up being dragged all the way to the county
hall downtown. I was one of the luckier ones, though. If you were arrested
someplace far away or if you fell into the hands of someone who'd been
holding a grudge against you, well, then you were just shot on the spot.
The atrocities those young men, thronging about in tens and twenties,

committed in their own neighborhoods and in town—they were . . . beyond words. When they brought me to the county hall I just sat there at first, kneeling on the floor. The place was teeming with armed youngsters—they kept coming in and out, in and out, and if your eyes happened to meet theirs, they'd jump on you and kick you senseless, beating you with their guns. I watched a member of the Women's League bleed to death on the concrete floor after one of them stamped her head into the ground.

Hey, you! Get over here!

A young man had approached us, but I couldn't tell who he was talking to.

I'm talking to you, you son of a bitch! he screamed, pointing right at me.

I staggered to my feet, my hands still bound behind me, and walked towards him.

Get in front!

He pushed me into a room. Inside were two men. One was standing by the window with his back turned. The other was sitting at a desk. It was Cho Sangho.

Well, untie the man's hands.

The young one who'd brought me obediently complied, untying my hands.

You may go now.

When the young man left, the man who'd been standing by the window turned around and came forward—it was my nephew, Yohan.

Uncle, what's happened to you? Sit down, sit down.

I wasn't myself at all. Still rather uncertain, I sat down and dropped my head—I must have looked frightful—I had dried blood all over my mouth and chin, and a clot of blood covered a tear in my scalp. My nephew handed me a bag of *Sŭngri** Biscuits—that was my meal. Cho Sangho sat there and watched as Yohan wiped the blood off my face with a handkerchief, but he didn't say much. I asked for a glass of water and I finally started to come to my senses after I managed to take a couple of sips.

What's all this about?

Yohan raised his hand, gesturing as if to physically shut me up. The Reds, they killed his father. Shoved him in the well.

---

* *Sŭngri*: a brand name; in this case, *sŭngri* is actually the word for "victory."

Enough, said Sangho. He turned to me.

I understand how it was that you became a committee member of the Christian League. You saved my life that day, sir, and today I will save yours.

That's how I survived. Thanks to Sangho and Yohan. They told me not to go back home. Yohan took me back to the county hall.

The worst will be over in the next three days, he said. Just stay put right here until we're done cleaning up the Reds. We can't say for sure who'll be making raids on your village.

What he had me do was cook meals with the womenfolk. So many people were brought in as prisoners over those three days. Whole families— women, elders, children—even newborn babies were being arrested. There was an underground air-raid shelter that'd been built during the Japanese occupation, and as soon as the war broke out, they'd dug a deep trench all around the building. As far as I could tell, the important Party members were all shoved into the air-raid shelter. All their families, women or men, young or old, were forced in there, too. All the younger men and women, the ones who'd been in the Democratic Youth League or the Women's League—they were taken to the police station and locked in the storage room. Families of soldiers and just plain farmers who'd happened to join the Party, they were all told to get into the trench in front of the Party building and stay there.

The men who were set to stand watch outside town caught some soldiers from the People's Army—stragglers, I guess—and brought them in. All they did with those men was ask their rank, regiment, and destination. Then they dragged them into the backyard of the police station.

There's something I have to mention here. When the sun set that evening, the sky was full of red dragonflies. I know you've heard it said that the sun is perfect at that time of year for laying the rice out to dry— well, we were well into autumn by then and the skies were crimson, ablaze with the setting sun. I think it was the day before the occupation forces were expected to enter. The public square where the police station and the county hall stood side by side is still wide, even today—the security forces, except for those who were left at the headquarters, had all gone out to guard the outskirts of town, and the rest of the boys had split up to roam around and find the Reds who were still hiding—so the streets were all empty. There were only four or five men standing guard at the air-raid shelter and the trench. Suddenly a group of Yohan's men showed up with two soldiers of the People's Army in their custody, still wearing their yellowish uniforms. The young man walking in front had one end of a wire in his hands. The other end of the wire had been pierced through the nose of one of the People's Army soldiers. The front of the soldier's jacket was soaked with the blood that ran down his face. I don't know if one of the guns was his, but the guy in front was carrying two. Behind them came the second People's Army soldier, who turned out to be a short-haired young woman. Who knows what happened to her military cap. She was being led by a wire that bound her hands together—the other end of that wire was tied to the waist of the first prisoner. She still had her uniform but she was barefoot. Four more of Yohan's men followed behind her.

They say they're brother and sister.

I could hear the guy who held the wire in his hands, speaking loudly to the guard in front of the county hall.

How many have we brought in today? This is already the fifteenth or sixteenth, isn't it?

Have they brought many in from other places, too?

Hey, why didn't you just take their guns and waste them on the spot? Why bother dragging them all the way back here?

They all went into the building. Quite a while later, the piercing screams of a young girl reverberated through the hall. It was getting quite dark by that point, and, well, they'd stripped those kids naked and dragged them back outside. They took them to the backyard of the police station. The short-haired girl had a small rear, and her legs resembled those of a sparrow. Wailing, she trailed after her big brother, her arms wrapped around her chest and her head hanging low. They disappeared around the fence, and I heard a couple of shots ring out. I came close to forsaking my God. Oh, but that wasn't hell, not even close. It was the following night that would shake my faith to its very core—and continue to do so for fifty long years.

❖ ❖ ❖

Ch'ansaemgol comes into view. The new highway leading into town passes below the mountain and, on either side of the road, the hillocks have been cultivated into orchards. In the orchard, small trees with neatly trimmed branches are heavy-laden with apples right on the verge of turning a perfect crimson. Nestled against the foot of a hill to its north, the village faces south. Near the lower road, pine trees and zelkova trees set off the red zinc roof of the Kwangmyŏng Church. The cross in the bell tower is clearly visible.

A group of about ten young men come marching from the direction of the town. They leave two people at the entrance to the village, and some others climb up the ridge of the hill that rises up behind the village. They are on the lookout for anyone trying to leave. The remaining handful start searching the houses.

❖   ❖   ❖

Johan

Right around the time Uncle was first brought in from Some, I set out to Ch'ansaem with a group of my men. I was in charge of the neighborhoods in Ch'ansaem and Palsan. As you can imagine, the ones I wanted to get my hands on most were Illang and Uncle Sunnam. The people who lived on the outskirts of town still had no clue about what had happened the night before, but if we were going to clear the area there was no time to lose. We wanted to try and capture the two men themselves, but if they were already gone we decided we'd bring in their families instead. We weren't going to let the same thing that happened in Chaeryŏng happen to us. We would either gain supremacy over the town from the very beginning or take the families as hostages so that the Reds wouldn't ever get the chance to really rally their forces.

I took the lead when we entered Illang's house. We've talked before about how Illang used to live alone in the village *sarang*, and for quite a while, too. After the land reform, though, when he became the chairman of our little People's Committee, he got himself a plot of land and built a house. He built it, actually, on the same spot the *sarang* had once been. The original structure had been nothing more than a thatched hut with one bedroom, almost like a shed, but Ichiro had his new house built with walls of cement brick; he even put up a decent slate roof. It was a two-bedroom house with a spacious office on one side. Without a word, I walked up onto the wooden floor ahead of the others. I could see that three large bundles had been packed—they were planning to flee at daybreak. It was still in the wee hours of the morning when I burst through the sliding doors. The whole family was asleep, lying side by side.

Wake up, you son of a bitch, I growled, my voice low.

I poked Illang's face with the tip of my gun. Illang looked up at me, his brows knitting up for a second, then sat bolt upright. His wife woke up, too. He'd married late in life, but his wife was still young. I knew her face. She used to work at the hot springs, doing laundry. They had a girl who was about three years old and a newborn baby.

Drag them out!

At my command, my men rushed into the room and hauled them all out into the yard. Illang's wife started to cry, and the children sat up screeching as if they'd been stung by bees.

❖ ❖ ❖

The county hall contacted us the night before. They told us we needed to evacuate—we were all going to fall back and retreat towards Sariwŏn the next morning. We were supposed to gather at the county hall with our families. We packed our bags before we went to bed that night—who knew they would attack so soon, before sunrise? I was asleep. Then I felt something cold and metallic poking into my cheek. I opened my eyes. The first thing I saw was Yohan's face. It just didn't look . . . human. His eyes had a weird glimmer and the cold-blooded smile on his face made all my hairs stand straight up. They dragged us all out into the yard while we were still half-asleep. My babies were crying. One of the men, the one who had my little girl—he just picked her up and slammed her back down. I couldn't tell if she was still alive. She just lay there on the ground, so quiet. My wife ran to her and something whizzed past me. I heard a thump. Right in front of me, my wife collapsed to the ground, blood seeping out of her cracked skull. I just gave up. It might sound strange, but I wasn't that scared. I wasn't even very angry. I was calm. The newborn kept howling, lying beside his mother on the ground.

Shiiit . . . I can't stand this fucking noise.

One of Yohan's men threw my baby, the same way he might kick a soccer ball—my child flew up into the air a little bit before falling back down to the ground a few steps away. Before I knew it I was up, grabbing for his throat. He shoved me off and I fell onto my back, but I was up again in an instant, trying to get to him. Everything suddenly went white. The whole thing was over in minutes. If only I'd died then, when I blacked out—then

I wouldn't have had to go through everything else. When I woke up and tried to rise, the way we all do when we first wake up, something struck me across the back.

Get up you stupid piece of shit!

It was Yohan, spitting the words out, standing over me, gripping a pick with both hands. I raised my head slowly and looked up at him. I'd known the children in that family since they were very young. I even knew their birthdays, their anniversaries. I hadn't been to their house for some years, not since liberation, but whenever Yohan came to visit at the *sarang* I always roasted him a couple sweet potatoes or taught him how to weave straw mats. I can't be sure, but I don't think I looked up at him with spiteful eyes. My eyes might have asked him how he could do these things to me— for one split second, he seemed to waver. He turned his face away, took out his revolver, and pressed it against my temple. I could see the firing pin of the gun, wide open like the teeth of a snake. I closed my eyes. He spoke.

You son of a bitch, you took our land—thought you'd be Party chairman for a thousand, ten thousand years, didn't you?

I could hear the others trying to stay his hand.

This son of a bitch was the chairman—he tried to enforce the Land Reform Order. He doesn't deserve such an easy death.

Listen, the others are going to want a turn with him, too—come on, let's take him into town.

One of the animals pounced on me with the end of a wire in his hand. I was still pretty dazed, but when he pierced the wire through my nose and tugged it, my eyes and cheeks felt like they were being torn apart. Every time he pulled the wire my face felt like it was bursting. Yohan spoke again.

All this is punishment, rained down upon you by our God.

Swallowing the blood that kept rising up in my throat, I gurgled, Believe in the God of Chosŏn.

I could hear Yohan laughing behind me.

Goddamn bastard. Still have breath to spare, eh? An illiterate fool, but now that you've listened to a couple of lectures you talk ready and smooth, is that it?

Just then, a shout rang through the village.

We caught the Mole!

Yohan turned to his men.

All right. Haul this piece of shit Ichiro back into town.

— And so I ended up living one more day, hanging on just long enough to experience that fiery hell.

❖ ❖ ❖

It wasn't me that saw them coming—it was my wife. She was in the yard hiding some of our food in a hole we dug the night before. Our house was pretty close to Illang's, but we were a little bit higher up. I'd been away from home for a few days, but when I got the order to evacuate from the Department of Defense, I came home to pack the things we couldn't do without and dig the hole so we could hide the more important stuff, like the sewing machine, our radio, and a bagful of rice. We didn't actually get to bed until after midnight. Then suddenly my wife was opening the door of the bedroom, yelling up a storm.

Men! Lots of them! They're coming into the village, and they've got guns!

I sprang to my feet, put on a shirt, and rushed out into the yard. I could hear crying and wailing coming from all over the place—it had already begun. My wife pushed me back inside.

Hurry, she hissed. You have to get out of here! It's those Jesus freaks.

I raced around the house into the backyard, tore the rough hedge fence apart, and fled. I ran for my life, tearing up the hill behind our house. I meant to go all the way over it, but the trails were so steep that I was soon stumbling, panting horribly. I was leaning up against a rock, trying to catch my breath, when I heard them yelling from down below.

Sunnam, you son of a bitch! We know you're up there!

— Come down or we'll kill your whole family!

How could I keep going? My wife, she wasn't even from around there. She used to be a worker at a sock factory in Pyongyang. All her life, she'd known nothing but hardship—she started working when she was twelve, taking care of her parents and her younger brothers and sisters. I met her at one of the Party training sessions. We both belonged to the lowest class, so neither of us had anything to our names but our bare hands. We had two children, a three year old and a tiny new baby, just like Comrade Pak Illang's little family. I trudged on back down. As soon as I got near my house, a couple of them rushed me, striking me on the back with the butts of their rifles. I fell to the ground.

We caught the Mole!

The shout seemed to come from far, far away.

❖ ❖ ❖

Uncle Sunnam's face was already soaked in blood from being beaten by several different men. By the time I got there, everything had already been taken care of. His hands were tied behind his back with a telephone cord, and he was on his knees. I glanced at him, but he dropped his head when our eyes met. I looked over the hedge fence and saw his wife squatting down on the ground, looking as if she'd been frightened out of her senses, blood streaming down from her nose. The older kid was right next to her, and the younger one was sitting on the ground. I guess they knew somehow that they shouldn't cry too loudly; they were just moaning quietly. Sunnam had played with us when we were all just kids, hanging around the neighborhood, and he'd never been directly involved in any village conflict—no one really had a personal grudge against him. Still, he'd been involved with the so-called peacekeeping troops in town from the very beginning, so everyone felt kind of intimidated by him. His wife was a member of the Women's League, but she'd always gotten along pretty well with the other women in the village. We hesitated.

Should we take them to town?

The man in charge of searching the house was the first to ask the question. We all knew, though, what would happen to them if we took them in. The young ones on our side had their eyes peeled for opportunities like these—they were dying for a chance to get their hands on a real Red. It didn't take me long to decide. All it took was two little words.

Shoot them.

A couple of men turned and ran back inside the fence. I heard them cock their guns. Then came the shots. I didn't look back. When the men shoved Sunnam, he fell into step, leading the way down the village road. We got to the village entrance. Illang, with his newly pierced nose and his party were waiting for us. The whole lot of us formed a line and began marching towards town down the new road. Wet fog spread out over the stream like a blanket of smoke. The eulalias were in full bloom, white against the stream banks. I was walking in front of Uncle Sunnam when I heard his deep voice address me from behind.

Yohan, can I have a word with you?

I just turned and looked at him.

What's the point of going all the way to town? Please. Kill me here.

I stopped walking. I wanted to put some distance between Illang's party, who continued on their way, and our group. I turned to the young men from Kwangmyŏng Church who stopped with me.

Let's finish him off here.

But he's a key figure—do you think that'd be wise?

We're going to be killing them all later on, anyway. Don't worry. Tell the guys up front to go on ahead.

Sending a man to the front to let them know what was going on, I took out a cigarette. I lit it and held it to Sunnam's lips.

Go ahead. Take a puff.

Greedily, Sunnam took the cigarette between his lips, inhaled deeply, and let the smoke come out his nose. I lit another for myself.

Well, you certainly are a sight to see—and to think how you used to go around with your nose stuck up in the air. You shouldn't have played the Red game.

Sunnam stood there without saying a word, just smoking his cigarette. He spat it out when it was only half done. With a deep sigh, he looked up at the sky. Tears streamed down his cheeks. Without facing him directly, I glanced at him out of the corner of my eye and said, Why the tears?

It's just the smoke.

My companions began to prod me.

Let's just get this over with and move on.

I spotted a utility pole along the stream bank. I turned to the boys.

String him up over there.

Was I remembering that time with the dog, that day I followed him down to the stream during the *Tano* Festival?* The guys unraveled one of the telephone cords they always had tied around their waists for easy access and shaped it into a noose. As one of the men pulled the noose down over his head from behind, Sunnam said, Yohan, can I ask you a favor?

---

* *Tano* Festival: traditional Korean festival held on the fifth day of the fifth month according to the lunar calendar.

What is it?

Please—bury me with my family.

I didn't answer. I just gave the signal to my men. They tossed the other
end of the telephone cord over one of the pins that stuck out of the utility
pole and pulled with every ounce of strength they had. With a strange
gurgle, Sunnam's body was suddenly up in the air, his legs flailing. At first
the men stood there and hung onto their end of the cord, but then they
just tied it off on one of the pins farther down and left it. We all hung
around for a while, waiting for Sunnam to die. Every time it looked like
he might finally be gone, his limp body dangling silently for a moment,
his legs would jerk again and the struggle would start all over again. Blood
oozed from the cut under his chin where the wire cut into his flesh and
trickled down the nape of his neck. I pulled my gun out from the waist of
my trousers and aimed at his heart. I fired.

❖   ❖   ❖

I did tell you, didn't I, that I was assigned to work in the kitchen at the
county hall with the womenfolk, right? And so I survived—just barely—all
thanks to Sangho and Yohan, but so many unspeakable things happened
during those three days that I can't even recall much of it. Meals were
cooked at two separate locations, the county hall and the police station.
They were short-handed so almost a dozen men my age had been recruited
to help out, and that was just for the kitchen I worked in. The women
and I were in charge of feeding the young men who came together in the
county hall meeting room. There were hundreds of people assembled in
the front yard, too, but the new recruits were responsible for cooking their
meals. The men in the meeting room were the leaders of the uprising, so
their meals were a little better—they got rice and soup and slices of salted
radish. The young men in the front yard were given plain rice balls. We
all made do with rice balls during the war, out there in the streets; you
probably already knew that, though. We'd just roll some cooked rice into
little balls with our hands. We used to dream of finding some salty side
dishes, or maybe just getting hold of some soy sauce. The cooks who made
the rice balls used to dip their hands in salt water before kneading the rice
to try and give them some flavor, but it wasn't the same.

Anyway, the women and I would put all the rice in a large wooden bowl and pour the soup into a bucket and take it all up to the meeting room. The place was full of faces I'd never seen before. I gathered that these were the men who'd come up from the South. Looking a bit more closely, though, I spotted some familiar faces scattered among them. I saw one young man who used to be a member of the church youth group and another who'd joined the Korean Independence Party. Picking up bits and pieces of conversation here and there, I realized they were all discussing the arrival of the U.S. Army. Apparently the Americans had just arrived in Haeju—they and the South Koreans were headed north, marching towards Sŏhŭng and Sin'gye. The men I was feeding weren't actual soldiers so they had no official rank, but they were all wearing American army uniforms and carrying brand new guns. It looked like they'd come in just before we brought them their dinner, so they'd probably arrived in town a little earlier that very evening—that would have been the sixteenth. They said that they were only the advance party. One of them recognized me.

Well, well! If it isn't the deacon!

I was so panicked and frightened that I didn't recognize him at first. He was wearing a military uniform, complete with field jacket, not to mention a cartridge belt and gun at his waist. It was one of those American guns that we used to call "Chickenheads."

It's me, Pongsu! Remember? I used to live here.

Finally, it clicked. This man with the pomaded hair combed all the way back—this man was the eldest son of the miller. He'd gotten into some deep trouble back home, after liberation. His father crossed the thirty-eighth parallel and went down South fairly early on, and all their land, including the mill and the brewery, had been confiscated. Until that day, I'd had no idea that he even knew Yohan. Just then, out of nowhere, Yohan stuck his face out from the sea of young men.

Uncle, you know Presbyter Choi Jang-no from the church in town, don't you?

Sure . . . we've . . . held revival services together, I answered vaguely, wanting to get out of there.

Pongsu joined in, You're still under forty, aren't you?

Yes, that's right.

Well, then you should join the Youth Corps. We need to form a branch of the Taeha Youth Corps here in our hometown.

Feigning inattention, I simply served the rice. The roar of conversation kept going strong as the men began to eat.

Hey, whatever happened to that guy who started the peacekeeping troops in your village?

You mean Ri Sunnam?

That's the one—he used to work as a handyman in the orchards, right?

Yohan finished that bastard yesterday.

Aw, c'mon—you guys should have left me my share—that son of a bitch was red through and through.

That was how I found out that my nephew Yohan had killed Sunnam. It's true that people killed each other out of spite during those hellish days to get even. But you know, it's also true that they all felt a kind of pressure to be merciless—they wanted their peers to think highly of them. If you showed any sign of weakness, if you had a single moment of indecision, well, then your whole ideology could be called into question. No one was to be trusted. There was even a joke that went around back then: that one's a watermelon—no, he's an apple—no, a persimmon— why, he's a green melon—ah well, it doesn't matter if he's blue, red, blue dyed red, or red dyed blue—anything that's got any color at all has got to go. When I went to clear the dishes after dinner, the young men in the meeting room were smoking. Sitting on a desk, Pongsu asked Sangho, Hey, Sangho, remember that guy who used to work as a foreman in my father's factory?

Sure I do. Isn't he the one that put your father through all that hell?

Whatever happened to that asshole?

Sangho snickered, We got him.

What about that piece of shit who was in charge of all the land reform in the northeastern districts?

Oh, that son of a bitch—you know, he'd actually made himself the chairman of the District Party Committee. We brought him in, too. Along with his whole family.

Pongsu hopped down from the desk. He kept touching the gun at his waist, grinning all the while, but I don't think he even knew he was doing it. I wasn't interested in being a spectator to such nonsense, so I hurried out of the room. Back in the kitchen I was washing dishes with the women when I heard someone crying out in pain in the backyard. Curiosity is strong enough to overcome fear, they say. Furtively, I wiped my hands on my pants and got up. One of the women looked at me.

Deacon, why bother? You don't want to see what's out there—whatever it is, you can be sure it's no festival mask dance.

You just keep your eyes and your ears shut. I'm going to go sneak a peek.

We, at least, had simply been told to cook—we really had nothing to complain about. It was the men they recruited later on that had to do all the real dirty work. They were the ones who had to deal with the countless dead bodies of all the people being killed in the backyard of the police station and around the county hall. The air-raid shelter and the trench were packed with people by then, just waiting to die, with no food or water. For the first two days you could hear the kids crying, but after that everything fell silent—there wasn't a single whimper. God only knows if they all dropped dead or what. Sometimes, when I walked by, I could see a couple of their heads poking up through the air shaft, which came up to about the height of my knees. Sir, please, give us some water, please, my child is dying of thirst. There were times I'd pass by, pretending I hadn't heard a thing, but whenever I could I'd get a bucketful of water and pour it gently down the shaft.

The backyard of the county hall was just on the other side of a wooden fence. I stepped up on a rock to try and look over it, to see what was going on. Dusk was setting in and it was getting pretty dark. I could make out a group of people standing in a circle around two big, whitish objects. Looking more closely, I realized the pale things were two naked men. Pongsu had unbuckled the cartridge belt from his waist; he was whipping one of them with it.

You dirty son of a bitch, pay up! Cough up all the rent you owe us, everything you haven't paid these past five years! Thief!

Abruptly, he turned to the other man and started beating him, too, shouting, And you! You were a fucking homeless piece of dirt and we took you in—we taught you, trained you to handle engines so you could make a living—and you have the *nerve* to tell us to give up our factory? The lowest mongrel is better than you! At least a dog knows to be grateful to its master!

Pongsu kept on thrashing them, his breath growing harsher with each passing moment. When one of the men, unable to take it anymore, made a run for it and tried to break through the human wall, the spectators kicked him back inside the circle.

Bring me some gasoline! It's in the car! Pongsu shouted, panting.

When the gasoline arrived, he poured it all over the whitish shapes as they quivered on the ground. It looked like he was giving them a bath. Moving as one, the circle of men stepped back a few paces as Pongsu reached over to strike a match. Throwing the match, Pongsu, too, sprang backwards. A tower of flame shot straight up into the air. I jerked my eyes away from the crack in the wooden fence. That was the beginning—the beginning of the Judgment of Fire in the book of Revelation.

❧ ❧ ❧

October 17. The U.S. Army arrives in the afternoon.

A regimental force of the First Armored Division moves into Chaeryŏng on its way north from Haeju. The main objective of their operation is to attack Pyongyang; they are not interested in mopping up the western regions. The temporary regimental headquarters stationed in Chaeryŏng dispatches search parties to Sinch'ŏn and Anak, which is located northwest of their route. A platoon led by Lieutenant Harrison of the U.S. Armed Forces advances to Sinch'ŏn. The regiment's intelligence officer has informed them of the Rightist uprising in the area, so a separate squad is sent ahead, riding in a jeep, before they all march into town. Everyone is relieved to see the flag flying from the county hall flagpole, not to mention the banner with "Welcome" spelled out in English. Unaccompanied by any combat units, the main force rides into town along the new road. They are courteously shown into the meeting room in the county hall. In the yard, young men armed to the teeth and a crowd of what seems to be their families have gathered together to welcome them. The Americans stay in the town of Sinch'ŏn for two hours. They contact the regimental headquarters in Chaeryŏng and request that rations, some medicine, and, most importantly, munitions such as bullets and grenades be brought to Sinch'ŏn. Approximately fifteen hundred men have assembled so far, but only about a thousand of them are armed. The regular troops, American and South Korean, continue their march north. They do not return until they retreat again the following winter. After the welcoming rally is over, it is announced that the defeat of Communism and the unification of Korea has become a reality. In the county hall, the Taehan Youth Corps and the new Autonomous Police are established, and a ceremony is held the following morning in the front yard to celebrate. Once the festivities are complete, the men return their attention to the air-raid shelter and the trench. The executions begin.

❖   ❖   ❖

For three days and nights, hundreds of us were crammed into that space. A solid iron door blocked the steep flight of stairs that led up to ground level. The air shaft near the ceiling measured about one span by three spans. There were two other rooms, one on each side, but the biggest was the room in the middle. The walls were concrete. The wind was soft, blowing in through the air holes in the ceiling.

From outside, all you could see was something like a chimney sticking straight out of a grass lawn. Young kids used to sit on it and let the goats graze while the grown-ups took care of their business at the county hall. They pierced my nose when they caught me in Ch'ansaem—the blood stopped after a while, but the next day my nose was so swollen—it was festering, I think. My throat still felt raw and split open. I know now that it felt so dry because all the blood from my nose had congealed in my inner palate. What I knew then was that I physically couldn't drink a thing.

I fainted while Sangho was swinging his pickaxe. When I woke up I was already in the air-raid shelter. All I could see at first were some feet. Someone was standing on my thigh. My arm felt loose, hanging weirdly from my shoulder. It looked broken. Ah, I thought to myself, my whole life I've had nothing, no name, no nothing; I've worked my fingers to the bone without ever getting a chance to stretch my back—but at least I've had these past few years. They make it all worthwhile. So many people were squeezed into that cramped room, more than you ever saw, even on a village market day. People just barely had room to sit down, let alone stretch out. It was late fall, but down there it was steaming. You could feel the hot breath of the people around you. Little children fussing for water soon tired themselves out and fell asleep. Many of them died in that sleep. Men took turns standing so the women could have room to sit down.

You know, I never hated anyone, not once in my entire life. For a bowl of

rice—maybe two bowls on a lucky day—I worked hard, and I kept wc
hard so that no one would have a reason to complain. And still, still I had
to watch as my own family was killed right before my eyes. That was when
I understood. If your heart isn't in the right place, you're no different from
the beasts in the forest. Overcome, I just stood there, staring at a patch
of blue autumn sky through the cracks in the air shaft. Out of nowhere,
a stream of liquid began trickling down the sides of the shaft. Thinking
some good-hearted passerby was pouring some water down to us again,
we crowded up to the shaft, our mouths wide open. Almost immediately,
one of the few who'd actually been able to get a mouthful stumbled back.

It's gasoline!

The streaming stuff was faintly pink in color—it was the kind they used
in cars. As the smell of gasoline filled up the small space, I noticed that
little streams were flowing down through the air shaft of the room across
from us, too. We all stood very still, looking up at nothing in particular,
our eyes wide open and our mouths agape. We stayed that way, completely
silent. Not a single cough. Suddenly a muffled, moaning sound, kind of like
the "oooh" a crowd of people might make, rose up all around us like some
sort of wind—and then, all at once, we were engulfed in flame.

❧ ❧ ❧

That first day, the eighteenth, and then the following day, the nineteenth—
all the way to the twenty-third—I think we all just went crazy. The dead,
well, they may have nothing more to say, but those of us who survived can
never go back to the way things were. You can't stay crazy forever, you
know. Time passes and before you know it you're alone, old, all your friends
have gone for good, and the world, too, has changed. Even then, though,
even if nobody else remembers, it's still there, deep down in your heart of
hearts. It was this land, this land where our mothers buried our umbilical
cords—this very same land that we dyed red with blood, transformed into
a place we can never, ever go back to, not even in our dreams. And that was
just the beginning—of the next fifty years.

Why the winter was in such a hurry that year has always been a mystery
to me. The first snow came down in torrents, covering entire hills and
fields. Of the defeated soldiers from the People's Army, crushed in Haeju
and Ongjin along the west coast, those who were quick and strong went

up into Mount Kuwŏl, just as the Christian Youth had earlier in the game. They became guerrillas, continuing to wage family feuds amid freezing winds.

I returned to Some. People in the countryside were afraid to go any distance from their homes. You never knew when you might make a wrong impression and get yourself killed. You see, for forty-five days, the killing and the dying continued. It was all over the place. Over thirty-five thousand were killed, they say, and for all I know that may be true. Especially since a great many stragglers who'd been driven to the southwest and separated from their units were cornered and slaughtered when the snow blocked the north road out of Sinch'ŏn. And then there were the guerrillas. They'd come down from Mount Kuwŏl for provisions, killing anyone who got in their way. Then, in retribution, members of the Youth Corps would search out the families of the guerrillas and kill them. On top of all that, the massacre of 400 women and 102 children was simple fact—the dead bodies were there to prove it, as were a few surviving children. One fourth of the county's entire population was killed—almost everyone in Man'gungni in Kunghŭng, more than half the population in Yongdangni in Onch'ŏn, and the entire male population in Yangjangni in Sinch'ŏn.

❖ ❖ ❖

In our village, too, the men who'd been to town established a branch of the Youth Corps. The whole thing was organized by the township. The guys set up a sentry post on the street and on the pass over the hill, and they made their rounds every night, going from neighborhood to neighborhood. Big Brother Yohan stayed mostly in town, coming home to visit once every couple of days. Once, in a car, he brought home a huge slab of uncut beef, saying they'd slaughtered a cow. Our family invited all the men from the Youth Corps, and everyone made a huge fuss as if it was some sort of festival day.

Just like any other winter, I went to play up in the mountains with Sunho and the other kids. We'd set traps along the ridge or wander around, looking for sparrows to catch with our nets. Sometimes we might even find a gray mountain hare caught in one of our traps. It was around the beginning of November, I think. As soon as I got up that morning, I set out for the mountain as usual to check my traps. We set them in three different places, so by the time I finished checking all of them I would get pretty hungry. The last trap was up at the very top of the ravine, so I made my way up the steep mountain path, picking my way through the rocks. The stream that ran through the ravine hadn't frozen over yet, and right next to my last trap there was still a little pool of water—it was the kind of place an animal might come to drink. Sometimes Sunho actually put as many as three of his traps around the pool, hoping we might get really lucky and catch a raccoon dog or a roe deer. Our traps were made out of bent wire, and we used sweet potatoes as bait, scattering barley or beans nearby.

Done checking my traps, I was turning away when I just happened to glance up into the deep forest behind the pool. There were people there. The first thing that registered was their shoes. Like Japanese *jikatabi*, they were cloth shoes that came up to the ankles. Every child knew that these were combat shoes, the kind worn by soldiers of the People's Army. My eyes fumbled slowly past the shoes to discover two soldiers asleep in an embrace. One had a cap on so I couldn't make out any facial features, but the other was a woman for sure—her bobbed hair spilled out across the grass. Lying beside them was a black leather case. It was only much later on that I learned all it held was a violin. I turned around, about to run away, when suddenly, with a resounding "Who's there?" something jumped on me from behind, forcing me to the ground. In an instant I was flat against the earth, the soldier sitting astride my back and pressing down on the back of my neck.

You—who are you?

It was a woman's voice. I could hear another woman call from behind, Stand him up. Let's have a look.

The woman who'd been sitting on my back got to her feet, still holding on to the back of my neck. I sat up, brushing the dirt off my clothes. Both women were soldiers of the People's Army. They wore the yellowish brown army uniform with the wide insignia on the shoulder and the baggy army trousers. Their lips were blue from the cold, and the stitching along their shoulders and the material around their knees were torn. Neither of them appeared to be armed. They were probably around high school age. Now that I'd sized them up, I found myself gaining a bit of confidence. After all, what could these girls possibly do to me, I began thinking. One of the two was small in stature and very thin—she would be, at most, two years or so older than myself. The other one, though, with her thick wrists and sturdy shoulders, might have been able to pass for something closer to twenty. Whatever the case, they both had twinkling black eyes, and it struck me that I hadn't ever seen such pretty girls in my village or anywhere nearby. The big one spoke.

Where do you live? Why did you come here?

I live down in the village. I'm here to check my rabbit traps.

They looked at each other for a moment, then the big one spoke again.

Did you come alone?

Yes, today I did.

Are there security agencies in your village, too?

I knew only too well what they were afraid of.

Sure. There's a sentry box at every alley.

The big one grimaced. Responding to the frown, the little one hurriedly pulled up her companion's torn pant leg and checked her feet. The big one's ankle looked awfully swollen.

Is it hurting again?

Yeah. I think I twisted it again trying to catch him.

Well, what do we do now? Where can we go from here?

There was a short silence. I was the first to speak.

Where are you from?

The South . . .

It was the little one who replied. The big one got up, broke a branch off a tree, and snapped off the twigs. Using it as a walking stick, she tried taking a few steps before she flopped back down on the ground.

Oh man, just taking a step hurts like crazy.

You know, this place—it's dangerous during the day. People come here for firewood, and for walks, too.

Oh! Really?

There's an orchard a little farther down. No one goes near there until spring rolls around.

The little one looked at me.

What's your name . . . student? You're a student, aren't you?

Yes. I'm in middle school—it's my first year. My name is Ryu Yosŏp.

She put one hand on her chest.

I'm Kang Miae, and her name is . . .

The big one, smiling for the first time, said a bit shyly, Hong Chǒngsuk. Yosǒp, you won't report us, will you?

Inform? No.

Why not?

I don't like people getting killed. Did you sleep here last night?

We've been here since the day before yesterday.

And you haven't eaten anything?

Acting tough like a man, Hong replied, Just water. That's why we were trying to stay near the stream.

You must be hungry. I'll go home and bring you back some food.

The two women hesitated for a moment and exchanged looks. Her face contorting anxiously, Kang Miae asked, Would that be . . . safe? If you're caught by a grown-up, you'll get in big trouble.

Are you afraid I might go down and report you?

It was Hong who answered.

No. We trust you, Yosǒp. Ah, do you like . . . singing?

Singing?

Later, when you come back for us—what song will you sing?

Let me see . . . do you know this song? *This is my Father's world, and to my listening ears . . .*

I then hummed the first bar. Kang's response was immediate.

Oh, that's a hymn. *All nature sings, and round me rings the music of the spheres.*

Promising them that I would be back with some food, I came back down the ravine. I was to start singing at the bottom of the hill when I returned and keep it up all the way to the top. At home I found both my parents, on this day of all days, going about their business in the main wing of the house. Of all places my mother could have been, she was bustling around in the kitchen, breaking dry twigs in front of the fireplace to use later when she cooked lunch.

Ma, have we got anything to eat?

Mother turned around to glance in my direction as I stood on the threshold of the kitchen.

Listen, these days we're lucky to have three square meals a day. I'm making lunch soon. Why don't you go inside and wait?

Instead of responding I just rushed around the stone fence and went over to the separate wing that stood behind the main house. Sister-in-law was in the last month of her pregnancy, so she spent most her time lying in her bedroom. I opened her kitchen door quietly, crept inside, and lifted the lid of the big cauldron. It was still warm, and inside was a big bowl covered with a piece of hemp cloth. Lifting up the cloth, I saw that the bowl was full of steamed sweet potatoes. Sister-in-law had probably steamed them for my little nieces to snack on. I took the bowl, hemp cloth and all, and got out of there. Shooting out of the house like an arrow, I checked to see that no one was watching and made a run for the hills. When I got to the ravine, I picked my way up through the rocks, thinking to myself again that the place really wasn't a very good hideout. When everything was said and done, they just really needed to move someplace more suitable. I began to sing.

> This is my Father's world, and to my listening ears
> all nature sings, and round me rings the music of the
> spheres.
> This is my Father's world: I rest me in the thought
> of rocks and trees, of skies and seas; His hand the wonders
> wrought.

I made my way back to the same spot, but when I got there the girls were nowhere to be seen—I searched all over, pushing aside the bigger branches and straining to see past the smaller trees. Finally, I let loose a great shout into the empty air.

Girls! Big Sisters! Where did you go?

Hush! We're right here!

Kang's face appeared from behind a big boulder, and then Hong rose up from a patch of clover bushes, much farther up the hill. As one climbed down the rock and the other walked out through the branches, I could hear them talking.

He wasn't followed, was he?

He's alone. I've been watching him.

Proudly, I offered them the bowl, still covered with the hemp cloth. Then, like it was some fantastic magic trick, I snatched the cover off with a flourish.

Help yourselves!

Wow! Sweet potatoes!

I sat a little bit apart from them, watching them with a distinct sense of satisfaction as they clutched the sweet potatoes in their hands and began stuffing their faces. A little belatedly, Kang turned to Hong.

Slow down, Big Sister, or you'll get indigestion!

Hong laughed out loud. Then, as her eyes met mine, she awkwardly held the half-eaten sweet potato out to me, still smiling broadly.

Yosŏp, you should have some of this, too.

It's okay. I'm going home for lunch soon—we're having rice.

Then, feeling a bit guilty about my thoughtless reply, I added, We should move out of here tonight. I'll bring you some rice too, later this evening.

After they'd finished eating, the two girls cupped their hands and drank from the mountain stream. For the first time, they both looked comfortable and lighthearted. Kang brought out the black leather case that she had left lying under the trees. I was expecting it to be full of guns, or at least something in that general category. Instead, she opened the case in a way that looked as if she were splitting it in two and took out a violin— something I'd only seen in pictures until then.

I had an accordion myself, but I lost it on the day I hurt my leg, Hong volunteered.

Yes, but you still sing very well, Big Sister, Kang said, bracing the violin against her shoulder and pressing down on it with her chin.

Are you Christian, Yosŏp?

Yes. I'm going to go to a seminary when I get older. Do you go to church?

I went to Bible school one summer—a long time ago.

With that, Kang applied the bow to the strings and began to play. The first song she played was the hymn I'd sung as I climbed up the side of the ravine. Unlike my voice, which had only just begun to change and so was wrought with unexpected squeaks and cracks, the fragile sound of the violin, trembling as the notes went lower and lower, touched me deeply.

Please, play something else. Just one more.

Kang and Hong thought together for a moment. Kang spoke first.

What about "Touch-me-nots"? That's one of my favorites.

Kang began to play, and Hong, her voice rather low and quite deep, sang.

Inside the wall, touch-me-nots bloom.
Standing there, so melancholy,
Endlessly long, hot summer days,
Always you bloomed so gorgeously,
Beautiful maids, maids pure and true,
Once smiled and played, welcoming you.

The violin seemed to sob more than ever at the crescendo, and the song's melody left me with a long, lingering aftertaste. My face burned, my throat soared, and, out of the blue, tears gushed out of my eyes. Sniffling, I wiped my face with my sleeve. Ah, suddenly, an entirely different world was opening before my eyes. Each of us must have been deep in our own thoughts; no one said a word. After a long silence, I asked them, What kind of soldier carries music instead of guns?

Well, you see, we're members of the Cultural Enrichment Corps. We go around from troop to troop and perform for them to cheer them up.

It occurred to me that these girls probably hadn't done a single thing to be ashamed of in this war. I was capable of making judgments, too, just like my big brother and his friends. I resolved then and there to protect those girls.

As soon as it got dark that night, I crept out of the house with a blanket and a basket of cooked rice. I led the girls down the ravine, taking them across the fields and into the orchard. The place was packed with the gnarled, twisty branches of the naked apple trees. I had a specific spot in mind—we'd used the place to set up the headquarters of our gang when we were little kids. It was a mud cellar, about six feet deep and roofed with thatched straw, set into the sunny side of the small hill at the far end of the orchard.

When we got there we lifted the straw cover aside and looked down inside. It was pitch black and impossible to see into, but a soft, warm earthy scent wafted up from inside. I took some matches out of my pocket and kindled a little resinous knot of wood from a pine tree, something we used a lot those days when candles were hard to come by. The whole cellar lit up. Tiny saplings, about as thick around as a finger, had been planted densely all over the room. In one corner there was a sprinkler, a small hoe, a shovel, and a bucket, all next to a stack of hay. I spread the blanket over the haystack. It looked spacious enough for two people to lie down. Sitting on the haystack, Kang Miae and Hong Chŏngsuk polished off the food—all I could find to bring them was some cold cooked rice and a bowl of *kimchi*. Reaching into their military jackets, they each took out a stumpy looking spoon, rubbed it a couple of times on their sleeves, and got down to business. They were the same kind of spoons we used in regular households, but their long handles had been cut in half to make them more portable.

Picking up a bucket, I went out to get some water. I walked down to the entrance of the orchard, where the trail cutting through the fruit trees met with the main road leading into the village. There, left over from the Japanese occupation, stood a run-down clapboard warehouse used for storing fruit. There was a water pump in front of the warehouse. I pumped water out into the bucket, together with a racket of rusty, squeaky noises. On the way back, carrying the bucketful of water, my heart began to grow warm. I had taken a great fancy to Kang Miae, so small and slender, just like a little girl. I believe it began at first sight.

I never went anywhere near the orchards during the day, only going to visit the girls at night. Each day it became harder to find food for them. Some days we had leftover rice, but often the only thing left after our meals were the newly washed dishes. Sometimes I'd go over to my brother's house and search out some more sweet potatoes. Other days I'd be reduced to scooping up some fresh beans from the cellar. I'd been taking care of the girls for eight, nine days maybe—not quite ten. It was only the middle of November, but snowflakes had already started to fall from the sky and each day was much colder than the one before.

❖ ❖ ❖

Before I actually did . . . what I did, I went home about three or four times. Once, I know, I went by car because I was delivering some food. On my other visits, I probably just took a bicycle. I think it was during my second visit home, around dinnertime or so, as I sat, for the first time in a long while, for a meal that Mother had prepared. Not really thinking anything of it, I said, I don't see Yosŏp anywhere.

Ha! Tell me about it. Who knows what he's up to—he goes out practically every night these days.

This may be the boonies, but it's still not a good idea to be roaming around after dark, especially not now.

I think the boy's just growing up. He puts away a couple of bowls of rice in no time at all, said Father.

A couple? Ha! It's a lot more than a couple! Yesterday he came back from one of his evenings out and practically inhaled all the leftovers in this house, said Mother.

Even then, though, I didn't think much of it. I headed back to our wing behind the main house to see my pregnant wife and my little daughters. I was on my way back out when I saw something dark lurking around the kitchen.

Who's there?

It's only me, Big Brother.

It was Yosŏp. Remembering what our parents had said, I thought I'd give him a hard time.

What the hell do you think you're doing, wandering all over the place these days?

Oh, well, my friends and I, we've set up this . . . clubhouse, and . . .

A clubhouse? How old are you? You're such a child! You've got no sense at all. Wandering around after dark these days is a good way to get yourself shot. There are no sides anymore—you got that?

Yeah, I got it.

Listen, Yosŏp, when I'm not around, you gotta take care of Mother and Father, especially now that your sister-in-law can't do everything. Boys barely a couple years older than you are out there right now, fighting, shooting guns. At night, you stay put at home. Understand? Answer me!

Yes. Yes, I will.

Later that same afternoon, there was quite a scene up at the county hall. Ch'oe Pongsu, the leader of the Youth Corps, had called Sangho to his office and was screaming at him. When I walked in, Pongsu immediately started yelling at me as well.

What in the hell is going on here? A member of the Youth Corps covering for a Red? Does that make any sense to you?

Looking from Sangho, who sat there hanging his head, to Pongsu and back again, I asked, What the hell are you talking about?

Oh, so, you didn't know either? The leader in charge of the northeastern districts has been reported and arrested—he was harboring a female Party member!

As we reached the one-month mark after taking control of the district, the level of official discipline began to crumble. They say it happened because our patriotism had been corrupted. Some of us began to extort property from the Party members, taking their lives as a kind of mortgage, and many of our men started taking advantage of the women. Rape cases became more and more frequent with each passing day, but we all just left each other alone, pretending nothing had happened. I turned to Pongsu.

Commander, are they saying that he acted dishonorably, as well?

I wouldn't really say dishonorable . . . she's a good looking one, a woman teacher, so I guess they probably fell for each other.

A female teacher?

Ah, what did they say her name was . . . I went down South in '48, so I don't know any of these new people.

For the first time, Sangho spoke.

You know her, too. Remember that teacher? Ms. Yun?

Oh, oh yeah, she used to board with the family who ran that store.

I see you comrades know her well. What's this bitch about, eh?

I'd only ever seen Ms. Yun from a distance, but you could definitely say that she had piqued my interest. Her hair was just long enough to put up in a ponytail and twist around to fall over one shoulder. She would wear a white *chŏgori* and a black velvet *mongdang ch'ima* that just covered her knees—very neat and gentle looking. I used to stop and gaze after her for quite a while whenever she happened to pass me on the street, inhaling her city fragrance. She must have used apricot-scented face cream; whenever she walked by I felt as if I were standing in the midst of an orchard.

I know her well enough—we lived in the same village. I believe she's from Haeju. From what I've heard, she's quite a decent girl—

Pongsu cut in.

According to the report I received, she made a speech at a People's Rally. Is that correct?

Oh, yeah, that's right. I remember she read something in the school playground, telling people to volunteer and join the army.

Well, now that everybody knows about it, we can't just let her go.

What's going to happen to the commander of the northeastern district? We will have to reinvestigate his dedication to our ideology.

My memory fails me, but I'm pretty sure we never ended up killing him. After all, he was on our side. The commander was, however, under "ideological investigation" for some time, which means he was probably beaten to within an inch of his life by the boys who used to be under his command—it's likely he ended up a cripple. I do know that the man was dismissed from all official posts. Who knows, maybe he took refuge in the South, going down with the mass retreat. Ms. Yun, on the other hand, was locked up in the storage room of the police station. Later she was transferred to a hot-spring resort run by the government. That was where I eventually helped her to rest for all eternity. It was better for her that way.

Anyway, after hearing the news I went back home for the night. Yosŏp was nowhere to be found, and no one knew where he might have gone. He did, however, show up again around supper time, so our entire family— my parents, my own family, and Yosŏp—we all got a chance to sit down together for a change and enjoy a meal. I decided to leave Yosŏp alone for the time being. After supper, Father and I talked for a while about what was going on with the war, especially on the front lines. Pretty soon after that I retired to our wing. The sun had set but it wasn't completely dark yet. Just having finished my business in the outhouse next to the fence, I was getting to my feet when I spotted someone walking across the cabbage fields. He was treading recklessly over the furrows, ignoring the tall, densely planted cabbages. He could have walked along the levee path, instead! I guess that's just how your mind works when you're a country boy at heart. I yelled at the top of my lungs, Hey you! What do you think you're doing?

The figure turned towards me, his voice dying away before it had even begun. It was Yosŏp. I walked out past the fence, shouting for him to come over to me. As I got closer, Yosŏp hurriedly hid something behind his back. Peering over his shoulder, I could see that it was some sort of bundle.

Turn around. Let me see. What have you got there?

I snatched up the bundle and opened it. Out came a gourd containing some cooked rice and a little china bowl filled with pickled radish and bean paste.

What is going on here?

I just brought it out to eat with my friends while we play.

All of a sudden, I remembered all the things my parents had told me earlier, about how Yosŏp had been inhaling bowls of rice and running around the village after dark. Thinking of what had happened at the office that day, a horrifying possibility dawned on me.

You little brat—tell me the truth! Where are you taking the food?

Grabbing him by the collar, I shook him back and forth, demanding that he speak. With a surprising amount of sincerity, Little Brother started rubbing his hands together, pleading his case.

Big Brother . . . this is a secret, just between us, okay? Promise you won't tell.

A secret? You little idiot! Do you have some sort of death wish? You want them to storm in here and kill our entire family? Who have you been hiding?

Girls . . . from the People's Army.

Girls? How many?

Two. They don't even have any guns.

Where are you hiding them?

Hanging his head, Little Brother wouldn't open his mouth. I knew very well that bullying him wouldn't do any good at that point. I changed my tone of voice and asked him again, gently this time.

Where are they? I won't hurt them, I promise.

He wiped his eyes with his sleeve—he must have been crying with his head bowed down. Getting impatient, I went on, imploring, You're so dense! Don't you see? If the neighbors find out, they'll suspect us! How can I help the girls if I don't know where they are?

I could tell he was right on the verge of bursting into tears as he finally blurted, I hid them in a dugout in the orchard, the one right over the hill.

I pushed him lightly on the back.

Well, go on then.

Wha-at?

How can they eat if you don't take them the food?

Big Brother, you mean, really . . . ?

And with that, I sent him on his way. I didn't go back to the county hall that evening. Much later that night, I went into the main wing of the house and saw that all the lights were turned off—obviously, everyone was asleep. I went to the stepping stone beneath the wooden floor and checked to make sure Yosŏp's sneakers were there nestled between the grown-ups' *komusin*. They were. He was back. Sticking a U.S. Army issue flashlight into my cartridge belt, I checked the magazine of my revolver to make sure it had enough bullets, opened up the chamber to check that, and set the safety. I was about to leave the house when I changed my mind and turned around. I went into the storeroom next to the house and went through the various tools instead—sickles, hoes, shovels, and so on. I grabbed a pick.

The little trail in the orchard was our playground when we were children. As we grew older, we would walk along it with the workmen, going out to help pick the apples. I knew every nook and cranny of that place. I approached the mud cellar without making a sound. Just as a precaution, I put down the pick, took the revolver in my hands, and released the safety pin. Holding the flashlight in one hand, I switched it on and shone it into the cellar. Startled by the sudden light, the two people who had been sleeping inside sat bolt upright, covering their faces with their hands. Aiming the gun at them, I spoke.

Hands up. Come on out.

Rustling around, they got up and climbed out of the hut. They were children, no older than high school age. I'd dealt with countless stragglers in town, just like these, so I didn't even bother asking for their ranks. I asked them the only thing that was important.

Anybody else besides you two?

No. Just us.

Where's your platoon?

We were separated a fortnight ago.

The smaller one had answered my questions, but the big one suddenly spoke up.

Are you a soldier of the National Defense Army?

That doesn't concern you. Kneel down over there. Hands up on your head, that's it.

The small one was hanging onto some sort of black bag or something, which was starting to bother me. Yosŏp told me that they had no weapons, so I knew I'd be able to take care of them myself without any problems, as long as I was cautious.

What is that? Toss it over here.

It's a musical instrument—a violin.

Toss it, I say!

The thing dropped to the ground at my feet with a resounding thud, flying open as if it'd been split in half. I picked it up.

So it is. A fiddle.

I'd seen peddlers in the marketplace playing "Yangsando" or "Hwangsŏng of Yesteryear," so I knew a fiddle wasn't anything special. I shook it a couple of times to make sure there wasn't anything inside it and tossed it to the ground. Then I crushed it with my foot.

In spite of myself, the shriek that burst from the lips of the little one startled me to the core.

Quiet! Before I take care of you both with just one shot.

Pulling them to their feet, I forced them to walk in front of me. With the revolver at my waist and the pick over my shoulder, I steered them down to the fruit storehouse, shining the flashlight to illuminate the path. I had them kneel on the slope with their backs to me. As I gripped the pick in my hands, the bigger girl, without looking back, said quietly, Let us sing.

With that, she started singing some sort of military song. Without a word, I let fly at the bitch, striking her body over and over again with the pick. She fell straight forward and rolled down along the slope. Brandishing the pick, I turned and swung, aiming at the small one. I missed. I think I must have hit her in the shoulder. She bent in half, screaming, then twisted back around to look me in the face.

Please, sir, let me live! Help!

I struck her again, and this time I caught her on the back of the head. That shut her up. I turned around and hurried away, going around to the front of the storehouse. The blood must have spattered—my face and the front of my shirt felt wet. I sat down in front of the water pump and washed my face and hands, then drank some water from my cupped hands. Still feeling kind of flustered, I went back home, got on my bicycle, and raced all the way back into town.

At the time, the only thought on my mind was that I had to get rid of them as quietly as possible, before anyone else realized what was going on. The bodies stayed there, sprawled out behind the warehouse, until some villagers discovered them and buried them. Yosŏp, of course, must have seen them on the following day when he took them their food. He didn't say a word about it, not for several decades—but then one day, he asked me if I prayed when I did it, in that moment. I, of course, answered that I had.

❖ ❖ ❖

December arrives. The U.S. troops and the National Defense Army are being pushed back. The Chinese Communist Army has entered the war. As the news that Pyongyang has been seized reaches the members of the Youth Corps and the security forces, they prepare themselves to retreat. They arrest all the people who have been under investigation, even those whose degree of participation was marginal at best, families of those who'd simply joined the Women's League, the Professional League, or the Democratic Youth League, and the families of soldiers. Some of the families are small units of survivors who have already lost the rest of their relatives. By now, trials are being held not just in town but in every village in the county. The cold-blooded killings at the storehouse in Wonamri and the slaughter at the reservoir and on the bridge all happen within a few days of each other, beginning on December 2. During the day they roam the streets to hunt men; at night they search the empty houses and gather together to drink. Many of the young men have collected quite a number of valuables and other items. They are waiting for a suitable means of transportation. They are eager to start moving south, even if it's just a few miles.

❖ ❖ ❖

After I delivered Tanyŏl and went out for a cigarette, I began to think. We couldn't just leave him there, and I thought maybe my older sister might be able to protect him since her husband was a Party member.

Let's name the baby Daniel. The Lord protected Daniel, even in the lion's den.

That can wait. The pain is killing me.

I realized my only option was to leave by myself. I left the house, telling my wife I was going to my sister's house to ask for help since she was in no condition to be on the road. My older sister lived in a neighboring village, Palsan, and my younger sister, two years my junior, had married a man in Unbong and settled down there. Since I'd missed the advance trucks that left the day before to stay and help with my wife's childbirth, it was crucial that I get at least as far as the pier in Haeju by the end of the coming day.

That was the final meeting point. By two o'clock, I could already feel the imminent arrival of dawn hanging over the mountain forests. The mist began to climb up over the ridges and spread itself out over the fields. The night was still but the air was icy.

Entering the village of Palsan, I managed to find my sister's house with a series of ready guesses. It was in a narrow alleyway bordered by a long stone fence on either side. A huge ginkgo tree marked what looked like the entrance—the stone fence simply ended, and the ginkgo tree appeared. I turned the corner, but as I stood facing the blind alley that led to my sister's house, a sense of uneasiness suddenly enveloped my entire body.

Despite the fact that it was the middle of the night, the wide wooden gate—rather fancy for a rural house—stood wide open at the end of the alley. It looked to be grinning ominously. I unslung the 30-round automatic carbine from my shoulder and held it at the ready. The front yard was empty and the house, two rooms built side by side, was dark. I went closer and called out softly, Sister, are you there?

No answer. I opened the door to one of the rooms. Sweeping the room with my flashlight, I found it was empty. The mattress was laid out, but the blankets had been thrown to the side, as if someone had just hurried out of bed. I thought I heard something at the back of the house. Aiming the rifle, I walked along the fence and went into the backyard. Something dark was squatting down, crouched close to the ground.

Who's there?

Without turning, the black thing muttered, What have we done to deserve this, what crime have we committed . . . ?

Brother-in-law?

Switching the flashlight on, I shone the light around the yard. A long skirt and a pair of bare feet were visible next to my brother-in-law.

Oh, God! What's going on?

Your sister. She's dead.

I'd seen so many dead bodies over the previous month that the scene itself didn't strike me as being particularly shocking. I just wanted to find out who had dared to do such a thing to Ryu Yohan's sister.

Who's done this?

Suddenly grabbing me by the collar as I crouched down next to him, my brother-in-law started shaking me back and forth, bursting into tears.

Who else but you and your kind would do something like this?

What? We did this?

That's right. Sangho was here. Lucky for me, I happened to be hiding under the floorboards.

I barely managed to get him off of me—he kept shaking me by the collar, hollering that the only way a farmer could get by these past few years had been to join the Party, asking me what deadly crime I thought he'd committed.

We thought since you were a vice-commander, we'd be safe—even in hiding, I wasn't too worried—and now, look! We've been struck by lightning!

That filthy butcher!

It suddenly occurred to me that the whole notion of this side and that side, of us and them—it was all over. It was no longer the Lord's Crusade. We were no longer fighting to overthrow Satan. We have been tested, I thought to myself, and we have been found wanting. Our faith was corrupted. My comrades and I—we'd become the endless days, days without light. What does that mean, you ask? We were sick and tired of living. At the least provocation, we would spit out, Fuck it, and kill whoever happened to be involved.

The decent-looking girls were taken to the resort at the hot springs, run by the social insurance agency. There were members of the Women's League, school teachers, and daughters of the enemy. The ones who'd been sent up from the South seemed to have plenty of experience—they were uninhibited and quite . . . knowledgeable. Since the resort catered to men from the Youth Corps, the security forces, and even the Autonomous Police, we didn't get into the question of hierarchy or rank despite the fact that we all had different official positions.

I never touched alcohol later in life, and actually that was pretty much the case in my youth, too. I did smoke cigarettes—I quit those in my old age. Pongsu, the leader of the Youth Corps, and Sangho both loved to drink, so they'd frequent the fancy restaurants together all the time. The two of them got along famously. When the war came to an end a month after we'd seized the whole town, we were confident that this new way of life was here to stay. There was a party every night. At first, I couldn't figure out where the men from the security forces went for their evening get-togethers. I myself finally ended up going to the resort only because Sangho insisted on having a farewell gathering to enjoy ourselves for one last time in our hometown. That was two days before we evacuated, I think.

The resort was an inn built by the Japanese in the old days. Inside the glass front door was a long wooden corridor, and every room had a sliding door made of rice paper and a Japanese-style tatami floor. When I entered the room I was greeted by half a dozen familiar faces. All around the table, sandwiched between the men, were a number of young women. The guys all acted fairly decently in the beginning—they behaved like gentlemen for a while. As they put back more and more alcohol, however, their language and gestures grew uglier. One man actually hit one of the girls. Then, after confirming something with the staff, Sangho turned to Pongsu.

Today's tasty side dish is a female school teacher.

What? You mean you brought her here?

She's standing by, in nothing but a bathrobe.

Hey, what about me? I want a go.

All right, all right, let's draw lots to decide the order.

I wasn't quite sure what they were talking about. Finally, as everyone started pouring out of the room into the hallway, I turned to Sangho.

What, is something interesting about to happen?

You should try it out, too. That woman teacher, Yun—she's here.

Here at the hot springs?

Well, hell, it's better than dying, isn't it?

I flinched away and sat back down at the empty table, all alone. There was a huge uproar coming from the corridor, the sound of men laughing raucously against the background of a woman's screams. I threw back two glasses in a row, though I never could hold my liquor. I stayed in the room for a long time before I finally walked out into the corridor, all flushed from the alcohol. As I walked by, I heard somebody moan in pain. I opened a sliding door and looked inside. Three men were sitting around a naked woman, holding down her arms and legs. A fourth man was on top of the woman, in the process of raping her. Swallowing the bile that rose up in my throat, I felt myself being drawn into the room—it was as if someone pulled me by a string. Pongsu must have already had his turn; he was still naked above the waist. Sangho's pants were down around his calves. Over his shoulder I could see the woman's familiar face. The string of her

Japanese-style bathrobe was unfastened and spread wide open across the tatami floor. I must have kicked Sangho, since he rolled to the side. Then I reached into my jacket, took out my pistol, and shot her. I shot twice, I think. I staggered out of the room, but no one came after me. The sound of the gunshots kept ringing through my head.

People who are leaving their hometowns usually have to try and hold back their tears; it's only natural. We, on the other hand—well, it's not that we spat on the ground and said good riddance, it's just that we all knew we would never return. The place was doomed to become a hell on earth, a place where only devils would be able to thrive. Or so we thought. After that day at the resort, I didn't see Sangho again. During those nightmarish days, though we pretended it wasn't so, we hated each other more than our enemies. I knew only too well that he shot my sisters in a fit of rage. We killed anyone we decided was our enemy, and that was no different, really. We killed anyone who'd joined the Party or the Workers' League—in fact, we killed anyone we could think up a reason for killing. That was why we hated ourselves.

As for Sangho, I returned the favor he'd done me. I had a pretty good idea of where Myŏngsŏn's family lived in the village of Palsan. Myŏngsŏn and Sangho had become very close as they worked together for the youth group at church. They had probably promised each other to get married when the war ended, or if they moved down South. Pistol in hand, I headed for Myŏngsŏn's house. When I got there, I knocked on the front gate. The second Myŏngsŏn's mother opened it I smashed her face in with the butt of the pistol. I ran into the front yard, rushed into the main bedroom, and opened fire on the roomful of girls. It turns out that Sangho was one step ahead of me, though. On his way through Unbong, he'd already slaughtered my other sister and her entire family. Years later, as I got older and older, I began to see phantoms. At first, I would scream out loud, dripping with cold sweat, but as time went by I would just sit there and watch them, as if from afar. I wonder—was it that way for Sangho, too?

9

The Fork in the Road

SEPARATION

❖

ALL RIGHT, ALL RIGHT. That's enough. Time to go.

The phantom of Uncle Sunnam spoke, and Illang, standing at his side, agreed.

Right. Let's go.

The other ghosts, both men and women, rose up quietly and began fading back into the darkness, disappearing like pieces of cloth quivering in the breeze. A voice, coming from someplace far, far away, reached Yosŏp's ears.

Those who killed and were killed are bound together in the next world.

It was Yohan.

Finally, I am home. Finally, I am relieved of the old hatred and resentment. Finally I see my friends, and finally, I can stop wandering through unknown darkness. I'm off. Be well, both of you.

They all disappeared. Silence descended. The darkness was gradually withdrawing; daybreak was on its way—outside the window, beyond the distinct shadows of the mountain ridge, the milky sky was growing clearer. Only Ryu Yosŏp and his uncle remained in the second-story room with the wooden floor. Yosŏp's uncle broke the silence.

"Those who needed to leave have left, and now the ones who are still alive must start living anew. We must purge this land, cleanse it of all the old filth and grime, don't you agree?"

Ryu Yosŏp clasped his hands together and began to recite a passage from the Bible he had memorized long ago.

> A time to love, and a time to hate; a time for war, and a time for peace. What gain have the workers from their toil? I have seen the business that God has given to everyone to be busy with.
>
> He has made everything suitable for its time; moreover he has put a sense of past and future into their minds, yet they cannot find out what God has done from the beginning to the end.

10
Burning the Clothes
BURIAL

SETTING OUT FROM his uncle's place in Some, Yosŏp and the guide climbed into the car and headed towards town. Cautiously, Yosŏp asked the guide in the front seat, "Would it be possible to drop by Ch'ansaemgol on the way?"

"There's someplace *else* you want to go, too?"

The guide grimaced, glancing at his wristwatch.

"We've got to be at the hotel by lunchtime."

"I was just wondering if we could have a quick look at the place as we pass through. . . ."

"I say, Reverend, you sure do have a lot of requests."

"I'm just curious to see if the place I used to call home is still the way it was back then."

"It won't be anything like the old days—everything's been changed by the introduction of the cooperative system."

"I'd be happy just to get a glimpse of the hill behind the village."

The guide laughed.

"We have no way of even knowing where Ch'ansaem is."

"It's in the Onchŏn township, so it'll be on the corner as we drive up."

At that, the guide consented quite readily, saying, "Oh, well, if that's the case, you can just tell us where to go."

Just as they had a few days earlier, they drove along the town's paved roads and empty streets. As they reached the outskirts of town and the rice paddies began to stretch out before them on either side, an open field ringed by the ridges of low mountains came into view in the distance. The orchard was exactly where it had been all those years ago. Standing along the ridges were the apple trees. Each fruit was ripening at its own pace, countless different shades of apples peeking through the green leaves.

"That's it right over there. Just stop at the corner of that road for a minute, please."

Stalks of corn lined the road, swaying back and forth in the autumn wind. Two-story duplexes made of gray brick stood at identical intervals along the hillside, surrounded by the orchard. Yosŏp was amazed to see that the village that had seemed so spacious to him as a child actually took up no more space than a small corner of the low hill. The levee where Yosŏp used to take the cow to graze had, at some point, been transformed into a cement embankment. Only the starwort blossoming by the cornfields was still the same. The tiny little flowers still seemed to be laughing out loud in the wind. Yosŏp stood there for a moment, looking up at the vast expanse of sky, then took the clothes out of the bundle he'd brought out with him from the car. The guide, who'd been smoking a cigarette off to the side, came up to him.

"What have you got there?"

"It belonged to my brother," Yosŏp replied, waving his brother's old underwear at the guide. "I promised my sister-in-law that I would help put some of her demons to rest."

"Ah, you brought them with you from Sariwŏn."

Yosŏp started off along the old levee path, cutting through the cornfields up to the base of the hill. The guide, having no idea what was going on, followed close behind. Avoiding the areas that were choked with weeds, Yosŏp chose a sunny spot where the dirt was visibly dry and crouched down to the ground. He reached down and gathered a handful of dirt.

"What are you doing?"

The guide seemed confused as he followed Yosŏp's gaze towards the patch of bare earth. Yosŏp answered him with a question of his own.

"You have a lighter, don't you?"

Apparently still unable to grasp what was going on, the baffled guide took out his lighter and handed it over to Yosŏp. Collecting a small pile of dry twigs from here and there, Yosŏp heaped them together and set the tiny pyre ablaze. The twigs flared up, crackling loudly. Above the flame, Yosŏp held the underwear that Big Brother Yohan had used to deliver his son Tanyŏl. The cloth fibers curled up, distorted, and the edges of the garment began to turn black, rapidly burning inwards. Holding it in his hand, Yosŏp turned the cloth over the flame, slowly, a bit at a time, so as to burn it all the way through. When all that remained was a square of cloth about the size of his palm, Yosŏp tossed the whole thing atop the miniature bonfire. It shriveled up and disappeared instantly.

Moving over, Yosŏp began to dig a small hole in the ground. After he scooped out several handfuls of dirt, the consistency of the soil became damp and mixed with leaves. He continued digging, and about a handspan further down, the soil became soft, pink, and tender. After sorting out all the little pebbles and patting the bottom of the hole down to make it firm, Yosŏp took out the leather pouch he'd been keeping on him. Untying it, he took out the *tojang*-shaped sliver of bone that had once belonged to his brother and placed it in the hole. He filled it back up with dirt. Just as one might do to put a baby to sleep, he kept patting the little mound of dirt that was left.

You're home now, Big Brother, were the words Yosŏp wanted to say out loud.

II

Matrix of Spirits
WHAT WILL BECOME

THE WIND BLOWS HARD. All the grass on the hillside is flattened in one direction; the tips of the blades tremble violently, as if they are being washed away by a powerful ocean current. Particles of dirt smash themselves against his face and earlobes as the wind pushes against his chest and thighs. Even the crows can't seem to fly properly. They flap their wings over and over but eventually, the moment they pause for even the briefest instant, they plummet towards the ground. The crows fall, but just as they are about to graze the earth they suddenly soar back up into the sky and disappear, flying swiftly in the opposite direction like a piece of paper blowing away in the wind. Their thin, naked branches shivering, the trees scream.

A long line of people, hunched over at the waist, all move in one direction. They look as if they are each dragging something extremely heavy behind them. The endless parade has no visible beginning or end. A winding path passes through the field, leading up into a faraway lavender mountain ridge. They do not speak. From here, only their backs are visible.

The sun is setting. Clouds soaked in twilight flow past. Just like the birds blown away by the wind, the clouds, too, stream backwards into oblivion. The reddish skies darken, and the moon rises like a piece of cloth in faded indigo. Under the moonlight, the parade of people moves on, making

231

slow progress. The high, steep path up the mountain ends at the peak. He can see the stripe of river etched in white and the lights of the village far below.

Like a bird, he soars up and over the scene. Below him a series of hills and a thin stream race by. He hears the cows moo in the distance and hears the hens cackle as they lay their eggs. He hears the people in the paddies, singing as they plant next year's rice crop. The fast beating of drums is superimposed on the buoyant, metallic sound of cymbals. He hears the mother call to her children.

Kids, time to eat.

❖   ❖   ❖

Once again, Reverend Ryu Yosŏp woke up from another early morning dream. It wasn't time to go yet. He pulled the curtains open and looked out the window at the deserted streets. The streetlamps remained unlit; Pyongyang was still covered in darkness. In the apartment complex across the road, though, several lights were on—around the middle and towards the top of the building. Has someone gotten up already to get ready for work? A car drove by, slowly, along the empty road. He gazed at himself as he was, reflected dimly on the windowpane. It was the face of the most familiar man in his whole world.

Farewell Guests

EAT YOUR FILL AND BEGONE!

Hamujagwi, the widower's ghost, *mongdalgwi*, the
    bachelor's ghost,
gorge yourselves—begone!
Kŏllipkwi, the ghost of the shaman, *sinsŏn'gwi*, the ghost
    of the blind,
gorge yourselves—be on your way!
T'ansikkwi, the ghost of the widow, *hogugwi*, the ghost
    of the maiden,
gorge yourselves—leave us!
Ghosts of the hanged, up in the mountain's drooping
    pine branches,
ghosts of the drowned, down in the bottomless waters,
hat'algwi, the ghosts of the women, shedding all those
    endless tears—
some died giving birth, some while still pregnant,
all clutching their rice bowls and mats made of straw—
their skirts always tucked, their hair all disheveled,
with scissors and thread still attached to their belts,
gorge yourself—begone!
Ghosts of those shot, pierced, even battered,

ghosts of those bombed by planes overhead,
ghosts of those burnt to ashes by flames,
ghosts hit by wagons, tanks, trucks, or trains,
ghosts made by smallpox, ghosts made by plague,
those made by typhus, consumption, or cholera,
ghosts still resentful, ghosts far from home,
all those who linger, each with its own tale,
today eat your fill, 'til your heart is content,
gorge yourselves—be on your way!
Behold today's feast, see our devotion,
the ghost of this land, the ghost of this house,
eat your fill and know when to be silent.
Fill your bellies, quench your thirst,
eat your fill and pack up what's left—
take it all with you, women on your heads,
take it all with you, servants in your aprons—
accept our goodwill, take some coin for the road
and be on your way, up into the heavens.

About the Author

◈

HWANG SOK-YONG is arguably Korea's most recognized and renowned author. Drawing artistic inspiration from his own experiences as a vagabond day laborer, student activist, Vietnam War veteran, advocate for coal miners and garment workers, and political dissident, he is embraced as a writer and champion of the people. His historical novel *Chang Kilsan*, an extensive parable about a bandit that described the contemporary dictatorship, was serialized in a daily paper from 1974 to 1984 and sold an estimated million copies in North and South Korea. In 1993 there was international outcry when Hwang was sentenced to seven years in prison for an unauthorized trip to the North to promote exchange between artists in North and South Korea. In 1998, he was granted special pardon by the new South Korean president. The recipient of Korea's highest literary prizes and shortlisted for the Prix Fémina Étranger, Hwang has seen his novels and short stories published in North and South Korea, Japan, China, France, Germany, and the U.S. Hwang was born in 1943 in Xinjing, Manchuria (now Changchun, China).